P9-DXM-983

A syrup maker who sticks to his guns . . .

"I can take a hint. No more news of the cooperative for you. No joining, no inclusion in the informational mailing list. No invitations to meetings."

"No nuthin'."

"I understand you feel strongly. Which brings me to my next question." I took a deep breath and reminded myself once again that I had wanted to be in charge.

"Someone damaged my car this morning while I was in having breakfast at the Stack."

"What's that got to do with me?" Frank bent down and tossed a piece of galvanized pipe as far as he could throw it.

"An anti-cooperative message was scratched into the new paint job."

"And you think I'd do a thing like that?"

"Considering your attitude toward participating in the co-op, the thought had crossed my mind." He heaved a cinder block next to the length of chain. It landed with a crack and sent a sizable chunk flying against my shin.

"I've had a thought just cross my mind, too. Beau!" Frank put two fingers in his mouth and whistled. My stomach dropped into my socks and my kneecaps turned into water balloons. Every junkyard needs a guard dog. Beau was on duty at Frank's place.

I started to run for the Clunker even before Beau and his drooling, snapping jaws hurtled into view.

HILLSBORO PUBLIC LIBRARIES
Hillsboro, OR
WITHDRAWN
Member of Washington County
COOPERATIVE LIBRARY SERVICES

Berkley Prime Crime titles by Jessie Crockett

DRIZZLED WITH DEATH
MAPLE MAYHEM

Maple MAYHEM

Jessie Crockett

HILLSBORO PUBLIC LIBRARIES
Hillsboro, OR
Member of Washington County
COOPERATIVE LIBRARY SERVICES

BERKLEY PRIME CRIME, NEW YORK

THE BERKLEY PUBLISHING GROUP
Published by the Penguin Group
Penguin Group (USA) LLC
375 Hudson Street, New York, New York 10014

USA • Canada • UK • Ireland • Australia • New Zealand • India • South Africa • China

penguin.com

A Penguin Random House Company

MAPLE MAYHEM

A Berkley Prime Crime Book / published by arrangement with the author

Copyright © 2014 by Jessie Crockett.
Penguin supports copyright. Copyright fuels creativity, encourages diverse voices,
promotes free speech, and creates a vibrant culture. Thank you for buying an authorized
edition of this book and for complying with copyright laws by not reproducing, scanning,
or distributing any part of it in any form without permission. You are supporting writers
and allowing Penguin to continue to publish books for every reader.

Berkley Prime Crime Books are published by The Berkley Publishing Group.
BERKLEY® PRIME CRIME and the PRIME CRIME logo are trademarks of
Penguin Group (USA) LLC.

For information, address: The Berkley Publishing Group,
a division of Penguin Group (USA) LLC,
375 Hudson Street, New York, New York 10014.

ISBN: 978-0-425-26020-3

PUBLISHING HISTORY
Berkley Prime Crime mass-market edition / July 2014

PRINTED IN THE UNITED STATES OF AMERICA

10 9 8 7 6 5 4 3 2 1

Cover illustration by Mary Ann Lasher.
Interior text design by Kelly Lipovich.

This is a work of fiction. Names, characters, places, and incidents either are the product
of the author's imagination or are used fictitiously, and any resemblance to actual persons,
living or dead, business establishments, events, or locales is entirely coincidental.

The publisher does not have any control over and does not assume any responsibility for
author or third-party websites or their content.

PUBLISHER'S NOTE: The recipes contained in this book are to be followed exactly
as written. The publisher is not responsible for your specific health or allergy needs
that may require medical supervision. The publisher is not responsible for any
adverse reactions to the recipes contained in this book.

If you purchased this book without a cover, you should be aware that this book is
stolen property. It was reported as "unsold and destroyed" to the publisher, and neither
the author nor the publisher has received any payment for this "stripped book."

Acknowledgments

Writing a book is an exercise in faith. I've been lucky enough to have a lot of people to thank for having faith in me during the process.

Thanks go out to my mother Sandy Crockett, who gets the funny bits; my sisters Larissa Crockett and Barb Shaffer, who call and ask all the right questions; and my children Will, Jo, Theo, and Ari, who are always happy to brainstorm new ways to bump off my imaginary friends. Thanks also to Philip Nadeau for his expert opinion concerning automotive restoration.

I would also like to thank my editor at Berkley, Michelle Vega, and my agent, John Talbot, for providing support and enthusiasm for the series. Also, I would like to express my appreciation for the beautiful work of cover artist Mary Anne Lasher-Dodge.

The other members of the Wicked Cozy Authors blog, Sherry Harris, Julie Hennrikus, Edith Maxwell, Liz Mugavero, and Barb Ross, have been an outstanding source of support for this book as well as life in general. I am so grateful to be journeying with all of you!

And finally, to my beloved husband, Elias Estevao, for making it all possible and for believing it's all worthwhile.

One

I slid out from behind the wheel and gently closed my car door. It had taken weeks for the local mechanic to repair my baby after it lost a cage match with a cassowary but it had been worth the wait. If anything, my vintage MG Midget was looking, and driving, better than ever. All those weeks of tooling around in the family's dreaded spare car, the Clunker, had been worth it. I gave the convertible's soft top a little pat and let my fingers run along the smooth shiny new turquoise paint, then headed into the most photographed building in New Hampshire for some breakfast.

To the best of all local knowledge, the Stack Shack is the only pancake stack shaped building in the world. It's been featured in travel magazines, cooking magazines, and even a book of odd buildings. The place is built with enough curves and layers to make any structural updates intimidating and costly, which is why Piper was able to buy it on the cheap when she was barely out of high school. She loves the Stack, which she knew she wanted to own and run ever since the first time her parents took her there for breakfast as a small child.

It's conveniently located just off Sugar Grove's main street with plenty of on- and off-street parking, which it needs. The Stack, as it's called by locals, is standing-room-only on weekends and holidays. It gets crowded to capacity on weekdays at breakfast and lunch, too.

The smell of fried potatoes and sizzling bacon filled the air. I glanced up at the specials written on a section of wall covered with chalkboard paint in the shape of a maple leaf. Piper stood behind the counter, a coffeepot in her hand, looking for all the world like she'd lost her best friend. Which I knew for a fact she hadn't since I was standing right in front of her.

"So what's good this morning?" I asked. Piper looked up from staring at the laminate counter in front of her like it held the answer to all the world's problems.

"Nothing." Piper always had a great suggestion for ordering off her menu. She never said *nothing*. If the special didn't seem all that special, you could be certain the pancakes would be.

"That doesn't sound like you. What's up?" I hoisted myself onto a stool at the counter and gave my friend all my attention.

"It's more what's down. Profits."

"At the Stack?" Business being slow at the Stack Shack was about as likely as successfully training a moose to ride a bicycle. The Stack had been profitable even during the Depression, when it had been built as a roadside attraction with the idea of separating a reluctant population from what little extra money they had. Things had only improved since then for the country and the Stack.

"No. Jill and Dean's profits." That made more sense. Jill Hayes and her brother, Dean, ran another sugarhouse in town, but their operation was much smaller than my own, Greener Pastures. Back at Thanksgiving Jill had lost her access to some trees she had tapped for years and it had cut way down on her ability to produce enough sap.

Her own property wasn't all that large and with forty gallons of sap required to produce one gallon of finished syrup, you needed to tap a lot of trees. It hadn't helped that last year had been terrible for production. You need warm days and cold nights to get the sap to really run and, unfortunately, Mother Nature had only been suffering from hot flashes. No sugar makers had done well and for those already running on close margins, it had been a disaster.

"Do they think they'll be able to hold on through this coming season?" I asked. Piper was plugged into what was going on in town because of her position as owner of the most popular eatery in Sugar Grove, but also because Dean was her current winter fling. Every year Piper has a winter romance and she takes it very seriously while it lasts.

"Dean was just in here talking about how tight things have gotten with the business and that they may decide to stop producing. He said he's trying to convince Jill to sell the property even before the sugaring season gets underway." Jill and Dean had inherited their land from their parents, who had died several years before in a car accident. Jill had finished raising Dean and one of the ways they had made ends meet was by producing syrup.

"I thought Jill said she was going to wait it out to see if the maple cooperative would make enough of a difference and then decide?"

"She wants to try to stick it out but she isn't sure if they can. Dean says the bank's sending threatening letters and if it weren't winter, the power company would have cut off the electricity for lack of payment."

"I knew their name was listed in the last town report as one of the owners behind on their property taxes but I didn't know things had gotten that bad." I was glad, and not for the first time, that the Greene family income didn't depend on syrup making. Greener Pastures was one of the largest producers in town. I was hoping we would grow to be one of the largest in the state.

"It is that bad. And they aren't the first family to lose their homes with all the economic mess." Piper was right. Sugar Grove, like so many other communities in New Hampshire, had been hit hard by the mortgage crisis. That was the reason I had decided to start a cooperative in the first place. By buying supplies as a group, all the sugar makers in town would be able to pay lower prices per unit on the things we needed, like taps and jugs and tubing. We were even going to be able to save money on office supplies. I had approached other sugar makers about starting the cooperative a week ago and, with one notable exception, they were all eager to participate. "Dean says if they sell, he's going to move out of the area." Piper fiddled with the silver hoop ring puncturing the corner of her eyebrow, a sure sign she was agitated.

I not-so-secretly harbored hopes that Piper would eventually marry my brother, Loden, but I didn't like to see her feeling miserable in the meantime. All I wanted to do was help. There had to be some way to get Jill some breathing room. After all, it was only a few more weeks until sugar season started.

"I'll talk to Grampa. Maybe we can think of something that would help." My grandfather has never needed money. None of us has, thanks to cheap ancestors and wise investments. That hasn't stopped Grampa from being a savvy businessman or a generous giver to causes he deemed worthy. Everyone in the Greene family has pet projects he or she sponsors and has found ways to make them self-funding. That's what I've been doing with Greener Pastures. What started as a family tradition is now a thriving concern that donates all post-tax profits to environmental causes. Grampa has done the same with many endeavors over the years. If anyone could help with this, it would be him.

"Great idea." Piper perked up just a little and flipped over a mug, filling it two thirds with coffee before sliding it in my direction. "Are you here for some breakfast? This is early, even for you."

I poured in a generous glug of cream from a cow-shaped creamer and spooned in enough sugar to induce a diabetic coma. With a metabolism like a hummingbird, I grab calories wherever I can get them, healthy or not.

"I was up saying good-bye to Mom and Lowell." My mother and my godfather had been seeing each other for some time without my knowledge. I was pretty upset when I first found out about their relationship but now that things were out in the open they were making up for lost time. For Christmas Lowell had surprised my mother by booking passage for the two of them on a cruise to the Caribbean. I hadn't wanted to get up at four that morning to see them off but I was still finding my way around their relationship and I didn't want them to worry that I didn't approve. So here I was, out in public, looking for breakfast at five thirty.

"Did they get off okay?"

"They did. Honestly, they were so cute it was sort of sickening. Mom made them matching luggage tags from recycled tarot cards and Lowell presented her with a hat so large it could be used as an igloo. He didn't want her to get sunburned."

"How long will they be gone?"

"Ten days. Lowell hasn't had a vacation in so long his suitcase had dry-rotted and they had to buy him a new one."

"I hope nothing crops up while Lowell's gone. It's hard to imagine Mitch being in charge."

"I can and if you keep talking about that, I'll lose my appetite."

"Well you wouldn't want to do that. The maple cranberry turkey sausage is to die for."

"Sounds like it would be perfect with some buckwheat pancakes."

"Coming right up." Piper buzzed on back to the kitchen and while I waited I entertained myself by spinning my stool around until I was dizzy. That's one of the perks of looking like a child. You can get away with a lot of behavior other adults would not. At under five feet tall and barely a hundred pounds on a fat day, I find people tend to underestimate my age. I may be twenty-seven but waitresses invariably ask me if I want the kiddie menu. Before I managed to make myself sick from all the whirling Piper brought out a heaping plate and I tucked in with a will.

The sausage was as good as she said it would be. I'd be willing to bet even people who think turkey sausage can't be a sausage at all would wolf it down and stick out their plates for seconds. The sweetness of the sausage complemented the nuttiness of the pancakes and made waking up that early almost worth it. Piper was sure to be out of the sausage before the end of the breakfast rush.

"Dani, isn't that your car?" Piper asked, pointing out the window. I turned my stool around again to see what was happening out in the street. Through the window, I could see my ex-boyfriend and current police officer in

7

charge, Mitch Reynolds, leaning over my car, with what looked like a ticketing pad in hand. I rushed out the door, still holding my knife and fork.

I squealed to a halt a few steps in front of the big ox. As much as I have no desire to ever again see him out of it, I have to admit the man did look darn good in a uniform.

"What do you think you are doing?" I asked, causing him to look up from the form he was filling out.

"Ticketing the citizen with the poor sense to go driving around with not only her headlights but her taillights busted out." Mitch pointed at the front of my car and then at the pavement. Little fragments of headlight cover scattered on the slushy ground.

"Busted! That can't be. I just got the car back from Byron." I felt my palms, wrapped around the flatware, becoming clammy with rage.

"Well, obviously, it can be. Look for yourself." Mitch smiled at me and his cheeks creased into double dimples. I walked around to the back of the car to check the taillights.

"Did you see this?" I asked, trying not to yell or, worse, cry. Someone had keyed my freshly painted trunk. The word *co-op* was written enclosed in a circle with a diagonal slash across it.

"I did. I thought it must be part of your fancy new paint job."

"Of course it wasn't. I don't even put bumper stickers on my car." Mitch did though. His personal vehicle, a four-wheel-drive truck with monster tires, was covered in so many bumper stickers that if it ever started to rust, it still wouldn't fall apart.

"You've got a couple of flat tires, too. Looks like it's back to the shop for this thing. You can call for a tow just as soon as I finish filling out this ticket."

"You can't ticket me because someone else vandalized my car."

"Watch me. Besides, I can't stop filling out the ticket once I start. Everyone knows that."

"So when were you demoted to meter maid?" I asked, batting my eyelashes in a way calculated to fluster and annoy. In a moment of lust-filled frankness Mitch had admitted to being completely gaga over lush, long lashes. As soon as I knew things weren't going to work out for us I had thrown away my tube of mascara.

"I wasn't demoted. Every cruiser has a pad of ticketing forms. You never know when you'll need them. Besides, do I look like any kind of a maid to you?" Mitch crossed his bulging biceps across his blue-clad chest and scowled down at me. Way down. It was one of the things I felt didn't work in our relationship. If that was what you'd even call it. Mitch and I had been out on a few dates, the first of which came about because my older sister, Celadon, had lied and said she was fixing me up on a blind date. When I came downstairs all dolled up, there was Mitch, a guy I'd known since before either of us could write in cursive. It ended up being more of a blind-rage date. The only perk was that he wore his uniform and everywhere we went we got great service.

I hadn't been sure how to tell him I wasn't interested and then one thing led to another and I went on more dates with him, until one night he started groping me in a way that would have meant we were married the year my family's house was built. When I asked him to stop, and had trouble being heard, I finally spilled the beans about never being interested in the first place. He was understandably hurt and broke it off there and then. I try to avoid him whenever possible but with the size of the town and the fact he works for my godfather, the police chief, it is hard to put such a policy into practice.

Then, of course, there are the ways in which he goes out of his way to run into me. Like this morning. If I fought the ticket, I'd just wind up seeing him again in court. I didn't like to pull in any favors with the chief but right about now I was at my wit's end. My insurance was going to skyrocket with all the points Mitch was racking up on my license. In the four months since the awkwardness in the front seat of a town cruiser, he had pulled me over sixteen times, ticketing me twelve. What he needed was a new woman in his life to take his mind off me and to express dismay at how much attention he was paying to an ex-girlfriend.

"Well you don't look like you know how to clean, that's for sure." I gestured at him with the hand that happened to be holding the flatware. His uniform was stretched tightly across his bulky chest, which highlighted his muscles but also showed off a streak of egg yolk running down the front, stark against the blue of his uniform.

"Are you threatening an officer of the law?" He dropped his gaze to the flatware roll in my hand, the napkin lifting in the stiff breeze and showing off the butter knife tucked in its recesses.

"You can't be serious." My heart began to slam around in my chest like a Super Ball on a trampoline. Mitch might actually arrest me. He'd pat me down for hidden weapons and then administer a cavity search back at the station. I would die of shame before my thirtieth birthday.

"I am. Put your hands on the car and hold still." Mitch put his ticketing pad on the hood of the cruiser and stepped toward me. I dropped the knife and fork with a clatter on the sidewalk and was preparing to place my sweaty palms next to the pad when the wind picked up even more. One strong gust lifted the pad like a dried leaf and sent it whirling down the sidewalk. Mitch raced after it, stabbing out a long leg, attempting to stomp on it before it blew too far down the street. He had gotten about half a block away when Myra Phelps pulled up in the town's only other cruiser. I wiped my sweaty hands on my jeans and tried to stop shaking.

Myra wriggled out from behind the wheel of the cruiser, dragging her purse along with her. "What happened here?" Myra kicked my car's front-right tire and the whole thing sagged even closer to the ground. "Lowell said Byron had finished with this just yesterday. Better than new, he said."

"It was, when I left it to go in for some breakfast."

"Lowell's been gone less than three hours and the town's already going to hell."

"I would have thought it was some random mischief except for this." I pointed at the back of the little car. Myra took a look for herself and clucked her tongue.

"Must be one of those militant animal rights groups I keep hearing about. They think all chickens should be free-range. You must have made them ornery by locking your flock up at night."

"It doesn't say coop, it says co-op. I think someone doesn't like the idea of the maple cooperative."

"Well that's just ridiculous. Who wouldn't want to save a bunch of money on things they need to buy anyway? Except maybe for Frank."

"If this is the sort of thing the cooperative is going to inspire, I'll be glad when Lowell gets back." We both watched as Mitch danced down the sidewalk still chasing his pad. "I'm not sure the current man in charge is up to any serious police work."

"Lowell asked me to watch out for that boy and to make sure playing chief for a week didn't go to his head."

"I think it's already too late for that. He just tried to arrest me for brandishing a weapon at him." I pointed at the flatware lying abandoned on the ground.

"Well he seems to be too busy chasing litter to worry about arresting you," Myra said as we caught sight of Mitch banging his head against a car bumper as he lunged at the ticketing pad. "Why don't you just call Byron to come get your car and then head on home before he catches up with you."

"I don't want to leave and get in even more trouble."

"I'll have a word with him. He's sure to come into the Stack. Sausage is the special today and he'll want to snag some before Piper runs out." Myra was the most informed person in Sugar Grove. She was the police dispatcher, which put her at even more of an advantage than Piper, news wise, but she also was interested in everyone's life above and beyond the call of duty. It didn't surprise me that she knew Mitch's breakfast preferences. It wouldn't surprise me if she knew which soap the pastor used, or the odds of any couple in town getting a divorce. "Take the cruiser. I'll have Mitch give me a ride back to the station."

"But what will you say?" I appreciated Myra's willingness to help but I didn't want her to fan the flames of trouble with Mitch.

"I'll tell him if he doesn't stop looking for ways to spend time with you, I'll have to tell his new girlfriend, Phoebe, what he has been up to."

"Mitch is seeing Phoebe?" That was music to my ears. A new woman in his life was sure to help keep him out of mine. And Phoebe was a nice person. Probably too nice to be interested in Mitch but I wasn't going to discourage their relationship if it meant he might leave me, and my driving record, alone. I decided if Myra was giving me a way out, there was no reason for me to stay standing outside catching my death of cold waiting for Mitch to come back and run his beefy hands all over me. I asked her to tell Piper what happened, then waved good-bye to Myra and hopped into the cruiser. I drove away as quietly as I could manage. I caught sight of Mitch in the rearview, his ticketing pad finally in his grasp. He was running down the street after me waving the pad and shaking his other fist.

Two

 I parked the cruiser next to the barn and walked along the worn path to the sugarhouse. The sugarhouse sits back near the tree line, away from the main house but not so far enough to be onerous when the snow starts piling up. You never know in New Hampshire if it will snow by Thanksgiving and stay white until past Easter or if you'll still be seeing brown grass after the turn of the year. I couldn't decide how I felt about it either. When the snow came early I felt the inconvenience of it, but when it was late everything looked so bleak and dead. Snow drapes the bare bones of the land in a way that highlights beauty. Dead grass and dry leaves just looked depressing month after month.

I headed into the sugarhouse gift shop to start a pot of coffee. I would want another cup or two if I was going to figure out what was behind all this on so few hours of sleep. I hadn't told Piper that although I had made peace with the relationship between my mother and Lowell, I still had trouble falling asleep. It was one thing to realize they had feelings for each other and that they went on dates. It was quite another to help your mother pack and to spot lingerie in her suitcase that caused you to blush. I don't think of myself as a prude but I don't think of my mother as having a sex life either.

I couldn't even talk to anybody about it. It wasn't as if chatting about something like that with your siblings seemed natural, no matter how close you were with them. And Piper wasn't an option. She had no reservations about any such thing. I once overheard her asking the pastor's wife about what the Bible had to say on the subject of threesomes. When she was explaining it to me later she made it sound like the conversation had started out about the Holy Trinity and had spun out of control from there.

While waiting for the pot to brew I started pacing around the gift shop. I grabbed a feather duster and flicked it over the displays of maple-themed plates and cups, maple leaf shaped napkin holders, and jugs of syrup. As I flicked and swished, an uncomfortable idea began to take root. What if I wasn't the only one to have experienced vandalism because of the cooperative? I hurried to the closet to put away the duster and pelted back down the path to the house.

I needed to talk to someone about my concerns and that person was Grampa. If anyone could tell me if I was overreacting, it was my grandfather. I tore along the back hall and found him, thankfully alone, in the library. Grampa's long beard was serving as a bookmark in a well-thumbed paperback with a Western-themed cover. I never knew what would catch Grampa's fancy in the book department. He was as likely to be caught reading a gothic romantic suspense as he was a snowblower repair manual.

This time, he was dozing. I wasn't sure if his beard got caught as he fell asleep or if he had time to park it in the correct page before nodding off but the result was the same. He was gently snoring away in a wingback chair beside the fieldstone fireplace. The fireplace had been built with stones from our own fields over two hundred years earlier. I sometimes thought about the passing of time and the passing of Greenes through this house when I bothered to slow down and ponder my place in the world every once in a while.

Grampa had been getting in the habit of nodding off more and more frequently lately and it gave me a cold squeeze around my middle to think about him one day being one of the Greenes who had passed on through the house and through my life. After my own father's death five years earlier those things weighed on my mind more than they might have otherwise. I paused in the doorway, unwilling to wake him. I stepped back from the threshold and the floorboards creaked. Grampa's eyelids fluttered open and he twisted his head in my direction, tugging his beard out of the book.

"Sorry to wake you," I said feeling guilty and selfish. Grampa had been up early, too, and I should have thought of that before approaching so loudly.

"Who said anything about sleeping. I was just resting my eyes." He gave me an exaggerated wink, as if to show off how energetic his eyelids now were. "Something I can do for you?"

"Well, since you're awake, there is." I told him about what had happened to the Midget and about the warning gouged into the trunk. "Now I'm wondering if some of the other members have suffered damage, too." Grampa twiddled the end of his beard between his thumb and forefinger.

"You've got to go talk this up with folks in person and find out. I'd start with Tansey because she's a big producer and will be flattered to have been thought of first. Then go over and talk with the Shaws. They'll understand about Tansey but won't appreciate being too far down the list."

"I'll have to stop at Frank's, too, won't I?"

"You will if you think he's the one responsible. He'll bark but he won't bite. And if he decides it has become controversial to become a co-op member, he just might join."

"Not if we're lucky, he won't." Just then Grandma appeared in the doorway.

"Do either of you have any idea why Mitch Reynolds is standing in the kitchen, saying he's here to arrest Dani?" Grandma asked. She sounded calm enough but she was rubbing the jade pendant on her necklace between her fingers like it was a worry stone. My father had given it to her for Mother's Day the year he died and in the years since she had polished it to a satiny gleam with all the rubbing.

"He can't still be mad about the cutlery. Myra said she'd make him see sense."

"He didn't mention flatware but he did say something about stealing a police car." My heart sank. If he was willing to arrest me for pointing a napkin-wrapped butter knife in his direction, what would he do to me for carjacking a cruiser?

"I can explain. Myra let me borrow it just to get home." Grandma shook her head slightly and compressed her lips together a bit. My grandmother may be a law-abiding citizen but she understands that sometimes the letter of the law needs a little work in the penmanship department. She took a deep breath and let it out slowly.

"I can't imagine how it happened but I'm afraid Lowell may have left his coffeepot on when he headed out of town this morning. How about if you drive his cruiser back over to his place and check?" she asked Grampa.

"I was planning to head on into town anyway. There are a few things I wanted to do to get ready for meat bingo tonight."

"I'll send Loden out to follow you in the minivan, just in case you need a lawyer." My older brother, Loden, was primarily a model-train enthusiast but he was also a card-carrying member of the legal profession. So far he had only used his skills on pro bono work for community members who couldn't afford a lawyer. I hoped neither Grampa nor I was going to be responsible for changing that.

"I'll keep Mitch busy with some coffee and a maple cardamom sweet roll while the both of you skedaddle. Dani, you aren't going to be making up any more mischief today are you?"

"Grandma, you know I never mean to make problems."

"I know. But you tend to attract trouble like black pants attract white cat hairs."

January in New Hampshire is no time to be riding around in a car with a busted heater. Pulling into the yard at Tansey Pringle's place drove home just how cold I was. I couldn't feel my legs as I tried to wriggle out of the Clunker. My feet, although wrapped up in a pair of wool socks and a heavy pair of snow boots, felt like two bricks. I hobbled up the porch steps and banged on Tansey's door. No one answered and I should have realized they wouldn't. Tansey wasn't ever to be found in the house during the day.

I traipsed around the side of the barn and on back to the sugarhouse at the rear of the cleared area in her yard. Smoked curled up out of a chimney desperately in need of repointing. A flock of Barred Rock hens waddled over to idly peck at my bootlaces. I knocked twice on the sugarhouse door, then shoved it open. Tansey never stood on formality and if you waited for her to answer, you'd stand around until nightfall. I was surprised to see Tansey with a notebook computer perched in her lap. From the sounds of things she was watching some sort of a video.

"Backwoods Bruce just put up his latest episode." Tansey pointed at the screen.

"Who's that?" I squinted at the small screen and saw what looked like the interior of a bomb shelter.

"The survivalist guy from New Hampshire."

"Never heard of him."

"Never heard of him! Well, you have been missing out for sure. Fortunately all his videos are archived online."

"Is that all he does?" In the video it looked like he was aiming his camera around at a specialty knife and waxing poetic about its superiority to other blades of similar cost. On the back wall of the cabin hung a topographical map of New Hampshire and a vintage vanity license plate declaring GEEZER.

"What he does is inform the public about the best ways to survive off the grid when the government collapses. At my age it doesn't happen too often but I tell you that man lights my overalls on fire." Tansey touched her finger lightly to the screen in what I interpreted to be an affectionate caress. I was both uncomfortable with knowledge concerning Tansey's turn-ons and encouraged by the fact it was still possible to get that worked up at her age. With my romantic life perpetually in the slow lane, I needed all the time I could get.

"His voice sounds funny." And it did. It was sort of mechanical and false.

"He uses a voice changer to protect his identity. The things he shares with the public could get him in trouble with the government and he can't be too careful. He tells the truth about big oil and out-of-control personal spending."

"Are you sure that isn't Frank Lemieux? Sounds like just the sort of thing he would say."

"I've rattled around in this body long enough to know it would not get stirred to carnal thoughts by Frank Lemieux, secret identity or no secret identity. But I know I'd give a year's worth of syrup profits for one date with Backwoods Bruce. They don't make men like that anymore." I didn't know about that. I'd started a slow moving romance with a conservation officer from the New Hampshire Fish and Game Department a couple months back. He was exactly the type of man Tansey was talking about. Minus the kooky ideas.

"That brings me to the reason for my visit."

"Romance? Have you come to your senses and are here to tell me you've decided to marry my son?" Tansey asked me this question every time I saw her. She'd asked it for years. Not that I am all that special. She asks it of my sister as well, even though Celadon is married to someone else already.

"Not today," I said. "I actually came to talk to you about the cooperative." Tansey hit the pause button on the video and shut the computer.

"I'm listening." She pointed at a pair of seedy lawn chairs set in the corner with a milk crate set between them as a coffee table, Tansey's office. She settled down into one and pulled a half-smoked cigarillo out of a rusty soup can and relit it. I wondered if I could somehow reposition the chair upwind of her smoke without offending her but nothing came to mind. I sat and tried not to breathe as I launched into my questions.

"I was wondering if you have had any problems since you said you'd join."

"Well, now you mention it, my knees have been bothering me more than usual."

"That's not exactly the kind of trouble I had in mind."

"I'm sure it wasn't. You never promised it would lower my costs and stave off my arthritis."

"So no troubles of any kind? No harassing phone calls? No one lurking around the farm?"

"What's this about, girl? You're starting to give me the willies."

"Someone vandalized my car this morning. They carved a message protesting the cooperative into the trunk."

"Well, ain't that a shame. Cute little thing it is, too, that car. I expect Knowlton would be happy to give you a lift until you get it repaired."

"Thanks, but I'll manage on my own."

"Suit yourself. But why you'd want to take your life in your hands riding around in something held together by duct tape and wishful thinking instead of Knowlton's truck I'll never understand." And she wouldn't either. Tansey loved her Knowlton like a child loves their favorite blankie. It didn't matter what he looked like or how he smelled, she couldn't see any of his flaws.

"So you're still on board then?" I searched Tansey's face for signs of resistance. She took a deep drag on her cigarillo and blew a smoke ring. I took it as a good sign to continue. "The damage to my car doesn't worry you?"

"I'm not going to let anybody get between me and my discounts. Besides, it was probably just kids letting off a bit of steam while the police chief is away." Tansey stretched out her legs and rubbed her knee much like my grandmother did her pendant. It made me wonder if her knee problems were of her own making. "Unless it was Frank."

"That's what I'm afraid of."

"You ought to be. They never made a tool for tightening that guy's screws." Tansey creaked to her feet and I hopped up as fast as was safe considering the condition of the chair. "Where you headed next?" Tansey asked as we popped out into the brightness of the day.

"I thought I'd speak with Kenneth and then head over to Frank's. I'm sure I won't get to everyone today but I figured since the three of you are the highest-volume producers I'd start with you." It was the truth as well as a bit of calculated flattery. Tansey prided herself on just how much syrup she boiled down each year, even though Kenneth always had quite a bit more. That was the reason I approached her first. She was touchy about how much more he managed to make and I wanted to keep her feathers smooth.

"Are you going to check on Mindy Collins?" I was hoping I could forget about her. Mindy Collins was quickly making herself as popular as turbulence on an airplane. Ever since Pastor Gifford had given her the job of church organist without hearing her play, she had been a burr under the community saddle. More recently she had decided to get into the sugaring business and was making a pain of herself in the process.

Her husband, Russ, was unemployed and had been for months. Mindy had decided to put her property to work for her and to make some much-needed money. Where once she had allowed anyone who wished to to tap maple trees on her property free of charge, now she intended to tap them herself. Several producers were still scrambling to find new sources for sap for the upcoming season.

The sugaring business can be quite lucrative on a good year and Mindy and her small family needed the cash flow. I didn't blame them but then I didn't need her trees. Fortunately my family's farm had more than enough trees to provide us with far more sap than we knew what to do with, even if the ratio of sap to finished syrup was forty gallons to one. People wonder why pure maple syrup is pricey but when I tell them how much sap it takes to produce enough for a stack of fluffy pancakes they seem happier to pay for it.

"I don't see how I can avoid checking on her. I feel obligated to check on everyone who agreed to support the cooperative." My stomach was starting to knot up. Controversy is my least favorite pastime. I don't understand reality TV shows or families that make a hobby of arguing then making up. I don't even understand how lovers' quarrels are supposed to spice up a relationship no matter how many times Piper tries to explain it to me as she's digging into a quart of ice cream, the tears streaming down her face.

"Maybe you'll get lucky and someone will have burned her sugarhouse down. It'd be hard sledding to get a pile of smoldering ashes inspected for a seal of quality by the state." Tansey flicked her own ash onto the dirt path.

"Or maybe she'll be scared off because of her kids."

"Here's hoping." Tansey raised a weathered hand at me in a wave as I slid into the Clunker and backed down the drive.

Kenneth Shaw's operation is about six miles from Tansey's as the crow flies. The weak January sunlight filtering through the grimy windshield halfheartedly warmed the air in the car and I arrived a bit less stiff than I had at Tansey's. Instead of chickens, the Shaws' bulldog, Bingley, careened out to meet me at the sound of the Clunker's muffler. His barking brought Nicole Shaw to her porch before I could open the car door.

"Morning, Dani. How about some coffee?" she asked. I nodded and gave Bingley a scratch behind his ears. I crossed to the porch and wondered how Nicole always managed to have the longest-lasting chrysanthemums of anyone around. That was the Shaw family in a nutshell. The longest-lasting, best-showing, best-producing everything of anything there was to have, do, or be. The Shaws were just that sort of people. The kids were voted most likely to succeed and prom queen or king. Kenneth and Nicole won any position they ran for in local government and they all had naturally straight teeth. Unfortunately they were also inherently likable so you couldn't even hate them for it.

I followed Nicole into a lemon-scented kitchen and wished my boots weren't covered in the dust from Tansey's place. She set a French-press pot on the counter and filled a kettle with water.

"Is Kenneth around?" I asked. "I have a question for him."

"He's in the den pretending to work on his book, I believe. Why don't you head back to talk with him while I finish brewing the coffee." She flashed me one of the smiles Kenneth was known to mention as the reason he married her and waved me away to the other side of the rambling colonial. The Shaws' house had been in the family almost as long as the Greenes' but it had an entirely different character. I walked along the gleaming pumpkin pine floored hall accompanied by an entire line of Shaw men's portraits glaring down at me, each more intimidating than the last. Their upper lips were so stiff you'd think Botox had been invented a few centuries before it actually was. At the end of the hall stood Kenneth's den, or lair as he jokingly put it.

"Come on in," Kenneth called out. I stepped in and looked around. The room always reminded me of a movie set. It looked so much like a country gentleman's office in a period English film it didn't seem real. Every plaid, every stripe, every wall-mounted stuffed duck oozed professional decorator. Kenneth's plaid flannel shirt even coordinated with the wallpaper. Every time I visited I wondered if he bought an entirely new wardrobe as soon as the room had been completed. "Well, Dani, what brings you here this morning?" Kenneth flashed me the smile that helped him win over hundreds of voters through the years. He pointed at a seat in front of the desk and I took it.

"I wondered if anything unusual had been happening around your property."

"What kind of unusual?"

"Vandalism. Odd phone calls. That sort of thing."

"Is this about what happened to your car?" Kenneth leaned back in his chair and tented his fingers.

"You've heard about that already?" Someone sure had been watering the town grapevine with liquid turbo grow.

"As the chairman of the select board I hear about everything sooner or later. I was just about to call your grandfather about this and ask if he felt it was wise to continue with your plans."

"No disrespect sir but my grandfather isn't the one in charge of the maple cooperative. That's why I'm here speaking to you." On the outside I hoped I looked calm and collected, cool as a molded gelatin salad, but on the inside I was quivering like one, too. The cooperative was a way for me to make my mark in the community and, believe me, it hadn't been easy to find some unstaked territory. Not with being the youngest in a family that helped settle the town more than two hundred years earlier. It meant more to me than I wanted to consider, especially as I sat in front of someone who could make it all fall apart.

"It doesn't seem possible you're old enough to drive over here on your own let alone to be running a business but time runs amok once you get past forty-five and you'd best not forget it." I stifled my annoyance at being reminded of my inexperience and youthful appearance. Kenneth Shaw's participation meant the most of anyone's and if he wasn't convinced he should remain in the cooperative, no one else would be either.

"I'll bear that in mind." I took a deep breath to steady myself and steered the conversation back to the point of my visit. "So, about the vandalism, have you experienced any?"

"No, not as of yet. But I am very concerned about this. The community has certain expectations of us. They look to us for an example. I am not sure participating in something that might be dangerous or expensive provides the right sort of guidance. I'll need to consult with Nicole before agreeing to anything. We will need a couple of days to think it over."

"I've already spoken to Tansey and she has agreed to continue her participation. But you go ahead and take all the time you need. The co-op will go ahead if there are enough members to drop the prices on jugs and things. If you want to support it, I'd be glad of your endorsement. If you don't, people will likely think you are nuts but there won't be any hard feelings on my part." I was right about the crazy thing. No one from a dyed-in-the-wool New Hampshire family brags about how much they paid for anything. It would make people think you were touched in the head if they found out you didn't at least wait for a sale or use a coupon. Bragging rights came in the form of telling how little you paid for something, never how much. It was tacky, uppity, and stupid to admit such a thing. If you absolutely could not get out of overpaying, you bemoaned the occasion 'til your deathbed and made a point to besmirch the merchant who dared to ask so much in the first place.

People in New Hampshire go to craft fairs not to buy things so much as to get ideas of what they could whip up more cheaply themselves to give as Christmas gifts. If he hadn't suffered any actual damage to his property, it was going to be difficult for Kenneth to resist the bargain, no matter how much of a show he made of talking it over with his wife before giving me an answer.

"I expect you are planning on questioning Frank about this?" Kenneth dropped his hands and leaned forward, looking like a seagull eyeing a piece of fried dough someone had dropped on the beach. Frank Lemieux had been doing his darndest to make Kenneth's public life a misery for years.

Every time Kenneth ran for an elected post, volunteered on a committee, or even attended a public function as a private citizen, Frank harangued him. It was almost as though they had a past-life rivalry because there didn't seem to be enough time in this one for so much hostility to get stored up. Generally Kenneth seemed to rise above it and that made Frank even more antagonistic. If Frank could be found guilty of something like this, it would be a coup for Kenneth.

"I'm headed over there next." I felt a little queasy just thinking about it but if I wanted to be treated like the person in charge of the sugaring business, I was going to have to take on the bitter jobs as well as the sweet.

Just then Nicole called out that the coffee was ready and Kenneth and I met her in the kitchen. We chitchatted for a few minutes about the likelihood of snow and where they were planning to go on their vacation. That's one of the good things about a tree farm. Nothing to milk, nothing to feed every day.

It's a long-term game not a short one but there is more flexibility for those who want to be stewards of one bit of land while still being able to see some other lands, too. The trees never hold it against you if you leave them to their own devices even years at a time. Of course if you let things slide too long, you have underbrush problems and trees of sorts you don't wish to grow volunteering their presence in the woods. But an annual vacation is something even the best foresters among us could manage. I said good-bye, scratched Bingley's ears, and headed west toward Frank's place on the outskirts of town.

Three

I had saved Frank for last for two reasons. One, he had already sent me packing the week before when I had felt obligated to ask him if he wanted to join the cooperative. He had to be asked because he was one of the primary syrup producers in the county, let alone Sugar Grove, but I had gotten an earful once he heard a state inspection was the entrance requirement. Frank was an antigovernment conspiracy nut. He had scoffed and yelled and given me pitying looks about my naïveté and gullibility but he hadn't thrown me out bodily. I had to believe he wouldn't this time. At least it wasn't a definite. I hoped.

Have you ever seen one of those illustrated storybooks with a drawing of the big bad wolf's house? That was Frank's place they used as the model. For years, before there was a town recycling program, Frank hauled things back from the dump and found ways to justify having them at his house. His house was sided with everything from old license plates to cast-off dryer doors. The entire place had been plumbed with used garden hoses repaired with duct tape when the need arose.

He had a homemade composting toilet that adults wouldn't speak of and kids on the playground whispered about more than how babies were made. While I admired his plans on behalf of the planet, I wasn't entirely sure leaving other people's garbage heaped up throughout the yard was actually a greener option than it sitting around rusting at the dump.

If only Frank's slovenly habits applied to his sugaring, I'd have had no need to visit. But it was one area he had shipshape. As much as people poked fun at Frank for his whacky ideas about JFK and aliens on the grassy knoll no one ever had a disrespectful word to say about his sugaring operation. Not even Kenneth.

Even from inside the Clunker I could hear the shouting. Frank is not an easy person to communicate with under the best of circumstances. I had picked the wrong time altogether if he was angry to begin with. I hadn't seen any other cars in the driveway besides ones driven by Frank and his stepdaughter, Phoebe. As much as Frank was not good to most people, he was good to Phoebe. Her mother died while Phoebe was in elementary school and pretty much everyone in town expected an aunt or grandmother to swoop in and cart her off to be raised by someone with some social skills and a working knowledge of child rearing.

But no one ever came. Phoebe's mother, Iris, had moved to Sugar Grove after her divorce with baby Phoebe in tow. She never really spoke about her family and folks assumed they must not be close. Phoebe stayed in the house on the hill with Frank and grew into a young woman. She was a grade behind Piper and me in school and tended to tag along with us like a little sister. I wasn't as nice to her as I should have been, mostly because, as the youngest in my family, I so rarely had the opportunity to boss anyone else around.

And with Phoebe, you could boss her around. She was sweet and wanted to do whatever anyone asked of her. It was so easy sometimes you almost wanted to provoke a reaction from her. I wasn't always the kindest child and am embarrassed when I think about it now. I've apologized a few times but it never seems to make me feel better, especially since she acts like she doesn't even know what I'm talking about.

But today, from the noises I could hear penetrating all the way into the Clunker, Phoebe was not about to be bossed around. Frank was shouting and, for once, she was giving it right back. The back window that wouldn't close let the sound of their voices in clearly. Whatever was wrong wasn't my business but I didn't want to stay if Frank was going to be even more unreasonable than usual.

"I can't believe you would do something like that. It's my business, too, and you had no right to go making that sort of decision without me." Phoebe's usually pleasant voice was shrill and louder than I had ever heard.

"I don't regret it one bit. That's no way to show appreciation for everything I've taught you." Frank sounded like he did regret something and was being defensive about it.

"That's because I don't appreciate this at all." Phoebe whipped around the side of the shed and came into view. Her blond hair streamed out behind her and I could see her breath puffing out in little bursts in front of her like unspoken words. I lifted a hand to wave but she blew right past like she didn't even see me. Frank was hot on her heels yelling and waving his arms around like he was limbering up for a trapeze act. Phoebe got into her little car and backed down the driveway without another glance at either of us.

I didn't know what to do. I was desperately hoping Frank hadn't spotted me when it became clear he had. He walked over to my window and tapped on it. I kept telling myself that no matter how many acres he had to hide a body in, there was little reason to think he would actually kill me, unless it was from my brain imploding from crazy-talk overload.

"If you're gonna eavesdrop on other people's conversations, you'd be better off rolling the window all the way down."

"I'll keep that in mind for next time," I said as I got out of the car and followed Frank a few yards down the driveway.

"It can't be good news that brings you all the way out here on that rickety piece of imported crap. And I don't expect you came here to listen to me having a bust-up with my little girl." Frank looked down the driveway and in an easier man I would have said he was on the edge of tears. It was a little scary. Scarier even than listening to him yell.

He folded his flannel shirt sleeved arms over his chest, resting them on his belly shelf like a pregnant woman. I took a deep breath and reminded myself if I hurried, I'd be passing the Stack restaurant just in time for lunch. Time to take the plunge and lay on the grease.

"You know it is always good news when I can lay eyes on your gorgeous mug. Give me a twirl and let me take it in." That shut him up. "I'm here to ask a question and before you start, let's get one thing out of the way right now. You aren't going to like it but I would appreciate it if I don't need to report anything rude to my grandfather about how you respond."

"Get on with it then." Frank liked playing cards and he was just barely back from being on the outs with Grampa over an incident that might have been construed as cheating if one played according to Hoyle.

"You haven't by any chance changed your mind about joining the co-op have you?"

"Have you decided to drop the state inspection requirement?" I had decided to make membership dependent on each sugarhouse passing the state's quality-assurance standard. I knew the price for the inspection was affordable and that it would ensure no one was aligning themselves with low-quality producers. Frank had actually looked intrigued about the cooperative until I had mentioned the state inspection.

"No, I have not. I think it is important that even if a producer is small compared to the others they would at least be able to claim equality in some way."

"Didn't your folks ever tell you about the time my father didn't pay for his parking tickets? Haven't you heard what happened to that woman nursing her baby in her own car? What about the cost of them passport cards for getting into Canada now? State inspection, my fat aunt Fanny." He picked up a baby car seat that looked like it might have been at home in a Ford Pinto and hurled it across the rutted cart track he called a driveway and off toward the tree line. I was beginning to wish I'd brought a witness. With a gun. Frank was rumored to have an arsenal of unlicensed and illegally obtained firearms somewhere on the property. He didn't believe in hunting licenses either and his smokehouse was usually busy curing a poached deer or preserving fish he'd decided to reel in without permission.

"Frank, you don't have to participate. This is just like one of those times when people offer me gum even when they know I hate the stuff. They feel like it's polite even though they know I won't say yes. I didn't expect you'd changed your mind but I thought it best to ask."

"You think it was polite to insult me by suggesting

some stranger with a clipboard should poke his nose into my inner sanctum? Into the alchemy that is syrup making? If that's your idea of polite, I'd pay to see you insult someone."

"I meant no offense."

"This place is already crawling with people poking their noses into my business. Just two days ago that damned Mindy whatshername sauntered in here begging me to tell all my secrets to the syrup-making business."

"Did you tell her anything?" Frank made great syrup and acted like there was some secret to his production. He hinted sometimes that it was the higher elevations on the hillside that made it so good. Other times he mentioned the type of wood he used to fuel the evaporator. He even had once suggested the old wooden buckets he used to collect sap imparted a certain special flavor to the sap and thus the finished product. No one took him seriously except himself as far as I knew, but Mindy didn't have any sugaring experience.

"I told her all sorts of things. None of it true but she didn't know that, the damned fool. I'm just afraid she'll keep coming back for more information and I'll never be rid of her. You know how womenfolk are. Always digging their noses into things that aren't their business." He hurled a length of chain close enough to my feet to make the point that he had remembered my gender and didn't approve. The only women he ever had a kind word for were his late wife, Iris, and Phoebe.

"I can take a hint. No more news of the cooperative for you. No joining, no inclusion in the informational mailing list. No invitations to meetings."

"No nuthin'."

"I understand you feel strongly. Which brings me to my next question." I took a deep breath and reminded myself once again that I had wanted to be in charge.

"Someone damaged my car this morning while I was in having breakfast at the Stack."

"What's that got to do with me?" Frank bent down and tossed a piece of galvanized pipe as far as he could throw it.

"An anti-cooperative message was scratched into the new paint job."

"And you think I'd do a thing like that?"

"Considering your attitude toward participating in the co-op, the thought had crossed my mind." He heaved a cinderblock next to the length of chain. It landed with a crack and sent a sizable chunk flying against my shin.

"I've had a thought just cross my mind, too. Beau!" Frank put two fingers in his mouth and whistled. My stomach dropped into my socks and my kneecaps turned into water balloons. Every junkyard needs a guard dog. Beau was on duty at Frank's place.

I started to run for the Clunker even before Beau and his drooling, snapping jaws hurtled into view. Before I could get my second leg safely stowed and the car door shut, Beau had his teeth sunk into my snow boot. I yanked as hard as I could and slid my foot out. Beau landed with a thump on the lumpy driveway, my footwear clutched firmly between his jaws. I pulled the door shut and threw the car into gear.

"I'll send your regards to my grandfather then, shall I?" I called through the crack in the window as I let out the clutch with my stocking foot.

Four

Byron's pants were hitching down and his shirt was hitching up as he bent over the guts of a car he was tinkering on. I've known Byron a long time, both as my mechanic ever since my father died five years ago and also as the town animal control officer. No matter how comfortable he might be with showing off his body, I wasn't comfortable with it at all. I cleared my throat and he stood up so quickly he banged his head on the hood. He must have whacked it just about where the hair on his head gave out and the baldness took over.

"Hey, Dani, you aren't here about the Midget are you?" He stood rubbing the spot on his head. "'Cause you look a bit wild. I know you're gonna want it back as soon as you can get it but I've got some other projects in line ahead of you."

"Nope. Something entirely different." Byron was right. I knew it wasn't even possible but I had hoped to come in and find him putting the finishing touches on a new paint job.

"Good, because I won't have it ready for you for another few days, at least. So what can I do for you?"

"I want you to do something about Frank Lemieux and his dog." My heart rate had slowed to just above normal but just saying so brought the whole thing back to my mind. I could feel my breath becoming shallow and my palms getting clammy.

"Has Beau been a bit playful again?" Byron wiped his hands on a greasy rag and smiled at me.

"He wasn't being playful. He was looking to exercise his jaws. On me."

"He didn't mean anything by it."

"Frank set him on me and he chased me across the yard, into my car, and all the way down to the main road. I don't call that playing."

"He was just fooling around."

"Frank's dog tried to use me as a chew toy."

"See, he was playing." Byron reached out a beefy hand and patted me on the top of the head. At well under five feet tall with freckles and a youthful glow, I have had a lot of people mistake me for a child. But usually they don't go so far as to pat me. Especially not if they actually know me and my real age. Being chased down by a dog was one thing, being patronized by the dogcatcher was another, even if I did trust him with my car. Now my dander was up, even if my height wasn't.

"Are you going to do your job or not?" I peeled his hand off my head and Byron stuck it in the pocket of his coveralls.

"Are you telling me how to do my job?"

"I'd never tell you how to work on a car but as a tax payer I can tell you I am not as happy as I would like to be with the local animal control officer. Why are you so reluctant to do something about this?"

"Did the dog in question keep chasing you after you left its own property?"

"No."

"Did the owner invite you onto the property in the first place?"

"Not exactly."

"Did anyone else see what happened?"

"I don't think so."

"You know I like you, Dani, but there isn't anything I can do. I could waste my time driving up there and giving Frank a warning but he will just tear it up in my face and say the government has no right to tell him what to do on his own land."

"But he can't just do stuff like that. Someone could be seriously hurt. Frank is not just a pain in the butt. He's a whack job."

"You might be right but he has his reasons."

"I think he might have been the one to damage the Midget."

"*No way* he'd do that to a car, especially a vintage one.

Besides, once you get to know him he has some good qualities."

"Name one." I hadn't ever seen anything from Frank to make that sound like Byron hadn't lost his marbles, too.

"He served in the military."

"So did a lot of people."

"He caretakes his land as well as your grandfather."

"I guess that's true."

"And he took care of his wife even though she was actually crazy." I didn't know Iris, his late wife, had been crazy. I knew she didn't get out much and that, Phoebe, never talked about her when we were in school together. It had been a bit odd that Frank, the stepfather, was always the one to come to open house events and school concerts.

"I didn't know that. What was wrong with her?"

"After Phoebe was born Iris fell into postpartum depression. Her husband left her after a couple years and she started having even more trouble. She couldn't bring herself to leave the house. Frank used to do odd jobs and she hired him to deliver firewood and to take her trash to the dump. One thing turned into another and he moved in. They got married a while later and he stayed with her through thick and thin after that."

"I know he and Phoebe are close."

"I almost think he was more invested in Phoebe than he was in Iris. I don't even think you have been more loved than that kid. And that's saying something." It was. With a family like mine there was no danger of not feeling loved at all times, More like feeling smothered by all the love. Stifled and overprotected. Watched with hawk-eyed fervor. But unloved, never. My family was so into giving me love they kept trying to marry me off to expand the love in my life to a whole new level. They were even more frustrated than I about how slowly my romance with Graham was unfolding.

"How do you know all this?"

"Frank's a friend of mine. We sometimes get together and talk over a few beers. I don't like the government in my business any more than he does."

"I had no idea."

"This may be a small town and you may be well connected but you don't know everything that goes on around here." I was about to feel insulted by the implication that I was a busybody when his cell phone rang. After a hurried conversation Byron hung up and grabbed his keys. "I've got to go."

"Someone need a tow?"

"Loose dog that needs rounding up. It might bite someone. Lock up when you leave, would you?" Byron grabbed his uniform jacket from the Sugar Grove Police Department and waved at me as he hurried out the door.

I headed back to the Stack. I had hardly made a dent in my break-fast when Piper had noticed Mitch ticketing the Midget. I was angry, hungry, and worried and needed a cup of coffee. And maybe some fries.

Piper, manning the counter as usual, took one look at me and called out an order of fries and a Reuben club sandwich to the cook in the back.

"Sorry about your car."

"I just can't believe it. Who would do something like that?"

"According to popular opinion, it was Frank."

"I'm not surprised. He was so hateful about the cooperative in the first place. As a matter of fact I went up to see Frank, Tansey, and Kenneth already, trying to do some damage control."

"So how'd it go with the three bears?" Piper was fond of fairy tales and referenced them often. She had storybook-themed tattoos all over her body, including one on her calf depicting the cottage from *Hansel and Gretel*.

"About like I expected. Tansey agreed to continue to participate. Kenneth was cautious and said he needed to consult Nicole. And Frank gave me his grassy knoll/alien speech and sent me packing with the help of his trusty hellhound. I just hope he leaves it at that and doesn't do anything else to rile people up and to make them drop out. The more participants, the better the prices will be for everyone."

"Frank's a wild card. You'll just have to wait and see." Piper popped the lid off a locally produced maple soda and poured it neatly into a glass.

"I'm hoping some other sort of scandal erupts to take his mind off the cooperative. Have you heard anything brewing around town?"

"Burton Cargill spoke up at the last zoning-board meeting and asked about decency ordinances in town."

"You mean like an adult-movie rental business?" I was shocked. Sugar Grove was such a clean-living sort of place I'd expect brown paper wrapped packages to spontaneously combust if they crossed the town line in the back of a mail truck. Who could imagine anyone going to such a place? My grandmother might die of shame just knowing it had been suggested. It would have to be aimed at tourists. Or Mitch. I could picture him stopping in while on duty, ostensibly to ensure no criminal activities were occurring and then confiscating DVDs for so-called quality inspections.

"Nope, a tanning parlor. One of the old ladies spoke up and said people ought not to be allowed to be naked in a public building in town under any circumstances. Should make for a nice piece in the paper don't you think?" Piper wiped the counter down with a vintage crocheted dishcloth from her vast collection. Anytime Piper is able to tear herself away from the restaurant, which isn't often, we'll head out to the nearest flea market, antiques shop, or garage sale for a bit of vintage kitsch buying. Piper has filled the whole place on the cheap with Formica tables, Fire-King mugs, and paint-by-number paintings by visiting the sales.

She lives year-round in a 1950s camper at the campground her parents own, a couple of miles off the highway. It seems like it ought to be drafty and miserable but my brother helped her put up some insulation and installed a propane fireplace. The whole thing is closed up tighter than a new pickle jar. It is cheap to heat, easy to clean, and cute besides. I envy her having her own place. She says I ought to buy a camper of my own and park it next to hers on the adjoining lot like a couple of old widowed sisters. I told her I already have a sister who is enough for one lifetime, maybe two. Still, the idea does have appeal.

"A tanning parlor? That's almost as bad. I think I'd rather have a smutty magazine stand. Those don't cause cancer and wrinkles like a pug. At least I don't think they do."

"Maybe wrinkles around the eyes and between the brows from the astonishment at what's between the covers but not cancer. Not that I've ever heard anyway."

"Although I guess you can't download a tan onto your computer the way you can download a lot of other stuff."

"How would you know about things to download, little miss prim and proper?" Piper asked. I was spared answering by the bell dinging for my sandwich. The cook, Charlie, must have realized it was for me because the sandwich was toasted to the very near side of burnt and a hillock of sweet potato fries threatened to erode right off the plate. Charlie and I agree about the superiority of sweet potato fries to that of any other sort and it has produced a lasting bond between us. Piper clattered the plate onto the long counter and asked a new question.

"So, will you be at meat bingo tomorrow night?"

"Have you heard who else will be there?"

"I will," I heard a voice say from behind me. A nasally

voice pitched just high enough to make you wonder if it was a man or a woman speaking. Knowlton Pringle. I'd been lucky enough to avoid him over at Tansey's since he was a late riser, and was the real reason I had visited her first. Avoiding Knowlton was both a hobby and an art form. He was known to turn up anywhere either my sister or I might be and it really didn't matter which of us he ran into. As far as we could tell from comparing notes, a Greene was a Greene was a Greene to him and he was determined to marry one of us. He hadn't even noticed when Celadon got married to her husband, Clarke. He just went right on pursuing her with the same vigor he had all along. I'm not saying Knowlton is a bad guy, but it is going to take a certain kind of woman to want to spend the rest of her life with him. My guess is a dead one.

Knowlton had been ahead of me by a couple of grades in school and had been in my brother Loden's graduating class. He lives with his mother, Tansey, on the family farm and is an acclaimed local taxidermist. I think his dream girl is probably one who would like to be stuffed and realistically posed after death. Every time he looks at me I can feel him thinking about how best to orient my arms and tilt my chin if he ever had the opportunity. He woke so late because he spends his nights wandering the highways and byways looking for roadkill to stuff. Little kids told each other ghostly stories at sleepovers about Knowlton, the man who wandered in the dark looking for the dead to carry home to his workshop.

He always smelled of something chemically that I secretly hoped was drugs even though I knew it was embalming fluid. Worse still, he stood too close when he talked to you and bent his face within inches of your own. His understanding of personal boundary space was not American in standard and I am not actually sure if it corresponded with any country on earth.

Knowlton has been on my do-not-call list since I was in the second grade. If this were a big city, I'd probably have taken out a restraining order on him years ago but it isn't and doing so would just be awkward. It would essentially mean neither of us could be downtown at the same time without violating it. Besides, his mother was someone I needed to support the cooperative and siccing the police on her son was not likely to inspire trust or participation.

Knowlton brushed past me, his flannel shirt embedded with animal hairs of unidentifiable sorts. I flicked something off my shirtsleeve that he deposited as he passed. Raccoon maybe. Or skunk from the scent wafting off him.

"Will I see you there, Dani?" Knowlton asked, wrapping his arm around my back as he went for the sugar.

"She'll save you a seat, I'm sure," Piper said, winking at him. She winked. She actually winked. I wished just once a creepy guy would turn his attention on Piper instead of all the interesting ones who were fascinated by her. Like the artists, photographers, and writers who made the pilgrimage to her family's campground. Or the nice guys with normal jobs who stopped in for pancakes and coffee and a helping of Piper's smile on their way to work several times each week. Like the road crew guys, the state troopers, and the men who worked at the ski lodge.

"Maybe I could reserve a table for us right near the front, by the ball cage. Nothing goes better with bingo than your best girl."

"I'd do that if I were you, Knowlton. I'd even put a couple of votive candles and a vase of silk flowers on the table for a little ambience." This time her wink was directed at me but I could still feel my sandwich turning to chalk in my mouth at the thought of everyone in town seeing me seated front and center with Knowlton. I never wanted to hurt his feelings; I just didn't want to marry him and nothing but a yes was what he was willing to hear from at least one of us Greene girls.

As a matter of fact, I would be willing to bet my favorite kidney his dream world included a harem containing both of us. I was imagining Celadon and myself in those floaty, floppy pants and midriff-baring tops when Knowlton helped himself to one of my fries. I am reasonable to a fault but I cannot abide fry snatchers. Especially ones I don't like under the best of circumstances.

"Since you use your fingers to stuff dead creatures you had better keep them out of my plate. Grab another fry and I'll cut one of them off." I wrapped my arm around my plate like a prisoner on a chain gang with short rations. Piper ran to the kitchen and returned with a new plate of steaming hot fries to go with my sandwich.

"That's one of the many things I love about you, your

feisty attitude." Knowlton leaned even closer and nudged me with his elbow, digging right into my ribs.

"Can I get a box for this, Piper? Suddenly I have a hankering to get back home." Piper nodded and reached for a compostable takeaway box from under the counter.

"You never said if you'd be at meat bingo."

"I'll think about it. If I'm not too busy getting engaged to Sugar Grove's most eligible bachelor."

"You know I love you, too, don't you?" Piper fluttered her eyelashes at me and it was impossible to stay mad. She looked just like a doll when she did that. Except for the tattoos and the blue mascara.

Five

 Celadon was in the kitchen, her arms elbows deep in dish-
water, a look on her face fierce enough to stop a
zombie in its tracks. The phone was clamped
between her ear and her shoulder and the person on the
other end must have been saying something Celadon
didn't wish to hear. I wished I had listened to the little
voice in my own ear that told me to use the side door
instead of the more frequently used back one. That voice
knows all and every time I don't listen, I regret it. This
was one of those times.

Celadon and I are pretty typical sisters. That is to say,
we love each other but frequently disagree about how to
live life or how to make a meatloaf or even what consti-
tutes appropriate clothing to wear outside of the home.
Tangling with Celadon after being chewed out by Frank

was not my idea of time well spent. I tried sneaking past but she lifted a soapy hand out of the sink and waggled it at me, scattering wrath and bubbles every which way.

Stopping and waiting for her to disconnect was far easier than dealing with her after she had tracked me down. She was always better at hide-and-seek despite my borderline freakishly small size.

"That was Mindy Collins. She was calling to say she wants Hunter to arrive for the camping trip a day earlier than previously planned. She and Luke need his help with some of the preparations before the rest of the squad arrives tomorrow."

"Why?"

"Some sort of emergency."

"Do squirrels have emergencies?"

"They do according to Mindy." Celadon clucked her tongue at her own mess and shot me a look like I was the one responsible for making it. "I need you to run Hunter over to her house. He's already packed so it is not a problem."

"But I'm already going to be late getting to meat bingo."

"I've got four pies in the oven and two cakes crumb-coated in the fridge needing a second layer of frosting. Those are all for meat bingo, too. I don't have time to even argue about this with you, let alone run him all the way to Mindy's and then down into town. You are going to have to take him."

"Where is everyone else?"

"Loden and Grandma have been busy all afternoon with Mitch. For some reason he seems to be looking for you. Grampa is out double-checking the meat inventory. That leaves you. You'd best get on with it or you'll end up standing Graham up."

"What do you mean?" Graham Paterson was the conservation officer I'd started seeing around Thanksgiving, when he had been based in Sugar Grove while rounding up a bunch of exotic animals someone was foolish enough to let loose. We hadn't been able to see much of each other lately since one of the other officers had been out with back surgery, and those ice fisherman weren't going to start policing themselves just to help nudge my love life into the fast lane.

Celadon grilled me daily for updates and was not too pleased with my lack of progress. She had wanted to see an engagement ring on my finger on Christmas Day and had not spoken six words to me until New Year's when one hadn't materialized. Her silence had been my favorite present of the holiday season.

"He called looking for you a couple of hours ago. I told him you would be at meat bingo and might have mentioned Knowlton would be there, too."

"Of course Knowlton will be there. He has a collection of troll dolls and lucky daubers he uses just for meat bingo." Knowlton is one of those people who wins every time he enters a raffle, plays games involving a spinner, or bingo in any of its forms. "What does it have to do with Graham? And what made you think you should stick your nose into my love life again?"

"You mean your lack of a love life? I am just trying to

give it some CPR. Nothing gets a man moving faster than a little competition."

"Were you trying to make Graham jealous? Did you tell him I was interested in Knowlton? You know that is so utterly false."

"What I mentioned was your previous relationship."

"What previous relationship? The one where he chases me and I run away screaming and feeling guilty for hurting his feelings?"

"I saw fit to fill him in on your history of habitual skinny-dipping with Knowlton."

"Being six years old and dunked naked into the same wading pool by your elders after a long day rolling in the dirt at a family picnic does not constitute skinny-dipping. At least not in any sort of a truthful way."

"Truthfulness is not going to help the situation with Graham move on to the next level." Celadon yanked the plug from the sink and scowled at the water sucking down the drain.

"You are altogether too involved in my personal life."

"Because you aren't involved enough." Celadon glanced up at the kitchen clock. "You need to get going if you plan on having time to change out of your work clothes and into something that looks like you are going on a date." Half of me wanted to bolt up the stairs and the other half wanted to drag my size-five feet. Dates were not my specialty and dressing for them certainly wasn't my strong suit.

When you are small enough to be mistaken for a fourth grader most of the time, dressing to attract adult men gets tricky. I'm twenty-seven years old and I still buy most of my clothing in the JC Penney children's department. It's not all bad. They have some really great deals in the clearance section. But it can be difficult to find something slightly sexy and definitely sophisticated in among the printed corduroys and sweaters with cartoon characters knitted into the pattern.

By the time I reached my bedroom I had settled on a pair of black trousers my mother had hemmed up by five inches for me and a black mohair sweater. At least I would be warm. The opera house was notoriously cold and meat bingo wasn't exactly a contact sport. At least not since Coleman Price moved on to that big bingo hall in the sky three winters ago.

I swiped a brush through my shoulder-length hair and slipped my favorite earrings into my lobes. A dab of lip gloss and I was about as ready as I was going to be. I wasn't too worried. Graham had seen me in a whole lot worse and no one in town would be dressing up too much for bingo. Or anything else for that matter. It's hard to find formal wear that goes well with snow boots.

I called out for Hunter and we hit the road. Even though I felt rushed, it was always a treat to go anywhere with Hunter. He's a great conversationalist and he thinks my jokes are funny. A lot of times people think we're siblings, considering how alike we look with our sandy hair and blue eyes, not to mention our height. Hunter may be only eight years old, but he's just a little less than a head shorter than me.

The plow had been by earlier in the day, winging back the snowbanks. Seeing over the steering wheel is a challenge for me. Double-high snowbanks were more than I could manage. Taking our lives in my hands, I was secure in the knowledge that if I got the both of us killed, Celadon would make it her business to scrawl ugly things in permanent marker on my headstone every Memorial Day.

No one was on the road and we reached Mindy's house without incident, covering the six miles in just under half an hour. On the way over I reminded myself that the right thing to do would be to ask Mindy if her family had experienced any vandalism. I really didn't want to. If you started talking to Mindy, it was a guarantee that you would be trapped for at least an hour. You just couldn't get away. And time was tight enough as it was without that. Besides, I told myself, if neither Tansey nor Kenneth had had any problems I couldn't imagine why Mindy would have. She was only just starting out in the business and had basically nothing to vandalize.

The walkway to the back door was shoveled out only about six inches wide. Even my feet had trouble getting through. If that was the Collins family's idea of a job well done, I had serious doubts about their ability to run a successful sugaring operation. All that sap doesn't just hop out of the trees and into jugs with price tags affixed. In response to our knock, Luke, Mindy's son and Hunter's best friend, answered the door, a gap-toothed grin spreading across his face. He tugged the door wide to reveal his siblings bouncing on the mismatched couches and spilling drinks on the shag carpeting. Mindy waved at me from the doorway to the kitchen.

"Dani, just the person I wanted to see. Are you still dating that game warden?" Everyone in town asked me the same question when they saw me. The reasons for each were different. Some people wanted to know because they genuinely liked Graham and wanted him to show up at events in town. They thought he provided a fresh face and pleasing personality to the mix. Others, like Tansey Pringle, hoped we weren't, so I could get back down to the business of letting Knowlton sweep me off my feet and onto a marital bed. Tansey was itching for wedded bliss for her only child so badly I wanted to pour calamine lotion over her head every time I saw her.

But many people asked because they thought my relationship, such as it was, with a conservation officer somehow made me an expert on all things wild and woolly. Or feathered. Or finned. As long as it was outdoors and remained free of domestication, a lot of folks thought the knowledge of its mysteries would have rubbed off on me over a couple of dinners, three movies, and six cups of coffee at the Stack Shack. Not that I was counting. I was betting Mindy was one of those people since she had never shown any interest in my love life before.

"We see each other when we can. As a matter of fact, I'm supposed to catch up with him over at meat bingo just as soon as I am done here." Maybe she would take the hint that I was trying to lay the groundwork for a speedy exit.

"Great. Could you do me a favor and ask him if he will come with the Squirrel Squad on our camping trip tomorrow? Russ threw his back out and can't help." Russ was always laid up in some way or another. I suppose that could have explained the shoddy job with the shoveling. It was also more than likely the reason he was having such a hard time getting a new job nearby. People in Sugar Grove were never too impressed with slackers. Russ had a well-established reputation as someone who wore slip-on shoes because he couldn't be bothered to work up the necessary effort needed for the kind that tied.

"That's too bad. Did he wrench it shoveling you out?" Mindy shook her head gently, a wistful look flitting across her face.

"No. He was bent over funny reaching for a beer in the back of the fridge. I came in carrying the groceries and found him slumped there with the fridge still hanging open. He said he'd been like that for a couple of hours. I guess he must have been there a while because he had managed to finish the beer, a half-gallon of milk, and two jars of jam. I had to head back to the store to replenish the supplies. He's been in bed ever since."

"Sounds rough. I can ask Graham if he would like to participate but I can't guarantee he'll even be available." I sort of hoped if he had time on his hands to spare, he would be wanting to spend some of it with me instead of a dozen kids but I didn't think Mindy and I were likely to share that wish.

"I would have thought you would have some ways of coercing him into doing whatever you asked." Mindy leaned in and winked at me. "That's how I get so much done around here." Mindy waved her plump arm like a game-show hostess pointing out the prizes. I looked around the room, at the walls with the paper half stripped, the bare bulbs hanging from the ceiling, and the television cabinet still in pieces next to a cardboard box and set of instructions.

I wondered if she was joking but I had never noticed humor being one of the senses Mindy possessed. From the look of things no one was going to be asking Mindy to write an updated version of *The Joy of Sex*. And I was a little shocked to hear such a thing from the church organist. I thought about tattling on her to Pastor Gifford just to try to get her to stop playing the organ. But I thought better of it. My grandmother always said while we knew the streets in heaven were paved with gold, no one knew if the street signs said things like Tattlers Row and what a shame it would be to have an address like that for all eternity.

"I'm not sure our relationship is at that point."

"Well then just do your best. I'm sure you'll think of something to convince him. If you're shy or need a few tips, just call the house. Either Russ or I could help you out." I couldn't imagine a world in which I asked a married man for advice about the sorts of things she was implying. My brain fogged over and my mouth flapped open and shut like a fish on a dock. Mindy misinterpreted my response. "Oh now don't get yourself all worked up being grateful; we'd be happy to help." She patted my arm and I felt contaminated, like I might have contracted moral leprosy. I heard myself promising to ask Graham to chaperone the kids just to change the subject and to make my escape.

Six

Meat bingo was being held in the opera house instead of the Grange because the Opera House Restoration Committee wanted the community to get a gander at what it was they were trying to restore. My grandparents, Celadon, and myself had all spent hours at the historical society and in the attics of various longtime townspeople uncovering photographs from when the opera house had been in its heyday. The opera house makes up the top floor of the town hall. Opera houses dot New England like alpacas. We have them but you won't find them everywhere. And anytime you do it feels special and nice.

A mill owner built the Sugar Grove Opera House in 1893 as a way to celebrate culture and the arts. In the intervening years, with the rise in popularity of other forms of entertainment and the decline of the mills, the beautiful old building, once a point of pride in the town, had fallen into disrepair. The clock in the tower still rang out the time because of a generous donation by the Greene family.

Some of that generous donation had come in the form of child labor provided by yours truly the summer before my freshman year of high school. Grampa had me working away with him in the guts of the clock room tidying up after the clock repairman and running up and down the stairs for endless cups of coffee and pastries from the Stack.

The only way I had finally gotten out of it was when I reported to Grandma I had found the repairman with his fly down and his tackle on display, relieving himself through the ventilation shaft in the tower of some of the cups of coffee I had fetched. Grampa was all for me continuing my work as I was sure to have seen similar things and worse from the bull he had in the back pasture. Grandma, however, said she would be fetching the coffee from then on. I'm not sure what she said to him but before the end of the week the repairman had finished the job he had spent two months fiddling around with.

Despite our history, I gave the clock tower an affectionate glance as I approached the building's heavy oak double doors with their time-smoothed brass handles. I climbed the stairs to the large space, thinking of all the shows and pleasant evenings that must have been enjoyed here in the past. Now most of the theater seats with their faded velvet upholstery worn smooth, have been removed from their rows facing the stage. Tonight they stood pressed against the walls, awaiting repair. This made room for the folding tables and chairs necessary for competitive bingo playing.

Often times the opera house is so empty it's creepy. Your imagination runs away with you and you start seeing shadows dart across the scuffed oak floorboards and hear rustling from behind the tattered curtains up on the stage that seems otherworldly in origin. Before you know it your heart is pounding around in your chest and sweat runs down your arms until your hands become slick.

But this evening the room was full of noise and hurried movement of a purely normal kind. If you can consider it normal for people to converge on a public place for the chance to win prizes of meat when they spell out *bingo*. The Opera House Restoration Committee sold bingo cards for a suggested donation at the door and the winners took home butcher paper wrapped packets of beef, pork, chicken, and venison. Everything was legal and above board and no one had to fuss with the state over gaming regulations.

It was a win-win and one of the most popular events in town. I searched around the room for Graham and spotted him deep in conversation with Tansey Pringle, the future paternal grandmother of my children, if Tansey had any influence with God. I generally did my best to avoid Tansey outside of our business dealings but Graham waved me over and I didn't want him to think I wasn't happy to see him. I crossed the room to the table where they stood.

"Hello, Dani. It's great to see you." Graham took a step closer to me and I wondered if he was about to embark on a public display of affection. I could hear the entire room suck in their breath at the same time and stare. I was surprised that my own thoughts bounced rapidly back and forth at that moment. Did I want him to kiss or embrace me in front of the entire town? Or would I rather we kept up the pretense that our business was private? Unfortunately any thoughts Graham may have had about his plans were driven off by the arrival of Knowlton.

"Hey, Graham, shouldn't you be out busting speeders on snowmobiles instead of in here slacking?" Knowlton and Graham had gotten along fine back around Thanksgiving. That was when Graham was in town for business not pleasure. But now that Knowlton viewed Graham as competition, things had gotten a bit frosty between them. At least on Knowlton's part. I wasn't sure how Graham felt and didn't think I had the guts or the right to inquire. It made things awkward every time they met up.

"Well, I've only managed to put in eighty-three hours so far this week but the opera house seemed like such a worthy cause I decided to take a night off. And the company was too appealing to pass up." Graham gave me a smile and moved in even closer. I held my breath and braced myself for impact. Which turned out to be Knowlton. He wrapped his slim fingers around my even slimmer upper arm and pulled me toward him.

"Dani, take a look at my newest troll doll. Now I'll be unbeatable." Knowlton was justifiably proud of his bingo winnings, raffle winnings, and ability to be the correct caller on any radio station contest he dialed in to. He was legendary in this narrow slice of life and it had gone to his head.

"I hope it brings you luck." I had to be polite. My grandparents were the meat bingo organizers and Knowlton was one of the most dependable donors. I got out of having to say anything else because Grampa was up at the podium clearing his throat into the microphone.

"If you could all grab a seat, we'll get started here pretty quick-like," he said. There was a scrambling and a hasty set up of troll doll altars and ceremonial dauber placement, at least by Knowlton. People spread out three, four, and even five cards in front of them and stared expectantly at the stage, where Grampa was polishing the bingo cage with a spotted handkerchief.

"We have a whole truckload of special things in store for you all this evening, with one outstanding offer amongst all the others." Grampa could afford to say this because he and Grandma donated all the meat to the event with one exception. "Piper has generously donated her Stack Shack specialty sausage. She's even offered to cook it right at the Stack if you win it." She had done the same thing for the last meat bingo session a few months earlier and the opera house committee had to hurry into the town office to print out extra cards because they sold out with people still in line. Grampa gave the cage a spin and the games began.

Knowlton did his good-luck troll doll pats and knuckle-cracking exercises and, unlike everyone else in the hall, he remained standing above his cards. I guess he wanted to stay light on his feet in order to maximize his chances of shouting out *bingo* before anyone else. The letters and numbers rang out in Grampa's clear, deep voice and cards were filling faster than a dirt basement during spring snowmelt. Some people, like Graham and I, were chatting but most were focused completely on the cards before them. All around pork roasts, racks of ribs, coils of kielbasa, and pounds of hamburg went to happy winners, an inordinate number of times to Knowlton.

As much as Knowlton is not someone I want to marry or even to have an extended conversation with under most circumstances, he does have some admirable qualities. I happened to know there were a great number of people who were better off for Knowlton's lucky streak. He and Tansey didn't eat a whole lot of meat themselves since there were only two of them. What most people didn't realize every time they groaned about Knowlton winning again was that he donated almost everything he won to the local food pantry. He just loved to win. He had almost no interest in the prizes at all. He didn't care about the tickets he won to concerts or to water parks in the lower tier of the state. He didn't need his oil burner cleaned or his windows washed. He just liked to feel like a winner sometimes, and who could blame him?

Finally after all the other packages were parceled out to good homes it was time for the sausage. Grampa announced a break before the last event of the night. People stood and stretched their legs and headed for the bathroom. I met up with Celadon as she was coming out of the ladies room and I was headed in.

"Did you get Hunter over to Mindy's?"

"Yes, I did." I decided not to mention Mindy's request about the camping trip. She would probably hear about it soon enough and I wanted to sort it out myself without any interference from her.

"I saw Knowlton over there with you and Graham before Grampa started calling the numbers. Did Graham seem jealous?" Celadon had her innocent look plastered across her face so I knew there was more to her question than mere curiosity.

"Knowlton made a beeline for us and clamored for my attention. I think he was more jealous than Graham."

"Well, I think that says a lot. I like Graham just fine but Knowlton has been all over the mere thought of you since your first breath. This new guy is traveling toward the matrimonial finish line slower than an arthritic snail crossing a spool of copper flashing. Maybe Knowlton should get a little more respect from you for his faithfulness."

"Stay out of it, Celadon. I mean it. If you don't butt out, I'll tell Mom there's something off about your aura and she'll put you on that celery diet again."

"You don't mean that." Celadon winced like she'd bitten her tongue.

"I do mean it and I will do it if I have to."

"Don't let me stop you from getting back to your dates."

"I think you meant *date*."

"I know exactly what I meant." Celadon turned on her heel and marched back toward the main room with her nose in the air and out of joint. I had a sneaking suspicion she had given Knowlton a similar line of incentive over the phone about my attendance at bingo as she had given Graham.

Even though the clunking of the plumbing system was enough to leave you deaf, I hid out in the bathroom for as long as I dared. I was stalling for time, trying to decide on the best words to use to ask Graham about the camping trip. I still hadn't come up with anything when I decided I was being ridiculous risking the loss of my hearing. I did what I had come in for in the first place and returned to the main room, surprised to see the folding tables used for the bingo cards rearranged in a whole new way.

The tables were lined up on two sides of the room, with Knowlton standing behind one set and Graham behind the other. Cards covered all available space. Knowlton was handing out his daubers to everyone in arm's reach. His collection was extensive and he remained convinced special daubers contributed as much to his luck as the troll dolls and ritualistic rubbing ever would.

Graham, on the other hand, had inspired pity among other members of the bingo brigade. They had lined up behind his table with advice and daubers of their own.

"What's going on here?" I asked Myra Phelps. Myra may have taken the night off from her police dispatch duties but she was never out of gossip mode.

"Your grandfather announced that you love Piper's sausage so much that you would probably follow the winner home and sit on their doorstep until they felt sorry for you and let you in to sample the goods."

"He what?" I felt my face flush and my flight-not-fight impulse swell up inside me.

"He sure did. I can't believe you didn't hear him."

"I was in the bathroom"

"That explains it."

"But that doesn't explain what happened to the tables. And the bingo competitors."

"Everybody bought out all the available cards. As a matter of fact your grandmother ran down to the town office and printed off a few dozen extras. Then everyone gave them to either Graham or Knowlton. There are far too many for them to keep track of themselves so everyone has chosen a favorite and is helping to mark them."

"They didn't." This was humiliating. It was one thing for your own family to get themselves tangled up in your love life, but for the majority of the town to weigh in as well was too darn much.

"They did. And I happen to know Bob Sterling is in charge of a side-bet pool. But don't go getting all worked up. It's all in good fun and the winnings will be split fifty-fifty with the opera house fund.

"I can't believe this." I couldn't but it was instructive. It was clear to see where everyone stood on the issue of my love life and whether they were on Team Knowlton or Team Graham. Myra finished talking to me and went over to join Tansey at Knowlton's table near Celadon and Pastor Gifford's wife, Lisette. Loden, Roland Chick, and Phoebe, stood near Graham. My grandmother wisely kept out of the fray. Grampa did his best to stir things up from the stage.

I headed over to where Bob, the only full-time EMT on the ambulance squad, was deep into a transaction with Dean Hayes. By spring Piper will have cast him off like an Icelandic sweater in a heat wave but for now they were a hot item. Why no one spent their time trying to get Piper married off instead of me I'll never understand. She's eligible, attractive, and runs her own business. She also might pay a contract killer to handle anyone who would meddle in her life the way people delighted in stomping around in mine. At least that was the kind of vibe my heavily tattooed, pierced, and purple-haired friend gave off and this probably explained the difference in how we were treated.

As soon as I approached, the two men stopped talking like little boys caught chatting during a spelling test. "So what's it that you two are talking about while everyone else is lining up the cards?" I noticed Bob slipping a wad of bills into his pocket.

"Dean was just asking me about the lawsuit I'm bringing against Frank Lemieux." Well, I expected him to fib but I didn't expect it to be something like that.

"What lawsuit?"

"He's taken over part of my property that adjoins his. He's planning on tapping it and he says it was his all

73

along. I have the place on the market and his behavior is ruining my sales potential," Bob said.

"What kind of behavior?" Frank would be intimidating if he took a notion to confront a potential buyer. I could see why Bob might be upset.

"I mean I hired a surveyor to come out and clear things up once and for all and he ran the guy off with a shotgun."

"So you filed a lawsuit?"

"What else can I do? I called the police but I didn't feel like it was enough. I've had a bunch of different hot prospects look at the place and then go on to buy something else. When I asked my Realtor why he said the buyers told him the guy next door threatened them and painted a clear picture of what he would do to dogs, adults, and kids that trespassed onto his property. There is only so much a man can take before he has to get serious about stopping a problem."

"I can see your point. I wouldn't want to be you."

"No one does. That's why I can't find a buyer."

"And that's the only thing you were talking about? I thought I saw you smiling, heard you laughing. I might have even seen a flash of cash changing hands. Did you just hire Dean to be your lawyer?"

"Oh look at that. Your grandfather's spinning the cage again."

Sure enough he was. The sound of the balls rattling got everyone's attention. Grampa asked if the crowd was up for a full-card session instead of just simple bingo.

"I am if you are. My luck's great no matter how we play," Knowlton said.

"I was never someone who thought they had too much luck until I ended up in Sugar Grove," Graham said. "But I feel like when I'm here I'm the luckiest guy around. So bring it on." He gave Grampa a little salute and nodded to Knowlton.

Grampa called number after number over the noise of the crowd. People shouted out "Got it" from all around the hall. Daubers were dabbing and people were giggling and I hadn't seen so much animation in the crowd in a very long time. Probably not since the shouting match at the town meeting the year Merton Spinks proposed we hire a woodchuck he discovered living under his front porch and whom he called Leon as the town administrator. Merton announced it couldn't do a worse job than the guy who had been occupying the position for the last four years. His comments had caused an animated debate and a lot of laughter.

Cards filled up fast and I could have sworn I saw smoke floating up from the bingo ball cage. Knowlton's breath came in small pants and every time one of Graham's rows filled across he yanked on the hair of the nearest troll doll. I felt sort of sorry for the little thing and wondered if it would be forced into an early retirement if he managed to snatch it bald. I wasn't sure but I guessed from Knowlton's patting that all the luck must be in the hair.

And then, when it was neck and neck with only one

blank space each for Knowlton and for Graham, it was over. Graham sprang up on the very tips of his toes, then sank back down, leaned right up next to my ear and whispered, "I'd be happy to share my sausage with you anytime." I was so flustered I heard myself speaking before I thought it through.

"Do you want to go camping?" There, I'd said it. I felt better until I realized I hadn't been specific about the details and who wanted him to camp. I felt myself blushing as I considered how his shared-sausage comment might pair up with a request for a sleepover. I felt like I had leapfrogged us over a whole bunch of dates and landed myself into a place that was much more forward than I had intended. I knew he was surprised by the way his eyes widened and then he stood up so straight it was like someone strapped jumper cables to his feet.

Before he got a chance to respond the crowd surged in between us. Graham's back must have been stinging from all the good-natured slapping it was enduring. I caught a glimpse of Knowlton slinking out the door. Tansey hurried after him carrying a box of his forgotten daubers and troll dolls.

I decided to wait for the crowd to die down before attempting to explain the camping invitation to Graham. It took quite a while, especially since most people were taking their sweet time heading home. I'd be willing to bet an acre of prime sugar bush that they were hoping to eavesdrop on our conversation. I would have waited for him in the parking lot but I was afraid Knowlton might be waiting there, too. He had looked so dejected leaving I didn't trust myself not to agree to a date just because I felt so sorry for him. Finally the crowd thinned to just those people involved in the cleanup effort. Graham crossed the room, a paper packet of sausage in his hand and a grin on his face.

"So about this camping trip," he said. "When did you want to go?"

"I don't."

"Has something happened to change your mind in the last fifteen minutes?" The grin left his face like it had never even thought about being there. In that moment I disliked Mindy Collins even more than I had when she was offering advice about my sex life.

"I think you misunderstood me and that's definitely my fault. I was actually inviting you on behalf of my nephew's Squirrel Squad leader. She needs another adult for the overnight winter camping trip tomorrow night. She asked me this evening to find out if you would be willing to help out." I could tell from the look on Graham's face that he was both disappointed and trying not to show it. It was a little flattering.

"I see. Tomorrow?"

"Yes. I totally understand if you aren't free or even if you don't want to do it."

"What time?"

"The kids arrive sometime after lunch at the Collins's place."

"I'll do it." The grin was back in full force.

"Are you sure?" All of a sudden it occurred to me that Mindy might take it upon herself to make the same offer of seduction education to Graham that she had to me. I wasn't sure I wanted him anywhere near her.

"I'm sure. I love camping, I'm free tomorrow, and I like your nephew."

"I'm sorry if I gave you the wrong impression."

"You can make it up to me."

"What did you have in mind?" My stomach fluttered and thrashed and generally made a nuisance of itself. I was torn between wanting to know what he would say and dashing out the door and down the steps before he could squeak a word out.

"I'm sure I'll think of something." Graham pointed his packet of sausage at me, gave me a light peck on the top of my head, and strode out the door.

Seven

Saturday morning breakfast at Greener Pastures is a thing of beauty. On weekdays we eat well. There is no shortage of home-baked goods and oatmeal or eggs. Sometimes someone even makes bacon and if you are up early enough, there will still be some when you get to the table. When we were all growing up, weekdays were school days and there just wasn't enough time to do breakfast justice. So Saturday was set aside as *the* day for life's most important meal.

Everyone gets to the table by eight with the sort of attitude generally reserved for religious occasions. Reverence is what Grandma's breakfasts bring out in the family when she has time to unleash her full culinary skill set. Her own mother, who was the cook for a logging camp as a young bride, had taught Grandma the way round the kitchen. Which meant she was taught to make everything from scratch and in generous amounts.

Considering how good a cook my grandmother is, the quantities manage to disappear no matter how much she churns out. When we were all teenagers Grandma baked at least three loaves of bread each day. The breakfast menu is always a surprise since Grandma didn't even know herself what she would want to create until she woke up that morning. So it was with eager anticipation I trotted to the warm and cozy kitchen and poured myself a cup of strong coffee. Stirring in a glug of maple syrup and a generous splash of cream, I asked if there was any way I could help.

Grandma may be a whiz in the kitchen but she is a teacher at heart. Every one of us is adept at whipping up a sit-down meal for forty. Well, maybe not the kids, just yet. Grandma starts in early teaching whoever is new to the family how to bake beans, frost a cake, or season a stew. Grandma believes everyone should know how to cook for themselves even if she prefers to do it for them. She's fond of mentioning that when she teaches one of us something her mother taught her, it makes her feel like her mother is still with us.

I know just what she means because I feel the same about sugar making. I can't remember a time when I didn't help in at least a small way during sugaring season. As soon as I was walking, my father would take me with him and point out his favorite trees. Which ones were the best producers, which ones needed the attention of an arborist. He showed me how to tap, how to boil sap down, and, most important, how to be a good steward of the patch of land we influenced. Every time I taste Greener Pastures syrup it is like he's still out there. Like I might just spot him weaving through the trees, running his hands over the bark on one, leaning up against another.

"No, you just sit yourself down and get ready to tuck in." Grandma waved a potholder at me and opened the oven door. A sugary, bready smell wafted out as Grandma attempted to hoist an oversized cast-iron skillet from its depths. Loden shot to his feet and took over.

"You just tell me where you want it and I'll move this to the table." He gave her one of the smiles I keep hoping will win Piper over and Grandma didn't make even the slightest protest. Celadon slipped into the room just as the pan reached the maple leaf shaped trivet and Spring followed in her wake, dragging her favorite blanket behind her. Grampa brought up the rear and took his place at the table, tucking a checked napkin into the neck of his shirt.

"Well, Olive, tell us how you've outdone yourself this morning." He rubbed his hands together and grinned.

"It's an experiment. I've made a version of those Dutch apple pancakes you all like so much." A cheer went up from the table. Grandma's apple pancakes were a thing of beauty. Puffy and eggy, with just the right balance between the tartness of the apple, the sweetness of the sugar, and the richness of the butter it made me want to tear up. But I didn't. I saved my energy for wrangling an extra piece. It was strange not to see my mother or Hunter at the table but it meant there would be more for the rest of us and that promised to be a good thing with Grandma womaning the stove.

Grandma wiped her hands on her vintage floral apron, moved to the table, and sliced into the pancake, dishing up heaping servings onto empty plates. I cut into mine with the side of my fork. I gave an appreciative sniff before popping a bite into my watering mouth. The apples I expected were replaced by sliced peaches. And nutmeg. The sweet flavor of brown sugar and the silkiness of butter in the sauce cascaded over the fruit.

I took a second bite and more nutmeg, stirred into the batter before baking, met my taste buds. I had never been so glad that my family was smaller on this particular Saturday than I was at that moment. I'm sure, eventually, I would miss my mother and nephew but with a breakfast like this one it was hard to imagine I'd regret their absence anytime soon.

I cleaned my plate and served myself seconds. I sometimes wish that I needed to watch my girlish figure or that my figure might have the hope of ever being something other than girlish but today was not one of those days. Today was about a super metabolism. I closed my eyes in order to better enjoy what was going into my mouth. Things were perfect. Until Celadon added her two cents.

"You know what would go perfectly with these? Those sausages Graham won last night at the meat bingo." I slowly squeaked open one eye and gave her a dirty look with it. She didn't seem to notice. "Any chance he's going to be traipsing down the stairs to join us for breakfast?"

"Celadon, don't tease your sister like that. She'll get around to managing Graham's sausage in her own time." Grandma gave me a tight smile and I wanted to drop through the floor. Loden started choking on a bit of pancake and all I could do was be grateful my mother wasn't here to contribute to the conversation. She would be sure to explain the innuendo to Spring, just in case, as a six-year-old, she managed to miss it.

"I'm just suggesting Graham seems like a great catch and that they looked pretty cozy last night. I thought maybe we might start planning a June wedding if Dani would find a way to turn on some more charm." Even caramelized peaches can turn to dust in your mouth given the right circumstances. I swallowed a swig of coffee to clear my palate.

Before I could say anything else the phone on the wall rang and I jumped up to answer it. I wondered who could be calling so early and then worried it was my mother and her psychic sense on the other end of the line eager to add her long-distance thoughts to the conversation.

"Dani, it's Jill Hayes. I was hoping you could come on out to my place this morning to take a look at something." Jill sounded angry. Her voice was pitched higher than usual and she was speaking so fast she sounded like she must have completed an auctioneering course.

"Sure. When did you want me?"

"Now." I looked around the table and noticed with

some regret the speed with which the pancake was disappearing. I also noticed the faces of the family gently leaning in my direction, their ears flapping and their eyes shining. I needed space more than I needed extra carbs.

"I'll be right over as soon as I dress my feet." I rang off and headed for Grandma to kiss her on the top of the head.

"Please tell me it was Graham calling," Celadon said. Our father always said she had a one-track mind once she was onto an idea. She wasn't going to let it drop until she got her way. Celadon had managed to get the school cafeteria to switch to locally sourced, organic food. She had started a program to provide transportation for seniors in town who could no longer drive and she had spearheaded a rails-to-trails program that turned miles of disused train track into hiking and biking paths. Now it seemed the entirety of her laserlike focus was on my marriage prospects. I was done for if I didn't steer clear of her to the best of my ability.

"Jill Hayes. She wants me to look at something up at her place."

"While you're out would you stop in at the hardware store and pick up some birdseed? We're almost out." Grampa took bird feeding seriously. He was like some people are about gas in their cars. When the seed barrel got half-empty he filled it up because you never knew what could happen. As far as I remembered we had never experienced a birdseed emergency at Greener Pastures but that might have been because of Grampa's careful planning.

Besides, that's what family is about right? Helping with the priorities of your loved ones even if they are not your own.

"Sure thing." I waved at them and dashed for the mudroom. It wasn't muddy or raining but I stuffed my feet into my rain boots because they didn't need tying and dashed out the door clutching the keys to the Clunker in my sweaty fist.

The road up to Jill's place offered a long look out over the town. Sugar Grove is quintessential New England. The roads wind, the river runs, the white church steeples stretch high above any other structures. Even at this time of year, when snowbanks were growing as fast as teenage boys, it looked beautiful to me. A gray squirrel skittered across a bare limb of a towering oak at the roadside. It would have been a lovely drive in the Midget. In the Clunker, it was something else.

In a lot of families kids end up with their car privileges suspended if they have done something wrong. That was never the case in my family. My mother decided early on that parenting a teenager who could drive him or herself to after-school activities and out on errands was a whole lot more convenient than parenting the non-driving kind. She saw no reason to punish herself because her kids' report cards or ability to make curfew was unsatisfactory. So instead of taking away car privileges, kids in trouble had to drive the Clunker.

It was easily the ugliest car in town, with its mismatched doors, bald spots in the upholstery, and a predominant paint color best described as earwax. It started on the first try only half the time, one window wouldn't roll up, and the heater never worked. Not that you'd want it to. At some point a skunk had sprayed while positioned just in front of the open window and had soaked the upholstery. Even after all these years, even with all the windows down in the summer, it was hard to sit in the thing. Just thinking about what it would have been like in winter with the windows mostly closed and the heater blasting made me want to gag.

And the worst thing of all about driving the Clunker was that it served as a general announcement around town that you were in trouble. My mother had gone ahead and spread the word to everyone she bumped into about Loden's unusual transport the first time he was sentenced to drive it. From then on part of your punishment was the public knowledge of your private business. I thought again about the person who had attacked my Midget and I didn't need the heater to get all warmed up.

Jill's place was on the outskirts of town and it took a good fifteen minutes to reach it. Jill was standing in the yard waiting for me when I pulled up. She looked about how she had sounded on the phone, hot and bothered, despite snow covering the ground. She didn't stop pacing even when I got out and slammed the Clunker's door.

"I think your cooperative idea is causing me a bunch of trouble." Jill crossed her arms over her chest as if to emphasize her words.

"Has something happened?" I felt sick to my stomach. Yesterday I had been angry about the damage to my car but also relieved no one else associated with the cooperative seemed to be experiencing problems. Maybe I had been too quick to set my fears aside.

"Follow me." Jill took off for her sugar bush, which is what sugar makers call their stands of sugar maples. I struggled to keep up. Jill's legs were longer than mine and she was fueled by rage. She was a hard act to follow but I managed to keep her in sight until she stopped abruptly near a magnificent old maple. I stopped next to her and looked where she was pointing. What I saw yanked a gasp out of me like one from a rescued drowning victim. Tears filled my eyes and I understood her anger completely.

"Girdled. And it isn't the only one." Jill's hands trembled as she stuck them into her pockets. I couldn't believe someone had done such a thing. The trunk of the maple in front of me was more than two feet in diameter. Someone had deliberately removed a four-inch wide strip of bark in a ring that completely encircled the tree.

Bark is more than a passive outer layer on a tree. It is the nutrient delivery system for the entire entity. If a tree has been girdled, as this one had, it could no longer use the pathways in the layers of the bark to move nutrients up from the roots to the rest of the organism. Someone had deliberately set out to kill that tree and was most likely going to succeed in doing so. Bridge grafting might save it but it was a lot of work and there were no guarantees that the graft would take. Any way you sliced it, it was a bad situation.

"I can't believe this. How many others were damaged?" I looked around and spotted another, and then another, from just where I was standing.

"Six that I've found. All mature specimens with no signs of disease."

"This is shocking, but are you sure it is connected to the cooperative?"

"I'm not certain but considering what I heard about your car, it makes me wonder if that could be the cause. I can't think of another reason."

"Any idea who would want to do it?" I hoped I wasn't going to hear what I was sure I was going to hear.

"Frank Lemieux. Somehow he heard about our money troubles and he offered to buy us out."

"That makes sense since his place abuts yours." It also would provide him with easy access to the damaged trees since he could have walked from his own property onto Jill's.

"He offered to buy it way back when our parents died but I didn't want to sell. I wanted to let Dean finish high school here. We had lost so much and I didn't want to lose our home, too. So I told him thanks, but no thanks."

"How did he take your refusal?"

"He wasn't too happy about it and he said the sugar bush would be wasted on us and that we were sure to make a dog's dinner of it. He hasn't spoken to me since, other than to yell about noise from my yard or stuff like that until he tried to talk business again last night."

"Did he make the offer to you or to Dean this time?"

"Both of us, individually. He ran into Dean at the hardware store and they got to talking. I guess Dean gave him the impression I'd love to entertain an offer. Frank pulled up here last night and offered to buy the place again. I thanked him and told him things were looking up because of the cooperative and that we would be hanging on to the property for at least a bit longer."

"Did he seem angry that you turned him down?"

"He got pretty loud and told me we were sure to regret our decision. He said something about not always being able to count on the trees producing all that well and that we would be better off taking the money now."

"But you didn't see him on the property after that?"

"I didn't catch him doing this, if that's what you mean. But somebody cut them up and I can't think of anyone else who would have had a reason to do this." Jill pulled a balled-up napkin out of her pocket and dabbed her eyes. I wasn't sure if she was shedding tears of sadness or frustration but either way I understood her pain.

"Has this made you change your mind about selling?" I really wanted the cooperative to work but I understood that Jill needed to do what she thought was right concerning her own circumstances.

"Hell no. If Frank thinks damaging my property is going to get me to sell to him, he's got another thing coming. If he did this, I'd burn the place to the ground, including all the trees, before I'd be willing to turn it over to him."

"What did Dean say?"

"He said maybe we should seriously reconsider putting the place on the market." Jill shook her head like she couldn't believe what she was saying, like she was surprised at how differently two siblings could look at a shared home.

"Is there any way I can help?" I wasn't sure how I could but it was always best to ask.

"I doubt it unless you can get Lowell back from his vacation with your mother to investigate. When I called this in to Mitch he told me he was too busy with real crime to worry about something so inconsequential as attempted murder of my trees."

"Did he say what kinds of real crimes?" I felt a nervous flutter in my stomach.

"Something about people evading arrest. Tracking down fugitives. Car theft. I was too upset to listen carefully." My stomach was right to worry. It didn't sound like Mitch had gotten over me leaving the Stack the morning before without a ticket and with a cruiser. I didn't want to be on anyone's fugitive list but certainly not Mitch's. And even more certainly with Lowell so far away and unable to help me out. I pointed the Clunker toward town. I wondered if Dean might have any answers.

Eight

Village Hardware is in downtown Sugar Grove. Right on Main Street between the barbershop and the bookstore. With a population of fewer than five thousand people, we are lucky to have so many businesses in town. A lot of communities all over New Hampshire are fortunate to have a post office and a couple of half-full churches. Because we are as far out from other towns as we happen to be, and because of a general interest in supporting the local small businesses, we have a grocer, a bakery, a florist, and a five-and-dime.

We have a restaurant that serves elegant dinners and several antique shops. We have a gift shop, a bookstore, a gas station, a mechanic, and a doctor's office. We even have an old-fashioned department store, named Bartleby's, where we've always shopped for school clothes.

Between what is available in town and what you can get shipped to you by shopping online, some people never feel the need to leave Sugar Grove other than for work or for a run to the hospital. Not that there aren't wonderful things in the big outer world but it is nice to be able to meet your needs without too much wasted gas.

Sawdusty smells and the vaguely metallic scent of chains and buckets of nails wafted toward me as I pulled open the door and stepped inside. Dean Hayes, his lanky figure draped as usual over the counter near the register, lifted his bony hand in greeting. What Piper saw in him I was at a loss to say. He was nice enough but I found him boring. He spent his time mooning after Piper and filling in sudoku puzzles.

I hadn't noticed any hidden depths to Dean myself but Piper assured me they were there. I think she was convinced he was mysterious because he had so little to say. I think he had so little to say because there weren't a lot of things rattling around in his head in the way of thoughts. He was decent looking in a ropey kind of way and his hair hung into his eyes rebelliously. Personally, I thought he was just too lazy to get a haircut often enough to keep it out of them. I doubted Piper's romance with him would last longer than the winter. I didn't think Dean was good enough for Piper but I didn't have to like him to want to help his business succeed.

"What can I help you with?" Dean asked, putting down his sudoku book.

"Birdseed. Grampa said you'd know what we usually buy."

"I can look it up in the computer. Anything else?" He looked back down at his puzzle like he hoped my answer would be no.

"The birdseed wasn't my only reason for stopping by. I was just up at your place talking with Jill. From the looks of some of your trees, you're having a bit of trouble."

"It's more than a little trouble. Trying to stay open is an exercise in throwing good money after bad. I've tried to convince Jill that we should sell but she just won't listen to me. She's determined to hang on to the place no matter what. I just don't understand it." He shook his head at me.

"Maybe the land means a lot to her. It's been in your family a long time."

"But it isn't doing any good. We just keep getting further behind every month. Selling's the only way out of the spiral we're in."

"You don't think the cooperative will help out your business along with everyone else's?" I asked.

"I know Jill does have hopes it will but I don't believe it will make a bit of difference. All participating is doing is drumming up false hope and delaying the inevitable. And devaluing our property while we wait to go broke." There wasn't really anything else to say so he looked up the birdseed I asked about and loaded it into the trunk of the Clunker. I had pried open the driver's door and dragged myself into the seat and was buckling the safety belt when

Knowlton loomed into view. He hopped out of his car and started waving both arms at me like he was directing flights at an airport.

I put my size-five foot down on the gas and peeled out of there before Knowlton could get any closer. I still felt guilty about how sad he looked leaving the opera house the night before. There was no way I could fend off his advances if he managed to get any closer to me with his hangdog look. I felt a little ashamed as I pulled out of sight, watching him still waving at me as I glanced in the rearview.

Already on edge, I jumped when I felt a buzzing in my pocket. In the privacy of my mind, I admitted I thought God had gone ahead and zapped me with a cosmic Taser for not being nicer to Knowlton. Then I realized it was just my cell phone set on vibrate. I was grateful it rang right as I pulled into the driveway at Greener Pastures. With a police chief for a godfather I'd heard enough horror stories concerning driving and cell phones but I thought I'd be safe answering in our own dooryard.

"Hi, Mom. How's the cruise going?" As much as I wished Lowell were home and investigating what happened to Jill's trees and my car, I decided right then and there not to be the one to spoil the trip. If Mitch decided to call him in, then there was nothing I could do to stop him.

"Delightful. You should feel what the sea air does for

the aura. Lowell's has never looked better," my mother said. That sealed the deal. No way was I getting the blame for tarnishing Lowell's freshly polished aura. "But that's not why I'm calling." She dropped her voice into the low tones she used for warnings and worries. It's like she thinks bad things won't actually end up happening if she warns in a whisper so evil can't hear. Like she doesn't want to give any ideas to the devil or karma or Loki or whomever it is that she credits with such things.

"So why are you calling then?" Not that I really wanted to hear her reason. My mother considers herself to be psychic and even though I don't want to, I sort of believe she is. She gets visions of things that end up being useful as you reflect on them later but have very little value ahead of time. It seems to me a lot of the practicality of a sixth sense would be having it actually make sense and in my mother's case, that's where it all falls apart.

What she really needs is a partner. Like Joseph, the guy in the Bible with the fancy colored coat and the hostile bunch of brothers. All kinds of people received images in dreams that weren't useful to them until Joseph came along and interpreted the meaning. Unfortunately my mother thinks she is the dreamer and the Joseph and, really, she isn't.

"I want you to say yes to a trip of your own. I see a change of scenery and heart-pounding adventure coming your way very soon. You won't want to say yes but you must. It will be a matter of life or death to someone near to you."

"I don't have any plans for a vacation. Things are too busy here right now and before you know it sugaring season will be on us."

"Just a short trip. Even an overnight stay. I'm thinking Sweden." I couldn't bite my tongue hard enough to keep the questions from spilling out.

"Sweden? Sweden is not an overnight trip from Sugar Grove. Or do you mean Sweden, Maine?"

"All I know is I see you rolling around in the snow over and over like those Scandinavians with the hot tubs. You know, the ones who whack each other with switches. Very stimulating for the system. Someone involved is wearing a fur coat. Like a Russian in an old movie. And I see Graham. He's looking on with a worried expression. Are you trying to make him jealous by seeing other men?"

"I am not even seeing much of Graham and I am certainly not going to Sweden and I don't want to discuss naked snow rolling with you or anyone else for that matter."

"Did I say naked? Although, that is intriguing. Just remember what I said. Say yes to the trip no matter how much you don't want to. It's a matter of life and death. And dress warmly. And don't forget to practice safe sex. If you're going to roll naked around in the snow, it can get a little difficult to remember to be practical."

"Mom, please stop talking about this."

"I've got to go. Lowell and I are scheduled for belly-dancing lessons in ten minutes. Give my love to the others." My mother disconnected and left me feeling unsettled. Conversations with her had always been difficult but ever since my father died they had gotten worse. She had become more insistent about sharing her gift, as she liked to think of it. I thought of it mostly as sharing her power to agitate but I supposed she couldn't help it. We all are who we are and aren't likely to be anyone else. At least not in this lifetime.

It had been much easier to discount what she had to say as crazy nonsense before last fall, when her sixth sense had gotten more honed somehow and she had actually given me a message that turned out to be somewhat true. Now I had a new message to think over and it wasn't sounding like a good one. Truth to tell, I was worried. She had said a matter of life and death. Despite the blatant sabotage and vandalism, no one had been killed over the cooperative and I found myself praying that it would stay that way.

I skulked up the seldom-used front stairs, trying to avoid talking to anyone lest a pair of plane tickets to the frozen reaches of the globe appear in their outstretched hand. I didn't dare look at a magazine for fear a vacation article would pop up before my eyes and I would be compelled to phone a travel agent. But no matter how hard I tried, I couldn't avoid something even more persistent than one of my mother's visions. Celadon.

My sister called out to me as I tried to slink silently into my bedroom. Her hearing is so sensitive I've often wondered if it was the result of a secret government experiment. She flapped her slim hand at me and pointed into her own room.

Back when we were kids I lived for the moments Celadon permitted me to enter her room. I almost never got an invitation, not even on my birthday. Now here we were years later and crossing her threshold was the last thing I wanted to do. Other than visiting Sweden for a good switching in a snowbank.

All I wanted was to flop down on my own bed and think. I wanted to think about the Midget, about the cooperative, and about who might be willing to hurt Jill's trees. Or maybe I just wanted to pretend to think about those things while actually taking a nap. But I followed her into her room instead because in the end it was just easier to do what she wanted than to argue with her.

"Which one of these looks the least like you are borrowing it from me?" she asked, reaching out a finger to touch the lacy edge of a peach-colored camisole. My sister has a passion for beautiful nightwear. She collects silky nightgowns and matching robes, peignoirs, and bed jackets. Ever since she was old enough for sleepovers she's maintained the very highest standards in nighttime outfits.

"I don't want to know why you are asking me this, do I?"

"You don't really want me asking Graham instead, do you?" Celadon picked up a spaghetti-strapped gown that looked like it was made out of meringue and a couple of dead swans. She pressed it against my body and clucked her tongue. "Mom should have taken you to an endocrinologist before it was too late."

"What does Graham have to do with your nightwear collection?" I pushed the fluffy bit of finery away from me and tried to make eye contact but Celadon was focused on the vast array of lingerie spread out before us.

"The camping trip, of course."

"Graham is unlikely to need your pajamas on his camping trip with a bunch of kids." I didn't need to be a self-proclaimed psychic like my mother to know something bad was headed my way.

"Perhaps you're right. Let's face it, Dani, in your case, normal avenues of seduction have not been leading to the altar. I think a less conventional approach is called for."

"What does that mean?"

"It means, you don't dress up. You don't do the dinner-and-a-movie thing with a lot of success. You get hives on blind dates. You're the only woman I know who has managed to require the Heimlich maneuver in a restaurant on a first date three different times."

"My throat is extra small. Things get stuck in there."

"You should have been born with a smaller mouth so there would be less of a loading dock for your chokable zone." Celadon tossed the nightgown onto the bed, where it joined the others. The state of her bed made me think about how often her husband was out of town on business. I don't think I would have wanted to sleep with her either from the looks of things. "No. Camping is by far the best way. And extreme camping conditions at that. Your wardrobe is perfect for the occasion and you don't even need to worry about spilling things on yourself."

"Camping!" I didn't mean to yell. My yelling tends to pitch high enough to serve better as a method of echolocation than communication.

"Mindy Collins called to thank you for getting Graham to agree to fill in for Russ today."

"How does this lead to camping? Or more important, you pulling out every item from your underwear drawer?"

"I volunteered you to help out, too. The two of you ought to be about equal to one adult with parenting experience."

"What? Why would you do that?"

"Can't you see that I've provided you with the perfect setting in which to ensnare a husband."

"What are you talking about? I don't want to ensnare anyone. I feel cheap and dirty and scheming just knowing those words went into my ear."

"Getting dirty is all a part of showing you're a good sport. I think it's best we play to your strengths."

"You think I'm a good sport?" I was surprised. I didn't feel like Celadon thought I was good at much and she chided me about my attitude on a near daily basis.

"What I think doesn't matter. Graham will think so if you just show up and act like a kid with the rest of them. I know that is something you can handle. Just don't choke on anything during the cookout. Although, come to think of it, Graham's in the protect-and-serve business. He might be really into saving a damsel in distress."

"I can't make myself choke at will." I stamped my tiny foot on the pumpkin pine floorboard and wished it made more of an impression. Celadon just sighed again and waved toward the door.

"I think you should know Graham is already downstairs waiting for you to be ready. He said he was delighted to hear you would be joining him and would be by to collect you before you changed your mind."

"He's here already? I haven't even had time to pack."

"He was downstairs chatting with Grampa about the merits of brook trout when I left him to search for something to spice up your evening." Celadon began neatly folding her lingerie. "And you don't have to pack. I had Loden and Grandma do it for you as soon as I got off the phone with Mindy. He loaded up all the camping gear and she packed your clothing. You should be all set to go as long as you remember how to put on your coat and shoes."

"I even know how to zip and tie all by myself." I was certain if I didn't get out of there soon I was going to say something that would require gift certificates for massages to repair. Maybe it was a good thing I would be away overnight.

"You can thank me later. I expect a full report when you get back." Celadon had a way of making even a date with a fun and attractive guy sound like it was a homework assignment. She could never be accused of being a romantic. Not that I thought of myself as much of one either. My taste ran more to a burger at the Stack Shack and a movie at the drive-in down by the lake than it did to candlelight dinners and gifts of jewelry.

"Maybe there won't be anything to tell." I wasn't planning to let her know even if there was. Celadon had a knack for ferreting out secrets and I knew I would be doing her a favor by allowing her to employ her considerable skills if I made her dig for whatever there might be to share.

"There had better be. You'd best get a move on. There's no telling what Grampa might decide to talk about if he gets into one of his expansive, storytelling moods." Celadon was right. As much as I loved for my grandfather to be happy, I wasn't sure I wanted him to amuse himself by telling Graham stories about my childhood.

I hurried out of her room before she could give me any further instructions or make any more demands and arrived in the kitchen just in time to hear Grampa starting to share his version of how I got my head stuck in the narrow crotch of a tree when I was three. He had made me hysterical by asking Loden to fetch the chain saw so he could get me out.

"In the end we just tickled her until she got all loose and floppy and she slipped her own head out just as easily as she slipped it in." Grampa beamed at Graham and then at me. "That's our Dani, always getting herself into trouble and then finding her way back out again using unconventional means."

"She does seem inclined to do things a little differently," Graham said.

"Some people think she's a bit eccentric, but don't tell her I told you so," Grampa stage-whispered to Graham. "She's a little sensitive about that sort of thing. Especially when good-looking young fellers like yourself are the ones hearing about it." Grampa creaked the maple antique kitchen rocker back as far as it would go without tipping over backward. He always did that when he got ready to kick his storytelling into high gear. That meant it was past time to leave.

"That's me, sensitive and eccentric. Ready to go?" I turned my attention from Grampa to Graham.

"I am always ready to go camping," Graham said.

"Even with a squad of squirrels?" I asked.

"I love kids. Someday I hope to have a whole squad of my own." He flicked his eyes over my frame briefly and I wondered if he was evaluating my hips and their birthing capacity. I felt like a failure. My hips are as small as the rest of me. As I looked back at him I thought of a Chihuahua giving birth to German shepherd puppies.

"Good attitude, young man. You can't work a farm without a crew. When were you thinking about getting started?" Grampa asked.

"We've got to go or those squirrels will have worn poor Mindy out if she has to handle them all by herself for long." I grabbed Graham's sleeve and tried tugging him toward the hallway. He didn't seem to be taking the hint.

"I was thinking sooner rather than later, sir. After all, no one is getting younger."

"You got that right. Why little Dani here is already

twenty-seven. Can you imagine that? Looking at her, she still seems seven instead of twenty-seven."

"I don't know about that, sir. She looks pretty grown-up to me." Graham winked and finally took the hint as I tugged on his sleeve again. I waved good-bye to Grampa and tracked Grandma down in the laundry room in order to give her a kiss while Graham loaded his truck with the camping gear and my clothing.

"You have fun, dear. I know you could use a little excitement in your life."

"I've had quite enough excitement with finding the Midget all carved up and trying to keep the cooperative afloat."

"That's not the kind of excitement I meant and you know it." Grandma adjusted my collar like I was about to head out the door to school looking like a ragamuffin.

"It's the only sort I seem to drum up and I guess I'll have to take it."

"I think there might be more out there in life for you to take if you just pay attention. Graham is a nice boy and he really seems to like you. I think even your father would approve. I know Lowell does."

"I thought you had your heart set on me settling down with Knowlton?"

"I have my heart set on you having a good life. I've always wanted all you children to be as happy as your grandfather and I have been. As happy as your parents were."

"I know. I want that, too. Which is why I don't want to be pushed into anything or to settle for less than perfect."

"Perfect doesn't exist, Dani. But good does. Kind does. Putting others first sometimes does. I think Graham may have all of those qualities. You could do a lot worse."

"Let's just see how the camping trip goes."

"Camping does tend to show a lot about a person. You should come home with more knowledge than you left with concerning Graham's core character."

"And whether or not he snores."

"And whether or not he likes children as much as he says he does. Kids can be pretty hard to like at two in the morning when they just won't go to sleep."

"Or if one of them vomits."

"A man who can handle childhood illness is someone to seriously consider. It makes up for a lot of other less wonderful qualities. Many's the time I wanted to hit your grandfather over the head with a teakettle full of boiling water, especially when he is driving." Grampa drives sedately and prefers backroads and scenic vistas. Grandma is a lead-footed speed demon and she finds him a trial behind the wheel. "But instead of assaulting him, I think back to your grandfather rocking a child with an earache, humming away good-naturedly for hours at a time, and I'll forgive him just about anything."

"I'll keep that in mind, Grandma, if a crisis pops up with one of the squirrels."

Nine

"I appreciate you being so nice about all this," I said to Graham as he navigated his truck down the rutted road to the Collins's place. I snuck a peek at him out of the corner of my eye. Truth to be told, I liked what I saw. His hands, gripping the steering wheel lightly but firmly, looked well groomed but not soft, like he worked with them a bit but washed them when he was done and knew how to use a bottle of lotion once in a while.

"I love kids and I love camping. There's nothing to be nice about." He looked over at me and winked one of his bottle blue eyes. "I meant what I said. This sounds like fun and I'm happy to help out." Graham reached across the bench seat and squeezed my kneecap. It tickled and it made me feel even more foolish.

"I just don't want you to think I put Celadon up to this or encouraged her in any way."

"You wouldn't be the first woman to use children to get close to a guy she liked." He smiled over at me and I felt less sure that he believed I'd had no part in us hurtling along the road to help out with the Squirrel Squad camping trip. If Celadon didn't manage to get me married off soon, she was going to make sure I died of embarrassment.

"I haven't used anything to get you to go with me. For all I know you called up Celadon and arranged this with her yourself. Maybe I ought to be suspecting you of planning all this." Like they always say, a good offense is the best defense.

"Celadon doesn't seem like the type to let much influence her besides her own thoughts and opinions. I wouldn't think you or I could persuade her to do any such thing."

"You've got that right." I felt a little better thinking he could see how Celadon had gotten us roped into an impromptu sleepover with no help whatsoever from me.

"It doesn't matter one bit how it all came about. I can't think of a nicer way to spend the evening than in the great outdoors with even greater company." Graham smiled over at me and I felt my stomach go all squishy and I knew no matter what Celadon had done I was not going to be able to hold it against her. At least not for long. Unless it started raining. Then all bets were off. Rain at this time of year was bound to be the freezing kind and I didn't have enough padding to sit comfortably in a wooden chair, let alone to survive the night covered in sleet. "Besides, there is absolutely no saying no to your sister."

"I've noticed."

"Is that why her husband makes himself pretty scarce?"

"He travels on business. A lot."

"Isn't that hard on the family?"

"I never really thought about it too much. There isn't any animosity. Celadon and Clarke just get along better when their marriage is filled with space. The kids have more attention than most by living all together with the extended family."

"Don't they miss their father?"

"They do. But with technology being what it is, they can video chat with him every day when he's away and that helps."

"Don't get me wrong, I think your family's great, but that's not my idea of an ideal marriage." There was an opening if ever I heard one. Was I going to step through it? My curiosity always leads me into awkward places.

"It isn't? A lot of men would love to roam around the globe staying in hotels and having adventures while someone else ensures daily life is in good shape back home. Whenever he talks about it, Clarke says he has the best of both worlds."

"That wouldn't suit me at all. I want to come home from a day at work, not a week away. I want to eat dinner with my family while they chatter about their day. I want to read stories to my kids and to tuck them in at night. And I want to sleep pressed up against my own wife every night." I noticed Graham's hands gripping the wheel a little tighter as he spoke. From the tension I was seeing there, I was sorry I had followed my curiosity. I tried joking a bit to lighten things up.

"What about business trips?"

"We don't have a lot of business trips with the Fish and Game Department but if it came to that, I'd take them with me. If you're going to see the world, why wouldn't you want the ones you love the most to see it with you?" And there it was, staring right at me. The real reason Celadon's meddling in my love life had always rankled so badly.

It wasn't that I didn't want to marry and have a family. It wasn't that I didn't want a man in my life. It was that I didn't want the kind of marriage she had. Taking advice about romance from her felt like I might end up with a relationship like hers. I wasn't resisting love, I was resisting Celadon's version of what it was. But Graham's version sounded like a perfect fit. My stomach got all gooshy and I suddenly felt shy and tongue-tied. This camping trip might turn out to be more important than I would have thought.

"I don't really know why." But if I thought about it, I guess maybe I did. I think maybe Clarke loved Celadon and the kids better from a distance or maybe not as much as they deserved to be loved. Maybe that was why Celadon was so tight and bossy and proper most of the time. Maybe she was covering a heart full of hurt and I hadn't bothered to notice.

"I feel sorry for your sister. She's too smart not to

recognize what is going on in her life and I'm sure it hurts her." For a man who worked more with nature than with other humans Graham sure was good at understanding how people ticked. I bet he was going to be great on the camping trip with all those little squirrels.

"I wouldn't tell her you feel sorry for her though. Celadon prides herself on being tough and correct. If you mention a vulnerability she's likely to resent it." I knew this from vast experience. Celadon was the one who was fine in a crisis or if she was injured until someone was nice to her. And then she fell completely apart. As in huge, heaving sobs and undignified nose dripping and red eyes. And then she got angry with the person who helped her to lose control. A happy Celadon was a steady breeze of energy. An angry one was a gale-force wind.

"I'll keep that in mind. Is this the place?" Graham pointed at a mailbox with a squirrel painted on it.

"That's it. Are you sure you're ready for this?" I asked as Graham pulled along the side of the driveway to let a throng of running children continue on their course.

"Everyone looks like they're having a great time already. Besides, what could go wrong?" Now he'd done it. For such a sensible man Graham didn't seem to have any idea about how things worked out when you tempted fate by opening your mouth too wide.

"Thanks so much for agreeing to help out," Mindy said as her eyes darted around the woods from one screaming Squirrel

Squad member to another. "Russ has been having a lot of trouble with his back and he just couldn't give me a hand."

"I bet he couldn't," I said, noticing one kid lifting a stick as thick as his arm above another child's head. Graham grabbed my hand and squeezed it.

"We're delighted to help. What can we do?" he asked.

"I need to get all these kids fed and then entertained for the evening before I run out of steam." Mindy's hair stood out from her head in angular clumps and she only wore one sock. I never thought of her as the best-dressed woman in Sugar Grove but it was easy to see that she had been through an ordeal.

"What were you planning for dinner?" I asked. I hadn't really eaten since breakfast and there was no way I wanted to risk starving to death out in the woods.

"I had decided on those aluminum foil packets that you tuck into the coals to cook, but now I'm thinking we ought to just give them cereal straight out of the box." Mindy pointed at the group of kids scrambling up trees and pelting rocks down on each other's heads. I could see how giving them any more fuel might be a mistake. Then again, hungry kids are even harder to manage.

"How about a safe campfire starting demonstration?" Graham suggested. "Kids love anything to do with fire. And the hunt for kindling and firewood will burn off some of that extra energy and work up an appetite."

"Are you sure you want them to know how to create something as dangerous as fire?" I asked.

"Trust me." Graham stuck two fingers in his mouth

and let loose with a whistle that rattled the few dried beech leaves still left clinging to the trees. All other noise stopped and the kids turned to see where the sound had come from. "Okay, kids, who wants to learn how to make a fire even when it's pouring and you have no matches?" Kids shot down out of trees and dropped sticks to the ground with a clatter. They flocked around him like birds to a feeder just before a winter storm is due. Mindy's shoulders crept down from around her ears and settled back below her neck where they belonged. I had never had a lot of use for her husband, Russ, and after seeing what he left her to deal with alone I was even less inclined to like him now.

"He sure looks like a keeper," Mindy nodded at Graham.

"He's certainly got a way with kids." Little people were hopping and crowding into each other to stand closer to Graham and the magic he was demonstrating with a bit of fluff and some flinty sparks. Just watching him there with my nephew, and thinking about the conversation we had on the way over, made me feel a few sparks of my own. He looked over at me and smiled an I-told-you-so smile, and I had to give him a thumbs-up.

"That's never a bad thing. A man who helps out with the family would be a real blessing." Mindy looked through the trees in the general direction of her house, where I expected Russ was sprawled on the couch clicking through the channels in search of the latest in reality TV programming. I felt sorry for her even if he was her choice. A distraction seemed in order.

"It looks like we might be able to manage a cooked dinner after all. What did you have in mind to put in the packets?"

"I have a bunch of pork chops, potatoes, and onions. And a whole lot of aluminum foil. I saw something on the Internet about making these but I've never done it before."

"Have you got any maple syrup?"

"I brought some for breakfast tomorrow morning. I planned to make pancakes. Why?"

"We make a similar type of foil packet meal sometimes at Greener Pastures. Let's do the potatoes separately. Then we'll combine the pork and onions and drizzle them with some of the syrup and some pepper before wrapping them up tightly. You just pop them in the coals to cook and everyone loves them." Mindy pointed the way to a cooler stocked with foodstuffs and we got started peeling, slicing, and wrapping while Graham charmed the kids and kept them busy.

Within a couple of hours dusk had fallen, Graham had pitched our tents, dinner had been eaten, and the kids were getting restless again. With the sun gone the temperature had plummeted and all I wanted to do was head for home. Or at least stay pressed as close to the fire as possible.

"How about hide-and-seek?" Hunter suggested to the other kids. Hunter loves hide-and-seek almost as much as I do. I play it with him, his sister Spring, Loden, and even my mother if she's not busy, on rainy days or in the depths of the winter when it is too cold to go outside. The family home is so large and full of nooks and crannies it seems like the place was purposely built for a good game of hide-and-seek.

The woods on Mindy's property seemed like an ideal place for it, too. The kids all hopped up and scattered and Hunter pressed himself against the nearest tree and began counting. I grabbed Graham's hand and ran into the woods.

"Don't pass the pink flags," Mindy called out. "Remember, Frank Lemieux doesn't like strangers on his property." I thought fleetingly of Frank's dog, Beau, and then the fun of the game drove all other thoughts from my head, even ones of losing toes to dog bites or frostbite.

The dark descended even more as we headed farther from the campfire. Stars sparkled in the cold night sky but they provided little illumination on the ground. Even the moon was just a sliver. Perfect for hiding.

"Do you want to split up or hide together?" I asked Graham.

"I think we should split up in order to keep a better watch on the kids. It's pretty dark out here and I don't want to end up on a search-and-rescue mission if someone wanders too far afield."

"Especially since this property borders Frank's."

"Who is this Frank guy? He seems to have made quite an impression on Mindy." I gave Graham the abbreviated version of the Mindy-Frank property line disagreement and longstanding animosity. I also mentioned how much Frank prefers his privacy and his low tolerance for intruders or the government. By the time I got to the part about Frank setting Beau on me Graham was scowling.

"Did you report the dog attack?"

"I went right to the animal control officer but he didn't want to do anything about it. He and Frank are friends and he seemed to feel like it wasn't that big a deal."

"Well, it will be if that dog bites a kid. Or a kid-sized adult." Graham squeezed my hand again before letting go. "Be careful and have fun." I waved at him and ran off through the trees to find a hiding space. The sounds of the others grew fainter until I could no longer hear Hunter counting or the campfire crackling. The smell of wood smoke still drifted toward me so I knew, while I was a good distance away, I hadn't entirely left the vicinity.

The snow wasn't really deep but it did add to the challenge of the game. Wading through it, even though it only came to mid-calf, made walking more difficult. It also left a trail of footprints for seekers to follow. On the plus side it made it easy to see if anyone else had passed your way. The pristine snow stretched out in front of me like icing on a wedding cake.

I walked and walked and finally crested a slight rise. Just as I reached the top, I heard growling. I felt the hairs on the back of my neck stand up and my stomach hit my ankles. Then I felt a shove from behind. The snow at the top of the rise was crusty and slippery. My feet shot out from under me. I tried to grab at branches as I slid past but Beau was on top of me before I could think.

Bits of brush stuck up from the snow and whacked me

in the face as I rolled over and over down the hill. The dog slipped and slid and rolled along with me. Out of the corner of my eye I saw Beau's dark coat flash past as he tumbled over and over, too. I landed at the bottom of the hill with a bang as I thumped against the side of a tree with low-hanging branches. Before Beau could double back and get his teeth into me I bolted for the tree and scrambled up into the crotch about ten feet off the ground.

My eyes had adjusted enough to the darkness that I could see a bit of movement on the ground below me. I covered my mouth with a mittened hand, hoping Beau wouldn't have any idea where I went if I was quiet enough. Logically, I knew dogs don't tend to climb trees but the instinctual parts of my brain weren't inclined to take chances. I held my breath and strained my ears, praying I wouldn't hear a thing.

There was a crashing, rustling in the woods coming from the direction of Frank's property. The sounds came closer and then I could make out Mindy's son Luke's tasseled hat just below me. He plodded determinedly ahead, moving past my tree and farther on into the woods.

"Gotcha." A voice cut through the still night air. It was rough and angry and too old to be one of the kids playing. And it wasn't Graham either. When I squinted I could see Frank standing in the pale light, waving a shotgun at Luke. The boy started flailing and fell back on his hind end in the snow. Frank took another step closer and pointed the gun at his leg. "How many times do I have to tell you people to stay off of my land?" Luke, silent until now, began to sob.

"You're not going to shoot me are you, Mr. Lemieux?" It was hard to tell what he was saying between the sobs but both Frank and I seemed to have understood him.

"I'm thinking about it pretty seriously. Nobody listens when I ask politely. Maybe taking a little action will get my point across better." Frank raised his voice to a holler.

"I'm sorry. It won't happen again. I promise." Luke sobbed even harder.

"That's what you said the last time I found you wandering around on my property. I think you need more incentive to remember next time." Frank raised the shotgun to his shoulder. I began climbing down the tree as quickly as I dared. I hoped I could startle him and knock him off balance so Luke could make a break for it.

"Sir, I suggest you lower your weapon." Now it was Graham's voice cutting through the night. Frank's face was awash in a beam of bright light from Graham's flashlight. He had his service weapon drawn and pointed at Frank, and the look on his face was capable and no-nonsense. I felt my knees giving way as I realized I wasn't going to have to figure out how to help Luke on my own. I clung to the tree, stayed out of the way and watched.

"I'm standing my ground. I got a right to deal with intruders on my property, especially ones who are interested in my sugaring secrets," Frank said.

"And I have a responsibility to protect the public. This

child may be trespassing but you will be hard-pressed to make a case for him being a threat to you."

"That kid needs to be taught a lesson, along with the rest of his family. Not a lick of sense in the whole bunch."

"Sir, if you don't lower your weapon, I will shoot you and then I will arrest you. You're worried about your privacy from an eight-year-old kid crossing into your woods. Imagine how much you're going to like it when every law enforcement officer in the area is trooping through your house and outbuildings shooting video and pawing through your possessions." Graham took a wider stance in the snow and adjusted his grip on his weapon. Frank stood with the shotgun to his shoulder for another second and then lowered it.

"The cops won't be there every time you forget your promises, boy. I'd be more careful next time if I were you." Frank whistled for Beau, who trotted over to his master, then backed up and vanished into the dark. Graham holstered his weapon, stepped to Luke's side, and pulled him to his feet. Luke buried his face in Graham's jacket and wrapped his arms around him. Graham embraced him back then looked up into the tree.

"Are you all right up there, Dani?" I scrambled down from my hiding place.

"I was already hiding up there when the hostilities started."

"I'm sure you were saving the element of surprise in case things got even worse."

"I was. I was going to jump on him if I saw him put his finger on the trigger."

"I know. Not that it would have made much difference. You're small enough that he wouldn't have been dissuaded even if you landed on his head. He would have flicked you off like a deerfly."

"Somehow I still feel like I was cowardly. Like I should have done more."

"A good police officer knows when he or she needs backup. In my professional opinion you did the smart thing. I'm glad I came along when I did."

"How did you know where to find me?"

"I was halfway down the hill already when you went tumbling past. You look pretty good for someone who was doing about thirty miles an hour down a hill. The way those bushes were switching your backside it was like you had insulted their families." Graham smiled at me and brushed some leaves off my jacket.

"Would you say that looked anything like I was one of those people in Scandinavia who heat up in a hot tub then roll in the snow before hitting each other with little branches?"

"Aren't they usually naked?"

"Well, yes. But other than that did you notice a similarity?" I felt myself blushing and I didn't want to pursue the conversation any more than necessary but all I could think about was my mother's phone call. Now what else was it she had said?

"Without you being naked, I'm not sure I can picture what you are saying. Do you want to go back up to the top and try again?" Graham asked, panting just a bit.

"No. It was hard enough coming down that hill with my clothes on. I'm not about to attempt it without them. You'll just have to use your imagination."

"Believe me, I am." Graham winked and I felt like I was in way over my head. Not that it takes much for that to happen at my height. Graham took me by one hand and Luke by the other and led us both back to the campsite. Luke burst into a fresh round of tears when he spotted his mother tossing another log on the fire.

"Are you hurt, sweetheart?" she asked. Graham and I both explained what had happened with Frank. Mindy's face glowed red in the firelight.

"That bastard. I knew he was crazy but I didn't think even he would go as far as that."

"I think he was just posturing. But I wouldn't cross his property line again. I think you need to keep the kids right away from there."

"I'll do more than that. If he even so much as speaks to one of us again, I'll kill him."

Ten

Considering what all had happened with Frank, it took some doing but after a while Mindy managed to settle down and all the kids got busy roasting marshmallows over a campfire burnt down to perfect coals. Even with the sugar rush, one by one the kids started nodding off over their toasting sticks and Mindy hustled them toward the tents. Mindy, Graham, and I took turns getting up from the warmth and light of the fireside to quiet the few restless kids. Before too long Mindy herself was dozing and almost pitched face-first into the coals.

"That's my cue to go to bed. Will you two be all right if I turn in?" Mindy raised her eyebrows at me and wriggled them in a way that I expect meant something but really just made her look like the whole camping ordeal had caused her to develop a twitch. When I didn't seem to catch on she tried again. "You won't be wanting a chaperone for whatever you'll be getting yourselves up to, will you?" I felt my cheeks flash with heat and not from the campfire. Not only did it sound like the church organist was encouraging fornication, the look on her face said she'd be happier to stay and help.

"I think we can handle things on our own." Graham's tone was no nonsense, like he'd slipped back into cop mode. Mindy took the hint and hustled off to her tent without another word, suggestive or otherwise. "You've got to wonder what makes some people tick," he said in a low voice, his lips pressed up near my ear as soon as the sound of Mindy's tent zipper buzzed through the quiet night air.

"She means well," I said, not sure I believed it.

"She was rude and I could tell she made you feel flustered." Graham scootched a little closer on the log we were sharing.

"She's had a tough day. You can't hold it against her."

"Yes I can. I'd prefer to be the one making you feel flustered." I swallowed hard, having no idea what to say. Piper would have thought of something sassy and flirtatious. Celadon would have stuck out her hand and asked him to show her a ring. Even my mother would have just started chatting about the way the stars were aligned for romance.

But me, I was tongue-tied and feeling so dizzy I thought I might just pitch over backward into a snowbank. It wasn't like I didn't think Graham was interesting. I just felt like we didn't know each other well enough to go pursuing the sorts of things Mindy was hinting at. Before I had to decide what to say I heard another tent zipper and a small head popped out through the flap. Then the rest of a small squirrel scout slipped out and looked at us from beside the tent.

Even from a distance in the dark the child's body language said misery. Slumped posture and heaving shoulders looked like sobbing to me. I scooched down the log and waved the child over to sit between us. By the time the little girl had reached us, the tears were streaming down her face.

"What's wrong, Molly?" I asked, giving her a quick once-over. She didn't appear to be missing any parts but with all the layers it was hard to be certain.

"I miss my mom," she plunked down between us and pressed her face into my jacket. It was a good thing my wardrobe was as low maintenance as Celadon had complained it was. Otherwise, I would have been worried about what the girl was depositing all over me. "I want to go home."

"I think you're homesick. You know a lot of people have that happen."

"No one else in the squad does." She looked up at me and I could tell she was embarrassed as well as sad. "The rest of them think I'm a big baby."

"Do I look like a big baby?" I asked.

"Kind of. Well, at least you don't really look like a grown-up."

"No matter how I look, I know just how you feel."

"You do?"

"I do. It happens all the time."

"It does?"

"Yup. As a matter of fact, when I went away to college I thought I would die of homesickness. I was so ill every day for the first two weeks of freshman year I couldn't eat and I couldn't sleep. I lost ten pounds." I wasn't just making up stories to make her feel better. I had been so ill I wasn't sure I was going to be able to stay. My roommate tried to get me to go to the infirmary but I couldn't let them call my family. My father hadn't wanted me to go so far away to school but I had insisted. At the time I felt like homesickness was my punishment for disappointing him by going against his wishes.

"You must have been really sad."

"I was. But eventually I got to like college and I had a lot of fun." At least until my father died of a heart attack at home in the sugar bush during my senior year. That had brought homesickness back with a vengeance. I lost more weight I didn't have to spare, too. By the time I got home for the funeral I was dehydrated as well since I couldn't even keep liquids down. But Molly didn't need to hear that.

"How did you fix it?" Molly wiped her nose on the back of her mitten.

"I decided that home would always be there and that the experience at college wouldn't. Just like this chance to go camping in the middle of the winter won't be something you can do every day. Home will be there tomorrow."

"So you are saying I should try to have fun while I can?"

"I've noticed telling other people what to do is usually a big waste of time. I'm just telling you how I solved my problem. You can try it if you want to." Molly looked at me and slid off the log.

"You really don't seem like a real grown-up."

"Thanks, I think."

"Will you tuck me back in?" Molly offered me her hand covered in the nose-wiped mitten. When I reached out to take it in mine it reinforced to me how much of an adult I really was. Back in college I probably wouldn't have been able to grab a hold of it without feeling squeamish.

"Sure thing." Two hastily invented bedtime stories later Molly was asleep and I was back on the log with Graham trying desperately to warm up. I was so cold I didn't feel anything but grateful when he moved in closer and draped his arm over my shoulder.

"You handled that really well," Graham said.

"I was telling the truth. I get terribly homesick. The whole family does. Why do you think none of us have moved out?"

"I think it's sweet."

"Molly's right. I'm probably not a real adult."

"Loving your family and feeling passionately connected to your home is nothing to be ashamed of."

"Sometimes I feel a little stunted and I'm not just talking about my height. Is it normal to be so attached?"

"I wish I knew." Graham turned his face away from

me and toward the fire instead. I was sort of glad. I wasn't
sure I wanted to see his eyes when he sounded so lost.

"Sounds like you haven't ever been homesick yourself."

"I haven't."

"Lucky you." I said it as a joke, trying to lighten the
mood.

"That's one way of looking at it." He turned back
toward me and I could see it was no time for jokes or for
clinging to a tree root at the shallow end of the emotional
pond. I decided if this relationship was worth pursuing,
it was time to let go of safety and discover where things
might drift.

"But it wasn't your way, was it?" I placed my hand on
the canvas of his insulated pants. Even through my mitten
and his trousers I could make out the warmth and close-
ness of him physically. I hoped my words hadn't ruined
the chance to feel close in other ways, too.

"You're right about that." Graham placed his hand over
mine and squeezed. "My mother was an alcoholic and
she lost custody of me for neglect when I was a toddler.
My father was never more than a stranger's name on my
birth certificate. By the time I was old enough to remember anything I was a ward of the state. I bounced around
from foster home to foster home."

"That must have been rough."

"It was. I never got to feel like any place was enough
of a home to get sick over."

"That explains why you want to come home to your
wife and kids every night."

"It also explains why I love camping. I went to camps paid for by the state during the summer for several years. I even worked as a counselor when I was older. At camp, everyone was only living there temporarily instead of just me." And right then, that's when my heart broke. From sadness, from shame. Thinking about the contrast between what Graham hadn't had any of and what I'd had in excess left a lump the size of a biscuit in my throat. I thought of how frustrated I had been lately with everyone sticking their noses into my love life and my business dealings and I felt sick. I usually thought of myself as a grateful person, someone who counted her blessings and numbered them in the thousands. But at that moment I just felt like a birthday girl who took a tire iron to a car because the gift was the wrong color.

"I wish I could somehow change all that for you. All kids deserve better."

"You know what they say. You have two chances to enjoy a happy childhood; by having one yourself or by providing one for your own kids."

"You're going to make a wonderful father one day."

"That's the nicest thing anyone has ever said to me." He squeezed me a little tighter. "You're shivering."

"I think I've turned completely purple."

"Your lips definitely have. Let's see if there's some way we can warm them up."

Eleven

 It was just past noon by the time I got home from Mindy's.
Even though the only body parts Graham had
tended to were my lips, I felt a little like I needed
to sneak back into the house. After all, I didn't want to
report anything to Celadon. Grandma was in the hall
when I opened the door. She took one look at me and
shook her head.

"Mindy called and told me about the confrontation
with Frank but you look even more worn out than she
sounded. You didn't stay up too late getting into mischief,
did you?" Grandma pulled a crumpled tissue from her
pocket, spit daintily in its center and reached out to rub
my face with it. "Why don't you take a hot shower and
put on some lip balm while your sister and I finish Sunday
dinner. We've baked a ham."

"With maple-apricot glaze?" My own spit started to spurt at the thought of it.

"But of course. Don't be long," Grandma said. I sprinted up the stairs to the second floor in search of a shower. With their pitch they would never meet code today but the stairs do help to keep my backside in shape. I feel grateful to the original builder every time swimsuit season rolls around. I may not have a lot on top but I don't have what you wouldn't want on the bottom either.

My bedroom stood at the end of the long hall. It was the least desirable when we were teenagers because it was the farthest from the bathroom. And it had the most places where the floorboards gave a warning creak when you tried to sneak in late. Back then I tried desperately to trade with one of my siblings but they refused.

Our bathrooms are old. Not harvest gold sinks old or even pink and turquoise tile old. They are indoor-plumbing-is-the-newest-thing old. The second-floor bath-room was actually scouted for a historical-movie set. The toilet flushes with a chain dangling from a box mounted to the wall. The tub is big enough to bathe three children at the same time. Can you guess how I know? Wasting water is a sin. Not enough of a sin to install a low-flow toilet, but enough of one to see no reason not to share the bathwater with someone if you shared the same mud puddle earlier in the day.

The shower is a handheld affair and makes for a bit of a juggle in the winter if you want to keep any hot water aimed at your shivering body while you shave your legs.

I usually just give up smooth legs for winter. Not only was it not worth the showering difficulties, it helped keep me warmer when I wasn't in the shower, too. A real win-win in my book. It was one of the few real upsides to being single in New Hampshire in the winter. No one could be relied on to start my car on a bitter morning or to scrape it after a storm but I didn't have to take anyone else's ideas of beauty into account when I made my personal grooming decisions either.

I wrenched on the taps and heard the creaking, groaning, shuddering that contributes to Mom's belief that the house is haunted. She keeps threatening to invite a team of crack paranormal investigators to come check the place out. I tested the water for temperature and shed my camping attire. I finished scrubbing off whatever had gotten on, then toweled dry and headed to my room for a change of clothes.

As in all the rooms in this end of the house, the ceilings were high and the light streamed through wavy, bubbled-glass windows. My room looked off toward the west and the vegetable garden, now tucked up for winter under a thick layer of shredded maple leaves. This part of the house dated to the 1870s. For around two hundred years, generations of family members put their own unique stamp on the house by adding wings and turrets and conservatories.

By the time my grandparents acquired responsibility for the place, they were all out of ideas for additions and turned to the landscaping and community projects. Which is why so many endowments have sprung up around town. We are always building something, even if it is only a castle in the air or a scholarship fund.

I grabbed my favorite old jeans and paired them with a pullover my grandmother had knit for me when I was twelve. It was a gray fisherman's sweater with chunky cables and ropey twists separated by swaths of seed stitch. The cuffs were starting to fray but I loved it and was only planning to hang around at home anyway. I fished around in the top drawer for some hand-knit socks to complete the cozy stay-home vibe I was feeling.

Halfway down the hall the smell of the ham tickled its way into my nostrils and hurried my feet. I reached the dining room and started pulling plates from the buffet. Glasses, silverware, and linen napkins were the order of the day. Pizza boxes and thick china were for the kitchen table, and that was nice in its place. But Grandma only allowed one thing on her dining table besides bone china and sparkling crystal and that was a sewing machine if the table in the craft room was too small for the project.

I had just placed the hot plates on the table when Grampa came in carrying the ham, glistening and brown, the crackling outer bits still sizzling from the heat of the oven. Celadon followed with a tea towel filled basket, slices of brownish bread peaking up through a gap in the fabric. My favorite, Grandmadama Bread. This is our family's version of the New England favorite anadama bread, which is usually made with molasses. We, of course, use maple syrup in its place. Hot from the oven and slathered with rapidly melting butter, there was not much on earth I would rather put in my mouth.

Hunter followed his mother with a platter of glazed parsnips and Spring brought up the rear with the butter dish. I hustled to the kitchen, sure there would be at least two or three more things that needed fetching. Scalloped potatoes wearing a cheesy browned crust on top released their fragrance on the counter. Grandma tucked a serving spoon into the dish and nodded for me to grab them. Within two minutes all available Greenes had been rounded up and Grampa was hard into saying grace.

By the time every far-flung loved one had been brought to mind and every blessing appreciated, the temperature of the cheese on the scalloped potatoes had dropped from boiling magma to something more akin to spring rain. The community should be grateful Grampa never felt the calling to enter the ministry. Once he got rolling the only thing that stopped him was my grandmother's gentle throat clearing, pitched slightly louder than a ticklish sound you might make at the beginning of allergy season. He'd once kept praying straight through the smoke detector because Grandma was away visiting a sick friend that day. The family joke went that Grampa would pray right through his own funeral.

We had gotten past the grateful words and onto the appreciative actions, full plates all around, when the phone rang. We don't answer the phone when we are at the table, so no one got up. Grampa doesn't believe in answering machines. He says anyone who wants to speak to us badly enough will simply try again. Anyone who knows us does just that. My siblings and I have gotten around the issue by having cell phones with voice mail accounts. The phone rang again five minutes later and the caller let it ring thirty times. I counted, so I know.

When the phone sounded again in another five minutes a twitch developed in Grampa's eye. His hands shook as he reached for the saltshaker. He knows the saltshaker is only there for guests since everything my grandmother cooks is seasoned just the way he likes it. That's how you could tell he was rattled, reaching for the saltshaker like that.

When it went off a fourth time he jumped up like his knees had never felt the cold of over seventy winters and grumbled his way out of the room. I could hear him stomping in the hall like the caller might get the hint. His telephone manners were not at their best when he lifted the receiver.

"Dani," he hollered, "it's for you." I looked at my plate and at my brother, niece, and nephew tucking into the ham with such intensity there might not be enough for a second helping by the time I got back if the call took longer than a speed-dating session. I stabbed an extra piece and plopped it on my plate, hoping that no one would dare to snatch it within view of Grandma.

I expected Grampa to glare at me when I reached the telephone table in the hall but instead he covered the mouthpiece with his gnarled paw and bent low to my ear.

"It's Tansey. She's all het up about some goin's-on up

at her place." He stretched the receiver toward me. "She said there was a problem and asked for you." I was baffled. When it came to people in town calling up with emergencies that required a Greene to straighten them out, I was never the one they called. Not even when they needed a babysitter. Why on earth would Tansey want me?

"Is that you, Dani?" Tansey sounded strained and a bit out of breath. I thought fleetingly of her heart.

"Yes. How can I help you?" I wasn't entirely sure I wanted the answer to that.

"Somebody's been messing around in my sugarhouse. They've left a threatening note. I think you ought to get on over here."

"Is this about the cooperative?"

"I'd rather you see it for yourself. And hurry up, why don't you." She disconnected before I could protest again or even say good-bye. I hurried back to the dining room and faced the curious.

"I've got to go. Tansey needs me to look at something at her sugarhouse."

"Is it something to do with the cooperative?" my sister asked, pausing her fork halfway to her mouth, a succulent bit of ham pronged deliciously in midair.

"I'm afraid so. She's asking for me to come right away. Please excuse me from the rest of dinner." I grabbed a piece of the bread to hold me until I could get back.

"I'll wrap up your plate and stick it in the oven so you can heat it up later." Grandma pushed back her chair, slid another piece of ham onto my plate, and followed me out of the room with it.

"You're the best, Grandma." I pecked her on the cheek.

"I know, dear. But it's nice to hear it anyway."

I slid into the driver's seat of the Clunker and eased down the driveway. The sun was growing dimmer by the minute. Gray clouds scudded in from the west and made the sky look like the batting from an old quilt, dirty white, lumpy, and gaping. I turned left at the end of the drive and made my way as quickly as I thought the old car could go toward the Pringle farm. I was worried about what Tansey had to show me. She had a lot of peculiar qualities but being a worrywart wasn't one of them.

Tansey sat in a busted web lawn chair in front of her open barn door. A bank of clouds blotted out the sun and made me wish I'd worn a coat. In my rush I just headed out in the sweater I'd been wearing. Tansey rose as I slammed the Clunker's door and waved her hand to motion me to follow her into the barn. Not even a greeting. For Tansey not to take the opportunity to yak my ear off meant something was definitely up.

On a cloudy, low-light day, the gloom in the barn took some getting used to. At first I could only hear Tansey shuffling around and creaking across the wide, rough barn floorboards. Once I could see, I wished I couldn't.

"What do you make of that?" Tansey stuck out her

sturdy arm, pointing a work-roughened finger at the far wall. Hanging from a rafter, by a noose, was a ratty old straw man that looked like a recycled Halloween decoration. One of Tansey's floppy gardening hats with the words *Pringle's All Natural Farm* embroidered onto the crown perched on the dummy's head. Someone had pinned a note to the dummy by stabbing an awl through a piece of paper and into its plaid flannel shirt. I took a step closer.

"If you don't want this to be you instead, you'll stay away from the Greene's and the cooperative." I read on the white lined notebook paper. It was written using black wide-tipped marker in all capital letters. The writing was messy, like someone had used their nondominant hand to print it. I felt sick. And a powerful feeling like a bad case of heartburn started bubbling up in my chest. Why was someone so opposed to the cooperative? The idea of anyone creeping into Tansey's barn and trying to scare her made me feel dizzy with rage.

"I am so sorry, Tansey. I'm sure this scared you."

"Scared me? No. Made me angrier than a bull with a snout full of cayenne pepper is more like it. I'm so mad I could peel paint with a look." I gave her the once-over and that did seem to be the case. The tension exuding from her was raw and fiery, not withdrawn. She looked ready to spring into action, not cower in a corner.

"When did you find this?" I asked.

"Just before I called you. I came out here after I was done with my chores in the other barn. I wanted to look at the supplies I might want to order with the cooperative when I saw this thing hanging from that beam. I turned toe and got on the horn to you."

"Did you come in here last night?"

"Nope. I had no reason to. All the critters are in the main barn, not it here. At this time of year it isn't a place I go more than once a day at most. In the sugaring season, sure, I'd be here all the time, but not now."

"So when were you here last?" I wanted to narrow down the time frame when someone could have gotten in without Tansey noticing.

"Before I went to the meat bingo. So early Friday evening it must have been. Maybe around four thirty or five o'clock. I was checking to see if I had left the cordless phone out here 'cause I wanted to call my sister."

"And this wasn't hanging here then."

"I would have been sure to see it if it had been." Tansey was right. It was obvious as soon as your eyes adjusted to the low light.

"So someone could have strung it up while you were at the opera house Friday night. Or anytime yesterday?"

"I expect so. I doubt I was home when it happened though. The dogs would have let out a fuss if anyone had come by and I never heard nothing like that." I wasn't so sure. Tansey had a lot of faith in her dogs' watchful prowess but they were getting on in years and I hadn't noticed them being as alert as they had been in the past. I also didn't think Tansey's hearing was what it used to be, so even if the dogs kicked up some dust she wouldn't necessarily notice.

Still, the time frame was narrowed down at least a bit. Everyone in town knew Tansey wouldn't miss meat bingo unless she was hospitalized. And Tansey hadn't even been born in a hospital. Friday night would have been a perfect time to sneak into her barn undetected.

"What did Knowlton say?" Knowlton, of course, never missed meat bingo so the person responsible would have expected to find the place empty. But if it had happened early maybe Knowlton himself was involved. Maybe he was playing a joke on his mother. The dogs wouldn't have barked at him and he wouldn't have needed to sneak onto the site. But he was too devoted to his mother to scare her like that and I would be very surprised for him to say anything bad about my family, especially considering how long he had been trying to marry into it.

"I don't expect he knows about this since I haven't seen him all day. I'm not sure what he's up to."

"That doesn't sound like Knowlton. If anything he tends to you almost too well." Part of Knowlton's problem in the romance department was the way he prioritized his life. Topping the list was spending time with Tansey, followed closely by his abiding love of taxidermy. Stalking Celadon and me came in third. Any woman would have to be content with whatever was left over.

"He's been making himself scarce since he lost at bingo to that game warden." Tansey gave me a look that said I had somehow rigged the bingo cage. "He keeps going on about how he'll never be able to compete with that other guy's sausage." There was no way I could respond to that so I changed the subject.

"I think you had better call the police and let them know about this. Probably you should try to locate Knowlton because if Mitch bothers to take this seriously, he is sure to want to question him, too."

"What do you mean question him? Like they would suspect him of wrongdoing?" Tansey stepped her stance wide and stuck her beefy hands on her matronly hips. I was glad I hadn't asked her about Knowlton's potential involvement.

"No, of course not. I just meant as a possible witness to anything odd that might have happened here. Anything that might help to identify who did this."

"Mitch's too busy singlehandedly running the police department to go worrying him about something like this."

"I'm sure he doesn't have anything more important to investigate than this." Maybe if he had something else to investigate, he would stop thinking about me filching a police car.

"There's nothing to investigate. We both know it was Frank, up to his usual rabble-rousing and troublemaking. This time he just got even more carried away."

"We can't be sure it was Frank."

"Who else has had one bad thing to say about the co-op? He's the only one in the whole town who tried to discourage it; the only one who didn't join."

"That doesn't mean he was responsible for this. Frank is difficult to deal with and a big blowhard but he hasn't ever hurt anyone as far as I know." I didn't want to fan her fire by telling her how frightened of Frank I had been when I went to recruit him for the co-op. Or how he had pointed a gun at Luke Collins the night before.

"Oh it's Frank. Of that you can be certain. He's been a mess for years and he's getting worse with age. The man won't even acknowledge he knows a body when he runs into them at the post office. And I do mean runs into. He crashed right into me the other day and didn't even grunt out an apology. Not even when he saw that he spilled my mail left, west, and crooked."

"If he's gotten as bad as you say, there's nothing we can do besides call the police."

"No matter what, I still know it's Frank and there is no way that crotchety excuse for a man is going to scare me off from the cooperative."

"I'm relieved to hear you say that. The rumors about this are sure to whip through the town faster than head lice at an elementary school. If you drop out, others are sure to follow and then there won't be a cooperative anymore."

"No straw dolly is going to keep me from saving money on my sugaring supplies. I work too hard for my earnings and any way I can legally save a bit is fine by me." Tansey had been barely scraping by on the farm ever since forever. Knowlton's father was never a part of the picture as far as I heard and she had to work the whole place alone. It couldn't have been easy and was probably one of the reasons my grandparents held her in such high esteem.

Tansey had been an older mother for a woman of her generation and Knowlton was something of a miracle baby. She was forty-five by the time he came on the scene and I expect she was pretty surprised by the whole situation. I know it caused a lot of talk in town. No one ever really figured out who Knowlton's father was. There was a lot of speculation but Tansey never talked about it and I don't think even my grandmother knew. I'm sure she never asked.

"You still need to give Mitch a call. I'll tell you what: If you get him over here to check this out, I'll go up and speak to Frank. I don't feel good about someone doing this to you and getting away with it."

"Now that's sweet, you know it is. That's just the sort of girl I want for a daughter-in-law. Knowlton's right to pursue you the way he does even if you are giving him a merry chase."

"That's nice of you to say, Tansey. Did you ever find that phone you were looking for? I'm not sure my cell phone will work out here." I wanted to get back home as soon as possible. Ham is fine reheated but I was hungry now and talk about Knowlton made me queasy instead of hungry. Besides, there was nothing to be gained by discussing any sort of romantic interest Knowlton had in me. Even if the threat hadn't driven Tansey from the cooperative, insulting Knowlton's eligibility just might.

Not to mention how much I wanted to be sure to take off before Mitch arrived.

"It's in my pocket. You'll go up to Frank's?" I nodded. "Well then, let's get the boy wonder over here." Tansey peered closely at the grubby handset and poked at the numbers. Even from a goodly distance, in a barn that acted as a wind tunnel, Myra Phelps's voice came through loud and clear. After telling Myra to let Mitch know she had a slice of her famous apple pie with his name on it sitting on her kitchen counter she disconnected without a good-bye.

"He'll be here any minute. I expect after what I hear about you stealing Lowell's police cruiser you'd rather be gone before Mitch shows up."

"I'd rather head over to Frank's than to run into Mitch. You should have seen the gleam in his eye when he saw me pulling out in Lowell's cruiser."

"That boy has loved slapping people in cuffs since he was just a bitty little thing. I remember him handcuffing Knowlton to the merry-go-round when they were in elementary school. Mitch gave the thing a shove and it dragged my poor Knowlton around three or four times before a teacher put a stop to it." Tansey shook her head slowly like she still couldn't believe it. I remembered the incident quite clearly.

Tansey would be distressed to realize how long it had taken for the teacher on duty to respond even after she spotted Knowlton whipping around the piece of playground equipment like a can tied on the back of a groom's car. Knowlton had a crush on the teacher and kept leaving gifts of dead creatures in her desk drawers. Maybe she thought the spinning would knock some sense into him. Or even better, give him amnesia. In the distance I heard the wail of a police siren.

"Okay, that's my cue to go. I need you to stall Mitch for a bit. He's sure to think Frank is involved and he'll head right up there and then I'll end up running into him anyway."

"I'll do my best to keep him here. That apple pie just might hold him for a while." Great. Not only was I going to be delayed even longer from my own lunch than I had planned, Mitch was going to be bellying up to some of Tansey's award-winning pie. I thought about asking her for a doggy bag with a piece for me but the siren was getting louder. I jumped into the Clunker and floored it. Which meant, I was barely down the driveway and around the bend in the opposite direction when I heard Mitch and his accompanying wail too close for comfort.

Twelve

 It was one thing to send a dog after me. It was another entirely to mess with my business. I'm a patient woman, probably even too meek and mild when it comes to confrontation. But if you manage to push the right buttons, my temper scares even me. Sabotaging trees, threatening the elderly, and sending out dogs to bite me were on the list of button pushes. I peeled away from Tansey's so fast the Clunker went airborne as soon as I hit the first frost heave. Even the car crashing back down to earth didn't convince me to take it slow and calm down.

All the way to Frank's place I rehearsed the sorts of things I would say to him. My fear of his dog went right out the window as the miles slipped behind me. By the time I pulled into his driveway and yanked on the emergency break, I had worked myself up into an under-five-foot-tall rage volcano.

Someone else looked like rage had gotten the better of him, too. Bob Sterling almost backed into my car as he reversed his own and took off down the driveway as quickly as I had come up it. I raised my hand in greeting but he just grimaced at me and kept both of his hands wrapped tightly on the wheel instead of the usual New Hampshire wave, which involves lifting just one finger up in acknowledgment of an acquaintance.

I wondered what could have gotten under Bob's skin as I raced up the steps of Frank's dilapidated porch, kicking aside a soda can and a bungee cord left in front of the door. I pounded as hard as I could on the door, flakes of peeling paint showered down with each blow of my fist. Frank's dog was the only one to answer my call. He barked and whined from the inside of the house and even jumped up on his hind legs to see who was out there making a fuss.

Despite my tough talk in the safety of the Clunker, I backed away as I noticed the dog was taller than me. But he was inside the house and I was safely on the outside. If Frank wasn't going to answer, it was likely he wasn't home. He wasn't exactly hospitable but he was eager to shoo people off his property. I went round the back of the house to see if there was any evidence of him there. Rusted cars and old oil drums poked up out of snowdrifts and brush. Some sort of a rusty engine sat in pieces on a splintery picnic table. But no sign of Frank.

I moved to the edge of the woods, toward where he might have entered if he wanted to sabotage Jill's trees. I stood silently listening for rustling or birdcalls that would indicate someone was nearby. I called out his name but no one answered. It occurred to me that Phoebe ought to be around here somewhere even if Frank wasn't. The last time I had been here they had been fighting but I hadn't heard that she had moved out or anything. And I had spoken to Myra since then so I would have heard. Myra knows all, sees all. With Myra around it is a wonder the police in Sugar Grove don't have a hundred percent clearance rate on cases.

Anger is not the most reliable form of fuel for me and I started to feel its strength ebbing away as I turned the corner of the house. A jay called from a tree above my head and when I looked up to spot it I noticed smoke rising from behind the sugarhouse. It was then I thought about letting myself into Frank's sugarhouse. I walked past the woodpile that had been dug into recently. Several sticks of stove wood stood out of line compared with the rest of the pile. A few pieces lay on the ground in front as though someone had left them where they tumbled when they hastily grabbed some wood.

I pounded on the door of the sugarhouse and waited more patiently than I would have expected. Then I thought about the trees at Jill's again and about the dummy swinging from Tansey's rafters and I tried the doorknob. I let myself in and crept cautiously forward.

Frank's sugarhouse looked nothing like the rest of

what I had seen of the property. Shelves lined the walls with things neatly lined up on top of them. Cupboards had doors with hinges that didn't sag. The floor was swept clean. Everything was just the way I'd keep it myself at Greener Pastures except for one thing. The room was hot. Too hot to be attributed to a normal heating system.

The smoke I had seen had to have been created by something and I was beginning to wonder if the sugarhouse was on fire. With more curiosity than sense I moved farther into the room, looking for the source of the heat. As I approached the evaporator the temperature shot up.

The evaporator in a sugarhouse can take many forms, from something cobbled together from found objects to state-of-the-art equipment. But the basic construction remains the same. You need a shallow pan with a lot of surface area suspended over a source of heat. In order to turn sap into syrup you need to remove a whole lot of water. During the sugaring season the evaporator ran almost constantly at Greener Pastures. But we never ran it outside of sugaring season. No one would want to waste the fuel. And it wasn't yet sugaring season. The nights were certainly cold but the days were nowhere near warm enough to start the sap flowing. I couldn't imagine why Frank would have had a fire going in his firebox. He might have had a lot of character flaws but being a spendthrift wasn't one of them.

"Frank?" I called out. "Are you in here?" I stepped around the evaporator with its empty sap pan and tripped, sending myself sprawling across the concrete floor. My elbow smarted and I'd ripped a hole in the knee of my only clean pair of jeans. I would have spent some time feeling sorry for myself on both counts if my attention weren't riveted on Frank. His eyes were open and staring straight at me but I was pretty sure they weren't seeing a thing. From the bits of bark trapped in the bloody dent in the back of his head I was more than certain he wasn't ever going to look at anything again. I scrambled back from his body and bolted to the other side of the evaporator. Sucking down deep hot breaths of the overheated air, I tried to tell myself to remain calm.

Apparently I am not much of a salesperson. By the time I got my fingers to work well enough to operate my cell phone and dialed Myra at the police station I was gulping down hiccupy gasps and had trouble making myself understood. She must have made out the word *Frank* and identified my number as the one calling. Myra may be a first-class gossip but she is an equally good dispatcher.

In under ten minutes Mitch was skidding the town's newest cruiser to a stop in Frank's driveway, lights and flashers both announcing his arrival. He burst in through the door, one hand on his gun holster. I took one look at him and after valiantly trying to hold it in, I burst into tears.

I'd like to say it was because of the lack of sleep, the stress of the cooperative, and the pent-up emotion of being so angry but I think I was just rattled. Thoroughly and completely rattled. Sure, I'd seen dead bodies before. People at funerals, people in movies, even a murder victim only a couple of months earlier but none of them had looked like they had been the victims of violence. I kept seeing the back of Frank's head with his fringe of graying hair matted with blood. Mitch wrapped his long arms around me and gave me a couple experimental pats on the back like I was a baby he was trying to burp. I pulled myself together and then pulled away.

"Frank's right over there." I pointed to the other side of the evaporator and noticed the baseball cap Frank always wore lying abandoned on the floor. Mitch crossed the room and squatted. When he stood back up he looked a bit rattled himself. It might have been the lighting but I thought he had a distinctly green tinge to his face.

"He's dead all right, that's for sure. Can you explain what you were doing in here?" Mitch took a step toward me and turned his back to the evaporator and to Frank. Maybe being aggressive was easier than feeling scared. Especially if you were in charge of a crime scene.

"I came to ask Frank about the sabotage to my car and to Jill's and Tansey's places. You know, the stuff you were too busy to investigate until pie was involved."

"With Lowell away I've had more important things to do than to worry about infighting between local businesses."

"Well it looks to me like the sabotaging just got to be your number one priority. Especially since Lowell is out of town. Maybe if you had taken it more seriously something like this wouldn't have happened."

"This isn't my fault. And you still haven't said exactly what you were doing here. Were you accusing him of sabotage or did you want to warn him it could happen to him, too?" Mitch crossed his arms over his chest and gave me the same look he had when he was preparing to pat me down in front of the Stack earlier in the week. It was a good question though. I hadn't even thought about the possibility that Frank's place could have been targeted, too.

"I was going to confront him. Just about everybody thought Frank was the one trying to warn people off the cooperative by messing with their properties."

"And?"

"And, after I saw the dummy in Tansey's barn I drove straight up here to tell Frank off. I was so mad I was getting light-headed on the drive over."

"Mad enough to kill him?" Mitch towered over me and I was glad to hear the ambulance in the near distance. He didn't look like someone I wanted to be alone with for much longer.

"I was mad but I don't think I'm even tall enough to have hit him. And I very much doubt I'm strong enough. Besides, the evaporator was heating away and Frank was on the floor when I arrived."

"You look like you've been in a bit of a tussle. Can you explain that?" Mitch pointed at the hole in my jeans and the scrapes on my hands.

"I tripped over Frank's body and banged myself up when I hit the concrete floor. From the bark I saw caught in the trough in the back of his head it looks like he was coshed with a stick of stove wood." I felt myself getting a little hysterical, like I might start laughing inappropriately. All I could picture was a maple tree uprooting itself and wandering over to hit Frank upside the head with one of its branches for girdling Jill's trees. That wasn't going to go down well with Mitch though.

"A likely story."

"It's the truth. That would explain the evaporator being on, too. I bet whoever killed him put the stick of stove wood into the evaporator and lit a fire in the box to destroy the evidence."

"You seem to know a lot about this for someone who claims not to have been involved."

"I doubt someone would need to be involved in this crime to make the same suggestion." I wished more than ever that Lowell was in town instead of frolicking on a cruise ship with my mother. Mitch had been looking for any excuse to get back at me for the failure of our lackluster romance. Suspecting me of murder was about as good a way to get back at someone as I could think of. While Mitch was not the smartest guy I had ever met, he wasn't dumb either. If I could give him some other viable suspects, he would certainly look at them, too. "Besides, there are plenty of people in Sugar Grove who hated Frank."

"That may be true but people have had problems with Frank for years. Why kill him now?"

"Last night Frank pointed his shotgun at Luke Collins for crossing his property line. When Mindy heard about it she threatened to kill him if it ever happened again."

"Did Frank threaten her kid again?"

"Not that I know of but I haven't been with her since this morning. Anything could have happened since then."

"Seems unlikely to me. You still seem like a better suspect since you're right here on the spot."

"What about Bob Sterling? As I pulled into the driveway this afternoon I saw him hauling out of here like his backside was on fire."

"Bob? What reason would he have to hurt Frank?"

"Bob was saying at meat bingo on Friday night that Frank's dispute about the property line was keeping him from selling his land. He was really angry about it."

"And he was here when you got here?" Mitch uncrossed his arms, which I took to be a good sign.

"He was. And from the sounds of things, he's about to be here again." The sirens of the ambulance had grown so loud I was certain it had arrived. Sure enough, the door to Frank's sugarhouse opened and Bob stood there with Cliff Thompson, the fire chief and part-time EMT.

"Keep that under your hat for now." Mitch tilted his head toward Bob ever so slightly then lowered his voice. "I don't want to have to slap the cuffs on Bob before he gets the body dealt with."

"Does this mean I'm not a suspect anymore?" I felt a glimmer of hope and lightness for the first time since tripping over Frank's corpse.

"Nope. It doesn't even mean I've forgotten about you stealing Lowell's cruiser. It just means you should be quiet. I'm sure I'll have more questions for you later. For now, I want you to wait outside."

Without another word, I scooted past Mitch and Frank and the others. I was glad to get out into the cold fresh air in the yard. I sucked down several deep breaths before I saw Phoebe rounding the corner of the house. She was coming from the direction of the woods beyond the clearing surrounding the house and outbuildings near the drive. Her pale blond hair was all pinned up on her head in a way I had never seen before. I watched as she spotted the ambulance and her pace quickened.

"What's going on here?" she asked.

"Phoebe, I have some very bad news for you." Frank, for all his faults, had been a better father to Phoebe than her biological one had ever bothered to try to be. This was going to hurt and having lost my own father, I understood exactly how much.

"Is it my dad?" Phoebe's already pale face lightened a few extra shades as any blood rushed to her vital organs. I knew that feeling, too. The one where your mind blanks, then your pulse races and your hands go all tingly as you think of all the terrible things that could have happened all in the space of a breath. Stress at that level is the ultimate warper of time. You think you conjured up absolutely every possibility for grief and you did it in a single second.

"I'm sorry, it is." Phoebe moved like she was going to go into the sugarhouse. I grabbed her arm. "You don't want to go in there."

"If he's hurt, he needs me."

"Phoebe, you can't help him. He's gone." I couldn't bring myself to say the word *dead* to her. It was so final, and so cruel.

"What do you mean gone?" Her pale blue eyes filled with tears.

"I found him in the sugarhouse. It looked like someone must have hit him on the back of the head with something hard." I didn't want to go into the details of the dent or the loose bits of clinging bark in the wound. She would be upset enough without having a gruesome image stuck in her mind's eye. I was going to have a hard enough time with it myself when I tried to sleep that night and I really didn't even like Frank. My father's death had been swift and not the result of violence and it still made me sick to think about him dying all alone in his sugar bush, his heart squeezing away and giving out long before his time.

"Oh no! It must have been Mindy. Or Kenneth Shaw. They both hated his guts. Dad told me about Mindy screaming about her Squirrel Squad yesterday and what would happen if my dad bothered the kids again. I have to tell Mitch. He'll know what to do."

Before I could answer, Bob and Cliff came out of the sugarhouse bearing a stretcher. Phoebe took one look at the figure lying on it covered in a sheet and started to wail. Mitch took her in his arms and rocked her back and forth gently like a small child. I couldn't hear what she said but I could see that he bent close to her ear. She nodded slightly and he released her from his embrace. He led her to the cruiser and held the door open while she slipped inside and slouched down in the front seat. He closed the door and headed for me.

"I'm going to need you to come down for a formal statement. Can I trust you to come into the station of your own accord?" Mitch asked.

"Of course. I'm not going to just run off."

"You've done it before."

"That was different. You were being petty and Myra told me she would explain about the cruiser."

"Lowell didn't leave Myra in charge of the department while he was gone, no matter what she is running around telling people."

"I bet once she hears about Frank she'll be glad you are the one with his butt on the line instead of her."

"Which is exactly why Lowell left me in charge. He knew I'd be up for whatever challenge came my way." Mitch had the speech down but the way he kept glancing around quickly and shifting his weight from one foot to the other like a recently potty-trained child said he was more nervous than he wanted to admit.

"Are you sure you can handle this on your own? Graham is a police officer, too, you know. I'm sure he'd be happy to help."

"I don't need any help. Not from Graham and not from you." Mitch stopped swaying back and forth and crossed his arms over his chest. Making him mad was the nicest thing I could have done for him. Anger had replaced nerves and he was ready to get down to business, if only to show me how much he didn't need anyone, especially Graham, to help him out.

"Not even help with Phoebe? I know how good you are with crying women." Mitch had left me alone in the movie theater on our second date because I had started tearing up when the main character's horse had to be put down. He was so flustered he had driven off and left me to find my own way home.

"The only woman I'm worried about is you and whether or not you'll show up at the police station to give a statement."

Thirteen

I waited in the police station for nearly an hour before Mitch made time to question me. I had no idea if that was to bug me or if he really had other things he had to take care of first. Either way, Myra had plenty of time to go over the grislier bits of Frank's death and to toss out theories of her own as to how he died.

"My money's on aliens," she confessed in a low voice. I assumed it was out of deference to Phoebe and not because she worried about what others thought of her belief in aliens. Myra was a UFO enthusiast who attended a local alien convention every year.

"You think extraterrestrials killed Frank."

"I do indeed. I think they planted some sort of chip in his head that made him spout all that antigovernment nonsense."

"But why would they murder him?" I was whispering, too. The whole conversation felt so disrespectful I was becoming queasy just listening to Myra, let alone participating.

"I bet the chip was malfunctioning and they had to dig it out before anyone detected it."

"You think an alien species that can build a craft and navigate a course into a distant solar system would hit Frank over the head with a piece of firewood to retrieve delicate technology?" Myra bit her lip then changed the subject.

"How's it going with Mr. Hot Stuff?" Myra raised her voice a bit like she wanted Mitch to hear her.

"I'm sure I don't know who you mean." I was getting prim, I could just feel it. You know how when Pinocchio lies his nose grows longer? Well, with me, my posture improves and I feel my buttocks clench and I suck in my cheeks a bit because my lips are pursing like a devout spinster with a mouthful of sauerkraut juice. My voice raised an octave and my fingers itched for something to do like stitching a sampler or tatting a doily. My mother would say the lying stressed me out so much it caused me to revisit a previous incarnation. Or maybe allowed me to channel a long-dead family member with better moral fiber than my own.

I expect if she was right, it was Myrtle Greene, the unmarried sister of the only pastor the family ever boasted. Her strict sense of decorum and behavior befitting a Christian is the stuff of family legend. If you ask me, Myrtle wouldn't condescend to channel herself in the first place. Such a thing would carry the stink of the occult. But if she did, she'd surely choose to filter through Celadon instead of me. After all, Celadon is the one who teaches Sunday school and I only manage to get to church at all one Sunday in three. I know because my grandparents remind the Saturday night before the third Sunday morning.

"That stud in the outdoorsy gear. You know, the game warden."

"They're called conservation officers now."

"No matter what you call him I'd be happy to let him measure my fish anytime." Myra is a winker, which makes me uncomfortable at the best of times. But when Myra does it, it takes on a leering, conspiratorial quality that leaves me feeling like a felon. This was not something I needed while sitting in the police station awaiting questioning in a murder investigation. Her eyelids were fleshy and droopy and covered in far too much sunset yellow eye shadow. When she winked it was like a blinking traffic light: Caution, caution! Not to mention if Mitch overheard anything complimentary concerning Graham it might put him in an even more combative mood. I needed to steer the conversation to another topic.

"I'm sure he would trust you to only keep regulation-length fish. After all, you are involved in law enforcement, too." Reminding Myra of that sometimes slows down the gossip train. Usually it doesn't, but it was worth a try.

"It's a good thing you've got that other guy chomping away on your bait. With how good Phoebe has been looking lately there isn't a lot of chance you'll be turning Mitch's head your way again."

"She looked pretty torn up at the house. She and Frank were so close and she was shocked." At least she seemed to be shocked. Then again, she and Frank had been arguing something terrible when I had stopped in to encourage Frank to join the cooperative in the first place.

"Well, of course she was. Phoebe's a decent girl. She loved her stepdaddy to pieces. Especially once her mother got so sick there at the end."

"Phoebe's had it rough. I hope she and Mitch are happy together." I meant it, too. If I were entirely honest, like channeling Myrtle Greene honest, I would admit that if Phoebe ended up with a happily ever after it would alleviate some of my guilty conscience about how I'd treated her when we were kids. One thing that prickled in the back of my head though was the possibility that she was dating Mitch just because I had, in the same way she had copied the way I dressed when we were in middle school. I hoped for both their sakes she was dating him because she really enjoyed his company.

"Things seemed like they were really turning the corner for her though before this happened with Frank. With her new hairdo and her wardrobe changes she was looking so nice and acting so much more confident. She's like a whole new woman." Myra was right. Phoebe had undergone quite a transformation in the last few months. It had happened slowly enough to not feel like a makeover like you see on television or in a magazine article but in the end the result was the same. Truth be told, Mitch hadn't shown any interest in Phoebe until recently and it may well have been because of her formerly mousy demeanor and complete lack of style.

"Maybe her new sense of confidence will help her to bounce back from Frank's death more easily."

"I hope so. She must've spent a fortune on her looks lately. It would be a shame if the expense didn't end up giving her a lasting boost," Myra said. I never thought of Phoebe as having a lot of money. She worked part-time at the local confectionery and gift shop in town, Sweet Treats. Her expenses couldn't be too high living at home, but still, she couldn't have had a lot of spending money. Retail just doesn't pay that much. I wondered if Phoebe had been arguing with Frank about money when I saw the shouting match between them. More important, I needed to decide if I should tell Mitch about Phoebe's argument.

Before I could make up my mind, Mitch popped his head around Lowell's office door and motioned for me to join him. He shut the door behind me and I was surprised to find myself feeling uncomfortable in Lowell's office. I had never felt uncomfortable there. Lowell's office had been like a home away from home for me, since not only had Lowell been the police chief in Sugar Grove all my life, he had been my godfather and dearest family friend all that time, too. For a kid who didn't get into trouble I had spent an awful lot of time in the police station. It just didn't feel right seeing Mitch behind Lowell's desk, especially the way he was looking at me across his steepled hands. I wondered if his posture was part of a course on intimidating body language. If it was, he should have earned an A.

"Tell me why I should believe you didn't murder Frank." No beating around the bush for Mitch. He was all business and all cop, which helped me to make up my mind about telling him about Phoebe.

"Did you ask Phoebe the same question?" The stunned look on his face made me feel a little more sure of myself. Now I was at least on an even footing.

"Why would I ask her a thing like that?" He dropped the steepling and gripped the sides of the desk like he was preparing to launch himself at me.

"Family always has a reason to feel sore about something. With no spouse in Frank's life, a child is a logical next person to investigate."

"What makes you such an expert?"

"I never said I was. But isn't there statistically a much greater chance a murder victim is done in by someone close to them. No one would ever say Frank and I were close."

"I know how to do my job."

"Since I know I didn't kill Frank and you seem to think it is possible that I did, I'll have to disagree with you there. You still ought to ask Phoebe why she was having a roof-raising argument with Frank on Friday morning. Did she happen to tell you about that?"

"What makes you say she was arguing with Frank?"

"I saw them, that's why."

"For someone who claims not to be too involved with Frank's life, you sure seem to be well informed. First Bob Sterling, now Phoebe."

"I went to Frank's place on Friday to ask him about my car. When I pulled up Frank and Phoebe were yelling at each other."

"That doesn't sound like Phoebe. She never yells. Phoebe's a real lady, unlike some women I can think of."

"Don't you think that makes it all the more suspicious? Frank yelled all the time. You could have used Frank's voice to blast granite ledge if you wanted to put in a new foundation. Phoebe would have been used to it. It wouldn't have provoked her."

"Don't you think that's pretty desperate of you, trying to implicate Phoebe? You must really want me back." Mitch shook his head at me like I was pitiable, like a butterfly with a crumpled wing. I felt myself beginning to boil over. Which is never a good thing. When I get angry I get all blotchy in the face. My voice gets even squeakier and I tend to punch the air with my tiny fists. Really, I look more like a child in the throes of a puberty-fueled fit than an adult woman with a right to be angry.

"It has nothing to do with any prior relationship you may have thought we had. I am never going to be more interested in you than I was when we broke up. Besides, I like Phoebe. I didn't even want to mention the argument to you but you just bring out the worst in me."

"Let's pretend for a moment that I believe you. What do you think the argument was about?" Mitch leaned back in Lowell's chair and actually flung his feet up onto the desk. I was definitely going to tell Lowell when he got back.

"I don't know from overhearing anything in particular. Phoebe yelled at Frank for sticking his nose into her business. Frank said she wasn't appreciating him. She agreed she didn't appreciate what he was up to and then she stormed off. I'd never seen her act like that before. And she was on the property, too, when I found Frank's body." The intercom on the desk squawked and Myra's nasally smoker's voice pulsed into the room letting Mitch know Bob Sterling had shown up for his interview and wasn't happy about being kept waiting. He said he'd be with Bob in a minute.

"You aren't off the hook yet, Dani, so don't even think about leaving town." Mitch pointed at the door. "You're free to go for now. On your way out tell Bob I'll see him." I wasn't sure how it was that I could simultaneously be both a suspect and a police department employee. I decided I wasn't and that Mitch could fetch his own suspects. As I reentered the waiting area Bob stopped his pacing and stepped toward me.

"Mitch called me in here to question me because of your tattling. I didn't have anything to do with what happened to Frank and I have a whole lot better things to do with my time than to be in here answering a bunch of insulting questions because a pip-squeak like you had to offer up opinions on stuff she knows nothing about." Bob towered over me and I was glad Myra was sitting right there at her desk. At least if Bob decided to rough me up there would be a witness.

"I don't owe you any favors. I'm in here because I'm a suspect, too. And you were leaving the scene in an awful hurry."

"There's no shortage of suspects as far as murdering Frank is concerned. There was no reason to single me out."

"You were at the scene. It wouldn't have been right not to mention you leaving like that."

"What about Knowlton? He was on the scene, too."

"I didn't see Knowlton. I only saw you. And Phoebe."

"Well, I saw him. He was skulking away into the woods just as I arrived. For all I know he killed Frank and then just sauntered off to round up roadkill like nothing ever happened."

"You said he might have killed Frank. Does that mean you never got to talk to Frank when you were there?"

"That's right. I pounded on the door until I thought either my hand would break or the door was going to. The only one I managed to rouse was Frank's damn dog."

"Was that why you were so angry?"

"Damn right it was. Frank's truck was sitting right there in plain sight and I was certain he was just not coming to the door because he didn't want to deal with me."

"Why didn't you go into the sugarhouse like I did if you were so hot to talk with him?"

"Because I've got better sense than you. No one pokes their nose around on Frank's property without an invitation. And no one gets an invitation. I had no desire to find myself at the business end of Frank's rifle. He hasn't been exactly quiet about his enthusiasm for the stand-your-ground legislation."

"Or maybe you did go into the sugarhouse and fixed your boundary-dispute problem once and for all."

"You just had better hope you and your whole family have no need for an ambulance anytime soon. If I'm the one on duty, I might just have my radio turned down when that call comes in." Bob shoved me out of the way with a large square hand and hurried to Mitch.

Back home once more I just wanted to reach out to someone I loved in order to talk over the chaotic events of the day. Luckily for me, the house is full of family. Usually, I was more likely to be looking for a quiet spot to gather my own thoughts than to engage, but when I needed to talk to someone I was spoiled for choice. I popped my head into the barn looking for Grampa but he wasn't around. I toyed with the idea of wandering up into the sugar bush to see if he was there but then decided the person I really wanted to talk to was my older brother, Loden.

Knowing him like I did, I was fairly certain he would be in his train room on a Sunday evening. Ignoring the grumbling coming from my stomach, I headed for Loden's special space. Loden's train room is housed in an addition unfortunately dreamt up by one of the more eccentric, and fortunately long-dead, members of the family, Verdant Greene.

Gripped by the Egyptology mania that swept much of the world at the time, Verdant built a pyramid replica on the side of the house. He was so thoroughly devoted to the authenticity of the space that he chose not to include such niceties as windows for light and cooling or a heating system of any kind for the winter. These design decisions, along with an entranceway modeled after a real tunnel into King Tut's tomb did little to endear this part of the house to anyone except Loden.

Family legend has it that, like an intrepid archeologist himself, at age two Loden had somehow toddled to the doorway and wriggled along the passage. An hour after frantically ransacking the farmhouse and adjoining fields in search of her missing son, my mother sat down in the far pasture to call upon her spirit guides for assistance. She claims she had a vision of Loden perched on a golden throne dressed in a loincloth. Moments later she burst into the pyramid to discover Loden contentedly sitting in the corner as though he owned the place. And he has, for all practical purposes, ever since.

I don't really give a lot of credence to my mother's spirit-guide story but I will say Loden's effect on the space is magical. He has turned the whole place into an extravaganza of miniatures. All of Sugar Grove is spread out in lavish detail. Loden has crafted all the buildings, down to the very last detail himself. He spends countless hours researching each new piece he adds to the display and then executes it with just as much care.

I may not like the accommodations but I love visiting

the pyramid because of what Loden has done with it. And because he is there. Loden never was the kind of big brother you feared. I think my tiny size made him unusually protective of me. As an adult I try not to take advantage of his instincts but as a kid on the playground his protectiveness was always welcomed.

I scooted through the entryway and landed at the other end eager to tell him all about Frank and my run-in with Mitch. He looked up from a small barn whose roof he was carefully covering in miniature shingles.

"So how did things work out at Tansey's?" he asked. Truth be told, I had mostly forgotten about Tansey and the threatening dummy in her barn. I told Loden about my visit to her and then my decision to head up to Frank's to confront him. When I got to the part about finding Frank with his head bashed in, Loden carefully set aside the miniature barn and gave me his full attention. When I mentioned being questioned by Mitch as a suspect, Loden started pacing the floor. Between the amount of space taken up by models and displays and the slanted ceiling, pacing was no easy feat.

"And to top it all off, Bob Sterling is angry at me for mentioning to Mitch he was leaving Frank's in a hurry at the same time I was arriving. He told me we had better not need an ambulance anytime soon up here at Greener Pastures." As I related the incidents of the day to Loden all of the emotion came flooding back at once. I felt lightheaded and sick to my stomach. My breath started coming in shallow pants and I worried I was about to pass out.

"Sit down, Dani. You look like you're about to keel over anyway." Loden pointed to a free corner and I squatted down in it and put my head between my knees. I felt him sit beside me and take my hand. Sometimes my family makes me crazy with all their interest in my love life or lack thereof and general meddling but at times like these I just felt grateful to have them. When my breathing slowed to normal and the nausea passed I had an encouraging thought.

"The good news is that with Frank dead the sabotage on the sugarhouses should stop. So I can get on with keeping cooperative members on board and placing supply orders."

"Are you sure that's a good idea? What did Mitch say?" Loden asked.

"I didn't think about it until just now. And besides, I'm not going to ask Mitch for permission to go about my business."

"How can you be sure Frank was responsible for what has been happening? It could be someone else. Which would make it a bad idea to pursue the co-op."

"Frank is the only one who raised any objections to the idea of the cooperative. He had to have been the one responsible." If I kept saying that maybe it would make it true.

"I thought of him as the embodiment of the Live Free or Die motto. He didn't want anyone telling him what to do and didn't much care what you got up to either. Given Frank's attitude toward the sovereignty of his own property, it seems out of character for him to damage some else's," Loden said.

"If not Frank, then who do you think might have done it?"

"I think you should consider Dean Hayes." Loden fixed his eyes on the floor, studying a spot on it with more interest than I thought it warranted.

"Why Dean?" I asked, but I had an idea why he would suggest Dean. Loden is a fair and levelheaded person but he has been not so secretly in love with Piper for years and years. He didn't even realize how much it showed until around Thanksgiving when I suggested he ask her to marry him. Loden is never a fan of the men Piper spends the winter dating and Dean was just the latest guy he wished would be permanently abducted by aliens.

"I heard him talking the other day at the hardware store about trying to convince Jill to finally give up sugaring and to put their place on the market. Dean sounded angry when he mentioned Jill refusing Frank's offer on the property."

"What does that have to do with the sabotage?"

"I'm just saying, who would be in a better position to girdle the trees than someone who lived on the property. He had legitimate reason to be in his own sugar bush and he would have known which trees to attack in order to cause maximum damage."

"Frank's property borders the Hayes acreage. He could easily have slipped onto their land without being noticed. The damaged trees are well out of sight of the house. And anyone who has ever tapped a tree could guess which ones would be most missed if they were put out of commission."

"All I'm saying is there has been a lot of damage to the sugarhouses around here and, with what happened at Tansey's place, it seems to be escalating. And we don't know if Frank was a victim of the same sort of thing or if he was killed for some other reason."

"No, we don't. Which means I would be foolish to put off finalizing the plans for the cooperative because the incidents might be linked to Frank's death."

"I think you are more foolish to pursue it until Mitch finishes the investigation."

"You can't mean that. It's Mitch we're talking about. He has never been in charge of the department for more than a couple of days before and he certainly hasn't been in charge of a murder investigation."

"Mitch may be unseasoned but that doesn't make him incompetent. I'm worried about you and about our own sugarhouse. Frank's death is no guarantee this is over."

"I'll take extra precautions but that's the most I'll promise. And while I'm busy with that, I think you ought to be asking yourself why you are so eager to suggest Piper's latest squeeze is a dirty rotten saboteur." I stood, gave him a bit of a wave, and scooched back out the passageway. I had some lunch I wanted to finish.

Fourteen

After a less than refreshing night's sleep I wanted to do something to take my mind off sabotage and murder. I really needed to replace the image that was bouncing around in my head of Frank lying facedown on the floor of his sugarhouse. I decided spending a little time in my own sugarhouse would do me a world of good. I had a bunch of paperwork to put together for the potential co-op members and I wanted to post a new recipe for a cheddar cheese maple spread to our website. Once a week I post a new recipe or article on green living on our blog attached to the site. I even started selling green products like stainless steel water bottles and cloth grocery bags with the Greener Pastures logo printed on them.

The back of the shop area houses a small office and I spent a lot of my time there ever since it was built the previous year. We always used to do the books in the main house den but as the business has grown I wanted to keep things separate for tax purposes. I also wanted to stop other people from using up all the sticky notes. Besides, once something was on a sticky note I needed to be able to find it again and in a shared office, peopled by family members, my notes kept getting stuck to the inside of a wastepaper basket more often than not. No one else liked the shop office as much as I did and that solved the problem.

I pushed open the sugarhouse door, glad to be in the familiar space. The rough wooden walls and long work-benches were worn smooth in places by generations of Greenes. Down under the bench in the corner my great-great-grandfather had carved his initials in the wall and when I was six I found it one summer day playing hide-and-seek with my siblings. When I shared my discovery with them, they laughed and said they both already knew about it. That's the thing about being the youngest in a family with a long history in one spot. There's no new territory to explore unless you make it up yourself or find a new way to look at a place already traveled.

Which was one of the reasons I was so committed to making the sugaring operation a success. Everyone had a niche to fill and a part to play in the family. Grandma and Grampa endowed the school. My parents had created an artist colony in a back parcel of land and hosted talented people who went on to win prizes in all fields of endeavor. Celadon set up a land trust that spanned hundreds of acres and received national attention. Loden used his law degree to run a free clinic out of our spare barn for neighbors who couldn't otherwise afford legal help in civil matters. What I wanted, more than anything, was to make my own contribution to the community. The maple cooperative was my first stab at doing just that. Coming up with ways to help my fellow sugar makers stay in business was one of the best ways I could think to be of service.

I wandered through the shop, running my hand over the stock and checking for dust. Not many people came to the sugarhouse at this time of year but we still did get the odd customer looking for something to give as a gift. Between Christmas and sugaring season, the only people who sought us out for purchasing were locals but I still wanted to make a good impression.

I made my way to the back of the shop and stopped short as I entered the small office. A drawer in the oak file cabinet sagged open and some file folders were shoved in like someone was in too much of a hurry to do the job neatly. I never leave things like that. I'm not compulsively neat but I can't stand to leave drawers hanging open. It looks like an unmade bed in the middle of your office.

Besides, how lazy can you be? It's not like a file drawer is all that heavy. Nor is it tricky to operate. No one who was authorized to be in the sugarhouse would have left it in this sort of a state. I took a last look around then sat in my chair and bent over the file drawer to retrieve the file containing the information for the cooperative.

The file wasn't where I thought I left it. I pulled open the other drawers and ran my fingers across the contents of each. Boxes of permanent markers, rubber bands, and pricing stickers sat neatly side by side but no files containing a list of contacts for suppliers or the contract I had created for members to sign were with them. Nothing whatsoever pertaining to the cooperative was there.

Deciding not to panic, I sat once again at the desk and booted up the computer. Or at least tried to boot it up. I pushed the power button on but no familiar sounds of thumping and whirring filled the small room. No moaning or a fan that sounded like a small plane preparing for takeoff greeted my ears. Just the sound of me cussing and the clacking noise I made on the keyboard as I tried to make it respond.

I climbed under the desk to check that the darn thing was still plugged in and that's when the bad news struck. Someone had neatly snipped the plug end off the cord and left it on the floor. I stared, confused at what I was seeing. No one had ever broken into our home in the more than two hundred years since my family had been given the land by the governor to settle the place. The closest thing to trespassing we ever had was Knowlton looking in the woods for things to stuff.

I wasn't even sure what to do. I banged my head on the underside of the desk as I struggled to back out. I wondered if there was any chance an animal had somehow gotten into the building and gnawed through the cord. I knew it was ridiculous but somehow it seemed preferable to a human being invading my space with malicious intentions.

I decided to check the stack of catalogs I keep near the wingback chair in the shop for anything I could use to rewrite the informational packets for the co-op members. Not only were the magazines missing, someone had taken the entire basket. Now there was no hope at all a wild animal was responsible. I also had to reconsider whether or not Frank was truly responsible for the sabotage in town. I hadn't been in the sugarhouse since Sunday morning.

It was conceivable that Frank had come by after that on Sunday when no one was looking and then returned home in time to be murdered before I found him at around one thirty. The time frame seemed tight but it might have been possible. At least I hoped it was, otherwise the saboteur was still out there and the problems for the cooperative might just be getting started.

I hurried out the door and considered locking it, then thought better of the idea. Firstly, I had no idea where the key could be found to open it up again later and secondly, I didn't like the idea of changing my life because of an unkind prank. Maybe I should have been more worried than I was but I shut the door behind me and hightailed it for the house.

I thought about calling the police but decided if Mitch hadn't been inclined to take the sabotage seriously before he had his hands full with Frank's death, he wasn't likely to do so now. I headed back to the house trying to decide if I should tell someone in the family about what I had found. I didn't want to tell Grandma or Loden whose voices I could hear laughing and singing in the kitchen.

It would just spoil their good mood. Grampa would bluster and complain about how much he hated the computer anyway and how glad he was it had gone and gotten itself killed. I noticed Celadon in the living room cutting out paper snowflakes with Spring and Hunter. The kids were actually sitting still and getting along so there was no way I was going to disturb that. It was as rare an occurrence as a flamingo at our bird feeder.

There was only one thing to do. I needed to procrastinate. I grabbed my keys and left a note scribbled on the chalkboard in the hallway to let the family know what had become of me. Breakfast at the Stack Shack was the perfect way to mark time until a decision appeared full-blown in my mind.

I chugged down into town, wishing once more Lowell were manning the police station instead of a deck chair in the middle of the Atlantic. My stomach rumbled as I thought about a hot stack of Piper's famous pancakes or an omelet the size of the moon filled with creamed spinach and sun-dried tomatoes. And coffee.

The damage to my computer should have killed my appetite along with my plans for the cooperative but somehow I managed to steer the Clunker into the only free parking space right in front of the Stack. I heard thumping overhead and looked up to see the local chimney sweep, Cal Donaldson, yanking his long brush in and out of the butter pat shaped chimney. It was a miracle he could stand up on the roof with the all lacquer the original builder had poured on it to resemble syrup. It hung down in permanent icicles all along the perimeter of the building, creating a hazard for the very tall as they went through the door.

I waved up at Cal before grasping the spatula-shaped door handle and walking in. A minute later and I was perched on a stool at the counter with a steaming cup of coffee in front of me and a whole list of breakfast specials and old favorites to decide among. Given the emotional ravaging of the last couple of days French toast seemed the best thing to set me back on track. Piper called out my order to Charlie in the back and leaned over the counter to look me right in the eyes.

"It was that bad, huh?" There was no fooling Piper.

"Finding Frank's body was grim. Telling Phoebe about it was even worse. The vandalism in town is escalating. I feel like I started something I should never have attempted." I added an extra couple spoonfuls of sugar to the coffee Piper plopped down in front of me, hoping it might sweeten my outlook.

"Don't say that. The cooperative is a great idea. I was talking about it with Dean and Jill just yesterday. Jill thinks the savings will amount to enough for her to stay open instead of selling." Now was my chance to put some feelers out about Dean.

"Did Dean seem as enthusiastic as Jill about keeping the business running?" I asked.

"What makes you ask that?" I thought I caught the barest bit of a scrunch between Piper's eyebrows. She is a great card player and keeps her facial tells to a minimum but it has gotten easier to notice the tiniest wiggle in that region since she got her brow pierced. Light glints off it when it moves. Dean hadn't been happy and Piper was hesitant to tell me about it. This was just one more way the week was going wrong.

"It just seems like the sugarhouse is more Jill's pet project than Dean's. I can see how he might be interested in selling the place if it meant he would have a nest egg of his own instead of all his assets tied up in someone else's dream." Here was where I was going to shift the topic just enough to relax her defense of Dean. "After all, things look like they are getting pretty serious between the two of you and maybe he would like to settle down in a home of his own with a family of his own before too long." Piper's eyebrow ring twitched again and I thought she looked just the slightest bit green around the gills. I know that look. It blankets my own face anytime Knowlton's eligibility is mentioned within the range of my hearing.

"I'm sure I don't know what you mean. Dean is a whole lot of fun but no one has said anything about settling down." Piper turned away to fetch my plate of French toast and side order of locally raised and smoked maple bacon. She banged the plate down with a bit more force than necessary.

"So I heard wrong about his interest in selling the property."

"No, you heard right." Piper wiped vigorously at an imaginary spot on the counter with the edge of her vin-

Jessie Crockett

tage embroidered apron. "He and Jill got into it a bit actually. She was so happy and he was a total downer. To tell you the truth, it showed me another side of Dean that I wasn't so thrilled to find out about."

"Jill called me up to her place on Saturday morning to show me a few of her trees that had been girdled. You don't think Dean wants to sell badly enough that he would girdle the trees to intimidate Jill into giving up, do you?" There, I'd said it. I busied myself with cutting into the toast, which was sliced so thick you could use it for insulation.

"As much as I wish I could swear I believed he wouldn't do a thing like that, I don't think I can." Piper stopped her rubbing and twitching and looked me in the face. "Dean is a lot of fun. He's a great musician and up for just about anything, which appeals to me. But I'm not sure I trust him to put someone else's interests ahead of his own." Maybe there was hope for Loden after all. It was my fondest wish that Piper and Loden would marry one day and that she would be a legal member of the family rather than an honorary one. Maybe I ought to put in a plug for my brother while we were being so honest.

"You deserve someone who would put your interests first. Someone whose moral compass matches your own and who you would never hesitate to believe in."

"You may be right but where would I ever find a guy like that?" A cold blast of air barreled into the Stack as Loden opened the door and gave us a wave.

"I think it might be a lot easier than you imagine." I

patted the stool next to me and Loden perched himself there.

"Kenneth called Grampa." Loden was generally a man of few words but the ones he used were worth listening to. If he thought he ought to drive out to find me and tell me something in person it was likely I needed to know.

"Is it about the cooperative?" I felt the French toast get heavier in my stomach as though there had been a significant change to the force of gravity.

"The Shaw place has been vandalized."

"No." Damage done to the Shaws' sugaring operation would be enough to single-handedly discourage people from sticking with the cooperative. If Kenneth pulled out, that might be it for my plans.

"Yes. Grampa said you'd be up directly to take a look."

"Grampa actually told Kenneth Shaw that I was the one to come deal with it?" I was thunderstruck.

All my life I've been trying to prove I was capable and should be treated with as much respect as anyone else in the family. Mostly, it has felt like I wasn't making any progress on that front. Being the youngest is always a challenge when it comes to respect and being sized like a Chihuahua hasn't helped any. And now, out of the blue, I was being entrusted with something as important as smoothing things over with Kenneth Shaw. I was beginning to rethink the value of being considered an adult. What is that old saying? Be careful what you wish for, you might just get it?

"I stood right there in the kitchen listening to the whole

conversation. Kenneth was worked up enough that I could hear his end of it, too. Grampa calmly explained that the sugaring operation and all aspects thereof, cooperative included, were under your authority and that you would be along shortly to see what should be done."

"Grampa used the word *thereof*? That sounds pretty suspicious to me." Grampa had a great vocabulary and was a well-educated and well-read man. But he wasn't flashy in any part of his life and that included what some might consider uppity speech.

"I may have paraphrased his exact words but it came down to that in the end. After he hung up with Kenneth he told me that after the way you handled the dummy crisis up at Tansey's he was sure you could take care of this."

"He said that?" I felt pricking behind my eyes, and as proud as I had been the day I won the school spelling bee back in the fifth grade.

"He did and he said you would get on it right away. So I offered to come tell you." Piper had moved down the counter to take a new patron's order. Loden kept his eyes locked on her from the safety of the backside of the menu.

"You could have phoned down to the restaurant instead of making the drive. It would have been more environmentally friendly."

"I could have but I had some business at the post office anyway and I never pass up a chance for breakfast at the Stack."

"Your timing is pretty good, too. I asked Piper if she

thought Dean could have sabotaged his own trees like you suggested and she said he might have done it."

"What's that got to do with my timing?" Loden looked like he was holding his breath.

"If she was in love with the guy, she wouldn't have said that. Dean's days as Piper's latest are numbered. I guarantee it."

"Maybe he's responsible for what happened at the Shaws', too. If he is, he'll go to jail for sure."

"Don't count on that working against him. Piper has a thing for bad boys."

"I know she does." Loden's shoulders sagged and he tapped his forehead with the laminated menu like he was trying to knock some sense into himself.

"She likes them, but she doesn't respect them in the long run. Patience and good character are your best strategies."

"And a sense of urgency is yours. You'd better get yourself over to the Shaws' before it gets any later or you'll have to explain things to two irritated old men instead of one."

"Kenneth and who else?"

"Grampa."

Fifteen

I crunched onto the Shaws' perfectly groomed gravel drive just five minutes later. It always felt like I was walking with muddy shoes across a white carpet when I drove onto their driveway. Or like I was deliberately messing up a Zen gravel garden. I could just feel a monk with a rake shaking his smooth head sadly at me with each rotation of the wheels.

Kenneth paced on the front porch. I unhooked my seat belt, a feeling of dread spreading from my stomach high up into my throat and down into my legs. Kenneth kept up his strolling vigil even as I crossed the dooryard. He looked good pacing, kind of presidential. If anyone could pull off looking good in a crisis it was Kenneth. I just wished I were hearing about it from a third party instead of finding myself in the middle of it.

I pressed on the Clunker's door and it was so heavy it shut itself with a banging that sounded angry when I never intended it. Kenneth stopped pacing and stuck his hands in his pants pockets. I hope he didn't feel chided. But I wasn't going to call attention to my puny arm muscles. Grampa always said they were about as big as a sparrow's instep. I got to be at least ten before I realized I was being insulted.

"Come on back to the sugarhouse," Kenneth said. That was it. No *How are you, Dani? How's the family, Dani?* For such a well-mannered man he was surprisingly abrupt. I followed his hurriedly retreating back. His long legs outdistanced me quickly and I found myself breaking into a jog to keep up.

The Shaws' sugarhouse was a lot like ours as far as function but very different as far as technology. The Shaw family had been sugaring for at least as long as the Greenes but where we were moving toward modern techniques and equipment the Shaws preferred to preserve the traditions of the past. Where we had a gift shop with hopes of expansion, they had a maple museum and a gallery of art and photographs documenting sugaring in New Hampshire through the ages.

"This is why I called your grandfather." Kenneth pushed open the door and held it for me. I looked around the room but saw nothing suspicious.

"I'm not sure what you mean." I could see from the way he rocked up onto the balls of his feet then crashed back down on his heels that he was feeling agitated and impatient but there was little I could do to help until he made things clearer.

"The museum." He pointed at the doorway between the main room holding the evaporator and the museum room. On the floor there was a steaming bucket full of suds. "Follow me." He raced across the room, leaving me to scurry after him. On the walls, where the photos and paintings used to hang, there were blank spaces and graffiti. Where a variety of buckets, spiles, and other sugaring paraphernalia normally hung or sat shelved there was nothing to see but sloppy scrawl.

I gasped, so startled to see the glossy wood walls marred by red paint. The Shaws' place was one of the most popular stops on the annual New Hampshire Maple Weekend open sugarhouses tour. One of the reasons was its cleanliness and pristine order. Kenneth supervised every aspect of the business himself. As the chairman of the select board, he had a standard to uphold and he did it without fail.

I stepped closer to the wall to get a better look at the writing but it really wasn't necessary. Even from considerable distance it was clear to see the nasty message.

"Cooperatives are for communists. This won't be tolerated in Sugar Grove. Pictures of your trees are missing. Join the cooperative and your trees will be next." I read aloud. "What sort of crazy nonsense is this?" I felt even worse now that I knew what the problem entailed. All I wanted was to help out the local producers, not stir something like this up from the bottom of the mud puddle. I regretted ever trying to get the cooperative going.

"The artwork is irreplaceable. The photos can be reprinted but it will cost me a lot of time as well as money to find the right negatives, get them developed and then framed and rehung. And I can't even begin to think about the wooden sap buckets and the tools passed down for generations of Shaws. It just breaks my heart." Kenneth hung his head like a small boy. I couldn't help but feel it was all my fault even though I knew the cooperative was a great idea and that I had nothing to do with what had happened here today.

"When did you discover this?" I asked, wondering if either Frank or Dean could be involved.

"This morning, after breakfast. I got home from my morning walk, had a bite to eat with Nicole and then came out here to do a bit of paperwork. And this is what I found. This awful mess."

"Did you find anything to give you some idea who did it?" I wasn't sure if I wanted him to have a suspect or not.

"Well, no. I didn't find a thing. I don't like to toss around names without proof but it seems like the most likely person to have done this was Frank." Kenneth's face was flushing red. I wondered if he was going to have some sort of coronary incident. I slipped my hand into my pocket to feel for my cell phone. If he started clutching his chest I wanted to be able to get someone here quickly. Although Kenneth's chances of getting some help from Bob Sterling might not be all that great if I phoned in a distress call.

"Frank's the only one who has said he wasn't happy with the co-op but I don't think he did this."

"No one else comes to mind. It had to be Frank." He stopped stomping around and looked me straight in the face. I gulped under his gaze. It suddenly occurred to me Kenneth must not have heard about Frank's murder. I was starting to feel like the angel of death with all the bad news I was spreading around the community.

"When was the last time you were in here?"

"Yesterday morning. I came in to check on things before church. Does it matter?"

"It would help pinpoint where people were when the damage occurred in order to figure out who could have done it."

"I can't say for certain. Like I said, I found it this morning."

"Depending on when it happened it might have been impossible for Frank to be responsible."

"I don't see how you can be so sure." Kenneth crossed his plaid shirt clad arms over his chest and widened his stance. He looked like he was trying to convince me I was wrong through stern body language. Fortunately for me, I did know exactly what I was talking about.

"I found his body in his own sugarhouse yesterday afternoon." Kenneth unfolded his arms and opened and closed his mouth like a fish gasping for air in the top of a dirty aquarium.

"What was it? A heart attack or a stroke? Something like that?"

"The police are treating it as a homicide."

"Hardly surprising considering what a disagreeable man he was but in any case that does seem to rule him out as the person who did this." Kenneth gazed around the room. "Why wasn't I told before now?" As a seated selectman as well as someone who volunteered for as many things as a member of my family, Kenneth was usually among the first to know about everything and anything that happened in town. Being out of the loop must have been almost as startling to him as hearing that Frank had been murdered.

"I expect Mitch has his hands full with the investigation. Lowell is out of town, remember? I'm surprised you didn't hear about it on the scanner though." The Shaws, like so many other people in town keep a scanner on most of the time. Anything they don't hear from a reliable local gossip they catch from the scanner. Accurate information is a form of currency around here and the Shaws are one of the wealthiest families in town.

"I expect you're right and I'm afraid the vandalism here, no matter how upsetting it is to me personally, won't end up being much of a priority."

"Tansey had some trouble herself before I found Frank's body and Mitch dropped by to look at things then. But, with Frank's murder I am sure he won't be bothering now. I think it will be up to us to get to the bottom of this ourselves."

"But I can't think of anyone besides Frank who would want to do something like this. Can you?"

"Didn't you have some trouble with Russ Collins a month or so ago?" It had been big news all over town and could easily explain the vandalism if Russ was the sort to follow through on a threat.

"There was a bit of a dustup. He was supposed to be refinishing all the downstairs floors."

"I heard there was a disagreement about speed."

"The disagreement was because there was no speed. None at all. That man couldn't be bothered to break into a trot if the devil was standing behind him with an electrified pitchfork."

"Did you fire him?"

"What else could I do? He did a poor job sanding the hall and made an even worse start on the living room. He left all his tools, equipment, and mess lying around our house for a month and a half. Finally, I tossed everything onto the back porch and told him we got someone else to do the job."

"So maybe he did this?" I looked around wondering if there was any way Russ would have found the energy to make off with so much stuff.

"Not a chance. He wouldn't have been able to muster the oomph for a job this big. The man took over a week to come get his own tools. I don't think he would have snuck into my sugarhouse to steal all of mine."

"Anyone else you had a dispute with recently?"

"No one comes to mind." I racked my brain for someone else, anyone else who would be interested in damaging Kenneth's property. Maybe it wasn't related to the cooperative. Maybe someone was just using that as an excuse to do the Shaws' operation some harm. I knew there was a bit of envy and tension where the Shaws were concerned. There always was with prominent, successful people. I decided to risk agitating him even more by asking about that.

"Was there any reason someone would want to do this to you and throw suspicion away from themselves by blaming the cooperative? Has anyone threatened you or caused damage here before?" My voice cracked like a fourteen-year-old boy.

"No. Of course not. We mind our own business and pitch in with what needs doing in the community. Everybody loves us. This is about the cooperative. It says so in screaming red paint."

"The message does seem clear but I think it would be best to explore all angles before accusing anybody."

"I'm not planning on accusing anybody. I want you to do it. This is all your fault, make no mistake. I wondered if this wasn't a too-good-to-be-true situation and it looks like I was right."

"I was only trying to help." My voice cracked again and my stomach felt sick at the thought of being on the wrong side of Kenneth.

"Now you have the chance to really be helpful by calling off the whole cooperative idea. It may not have been as good as you thought in the first place."

"Stop the cooperative? You've got to be kidding. It will save so much money for everyone involved."

"Whoever did this is threatening my trees. You, of all people, understand what that means." Kenneth got even redder. He started rubbing one hand against the other.

"I can't stop the cooperative without talking to the rest of the people who want to join. I think people will have to decide for themselves if they want to continue to participate or not."

"I am sorry to tell you this Dani but I am going to withdraw myself and encourage others to do so too before something even worse happens to my property." Kenneth had the same look on his face he always wore just before bringing down his gavel at a rowdy select board meeting.

"I understand. You have to do what you think is best for your business. But I hope you will give me a little time to try to get to the bottom of this before you start discouraging others from participating. I promise to see if I can figure this all out before anything else happens."

"And how do you propose to do that? Mitch's got his hands full with investigating what happened to Frank and last I heard you weren't exactly in a position to ask him for any favors anyway."

"I'll do my best. That's all I can tell you. If that isn't good enough for you, there isn't anything else I can say." I looked up at him, my best tough business look on my face. Maybe he would back down if I just didn't show any fear.

"I'm sorry, Dani, but I just can't risk waiting until an amateur gets to the bottom of a crime. I am pulling out and will be advising everyone else to do the same." He shook his head slowly back and forth, staring at the wall in front of him. I just didn't know what else to say. I couldn't offer comfort for his loss and I wouldn't back down from my plans for the cooperative. I decided the only thing to do was to find the saboteur and Kenneth's missing items. If Loden was right, it might even lead to the killer.

After my discouraging conversation with Kenneth I was looking for someone to blame. I thought automatically of Russ Collins and Dean. I know I thought of Dean because Loden had already suggested him. I'm not proud to admit it but I thought of Russ because I didn't like him. I felt like a bad human hoping a family man might be a criminal but I didn't think from the looks of things around his property it was likely it would make much practical difference if he spent time away in jail. After all, from the disheveled state of his driveway he wasn't doing much work around the house.

I knocked on the door at the Collins's place but no one came to answer it. Mindy's minivan wasn't in the drive but Russ's sedan was sitting there, snow still pressed up against it from the last storm. I wondered if he was just too lazy to come to the door. I banged again slightly harder and then pressed my face against the glass hoping I might see something to let me know if he was actually home.

I heard a voice calling faintly from somewhere in the house and I took that as a sign to let myself in. After all, the Collins family only had cats, no dogs. After the terrors of Beau I thought it unlikely I was going to be intimidated by a tabby. As I entered the hallway littered with shoes and backpacks I heard the voice call out again.

"I'm in here but I'm not getting up." I followed the sound and ended up in the cluttered living room. Russ lay stretched on the couch, the remote in his hand, a bowl of what smelled like barbecue-flavored chips perched on his stomach. "Dani, what a surprise. Did you forget something after the campout?"

"No. Actually, I wanted to ask you about getting a quote for a job we need done up at Greener Pastures." I noticed Russ scootching up just a bit, like he had forgotten his back trouble.

"What kind of a job?"

"I'm thinking of expanding to add a screened porch to the sugarhouse shop so we can serve afternoon tea in the summer. I thought of you immediately." Which wasn't true. I had thought of Wesley Farnum, the master builder the Greene family had trusted with everything for years but telling him that wasn't going to help get the answers I wanted about the vandalism at Kenneth Shaw's.

"Sounds like a good-sized job. When were you thinking of starting it?" Russ forgot his back a little more as he turned a bit to look at me.

"That will depend on the weather of course. It would be an outside job after all. So the snow will be a factor."

"And frozen ground."

"And you'll be too busy with the sugaring this year to mess around with a building project. So after the sugaring season is over, I'd say."

"Of course."

"So are you interested?"

"Of course I'm interested. A man has to provide for his family, doesn't he?" Russ dug into the bowl of chips and stuffed a handful into his mouth.

"I hate to do this but I'll need to ask for references."

"But you know me." He was right about that. I knew he wasn't likely to get any good ones from anyone in town but after filling in for him on Saturday night at the Squirrel Squad campout it was a pleasure to watch him squirm. Besides, how better to introduce the dispute with Kenneth and the possible vandalism.

"Of course I do, but it's a matter of evenhandedness. In a small town like Sugar Grove it's easy for people to get hurt feelings, especially where business is concerned. I always ask everyone so no one can be offended."

"How big a job did you say it would be?" Russ popped some more chips in his mouth and ground them around with his mouth hanging open.

"I was thinking maybe eight hundred square feet, possibly a bit bigger. And we'll need steps, railing, and garden beds built in along the front to blend it in with the surroundings. Visual appeal is a big part of the success factor for this type of venture." Unfortunately I could almost see the spit forming in his open mouth as the numbers he was adding up in his head were making it water.

"I guess I could rustle up a few references. It sounds like the project could be worth my while."

"Something from one of the other sugarhouses would be especially helpful. Didn't you do some work for the Shaws not too long ago?"

"I know I haven't done any work for him in his sugarhouse."

"I'm sure Kenneth mentioned you were doing work for him. He said something about it the other day when I was there talking to him about the cooperative. I just wish I could remember what the project was."

"I'd have to look over my records." Russ slid back down and drew the bowl of chips up higher on his chest, obscuring his face a bit.

"I know. I remember now. It was a flooring job wasn't it?"

"Oh, that's right."

"I think I heard maybe it didn't go so well." That got Russ's attention.

"Where'd you hear that?"

"Kenneth mentioned it himself."

"Did he tell you he pulled out after I had already spent time on that job? He refused to pay me, too. I ought to have sued him, put a lien on his property."

"Why didn't you?"

"It wouldn't have been worth all the legal fees. But one day someone's gonna show that guy."

"What do you mean show him?"

"I mean, someone is gonna take him down a peg. He struts around like the king of Sugar Grove. Being a selectman doesn't entitle you to lord over everyone else. Having more money than a dog has fleas doesn't either. That guy needs to be shown he can't just push people around and get away with it."

"Maybe someone already has taught him a lesson," I said, wondering if I really ought to spread the gossip about the Shaws' museum or if I had better remain quiet. I decided if Myra heard about it, and she would have, everyone else would, too.

"What kind of lesson?"

"Someone stole most of the items in his museum and scrawled graffiti on the walls where the art hung." I watched his face carefully for signs of guilt. I'm not sure if he looked guilty but he certainly seemed pleased if the smile splitting his face from ear to ear meant anything.

"That sounds like just about the best way to stick it to the old boy. I wish I'd thought of it myself." Russ completely forgot about his back injury and popped straight up and leaned toward me.

"Are you sure you didn't think of it?"

"What are you implying?"

"The police are going to be looking for someone who had a dispute with Frank and you are bound to be at the top of their list."

"Why me? There had to be tons of people with a problem with Kenneth. What about Frank? He hated Kenneth's guts."

"The time frame for Frank to have done it is pretty tight. Frank was probably dead too close to the time the vandalism occurred."

"Are you sure?"

"No, I'm not absolutely positive but it would have been nearly impossible. Where were you on Sunday?"

"I don't have to explain myself to you."

"Of course you don't. But you will have to tell Mitch where you were. And if you don't tell me, I'm going to mention to Mindy how glad she must be that your back is completely healed. I'm sure she has all kinds of things you could be doing around here. I hear another snowstorm is due in and it looks to me like someone needs to do a better job shoveling a path to the house."

"I was here the whole time."

"Are you sure? Did you sneak out for snacks like one of those bags of chips?"

"No. I was here from Saturday afternoon until now."

"Thanks for that, by the way. I can't think of anything I would have rather been doing than filling in for your sorry, lazy self at a winter campout."

"I was happy to get out of it, I can tell you. It was nice to be at home having a bit of peace and quiet for a change. You don't know what it's like around here with all the kids running around and yelling nonstop."

"You didn't leave for any reason?"

"How could I? Mindy might have seen me or heard about it from someone else and then I would have had to have helped with the campout."

"No chance you could have snuck off?"

"Mindy was right on the other side of the property. How could I risk her coming to check on me or sending one of the kids?"

He was right about the risk of being spotted. But what if Mindy did know he was faking his back injury? What if she was giving him a way to take care of his grudge against Kenneth? Or even worse, what if he was the one who killed Frank? If he didn't have an alibi for the time of the vandalism up at the Shaws he didn't have one for the time of Frank's murder either.

Sixteen

With one of my preferred suspects questioned I decided to turn my attention to the other. In light of my earlier conversation with Piper I was especially eager to speak with Dean. If his girlfriend wasn't even sure he didn't damage his property to serve his own ends, then I felt he merited careful consideration. The fact that he stood between Loden and Piper only made me more eager to chat with him.

But I still needed an excuse to ask him about his whereabouts yesterday afternoon and evening. I knew he couldn't have been working because the hardware store was closed on Sundays. And I knew he didn't go to church but that would only have been in the morning anyway. I wished I had known about the timing of the vandalism at Kenneth's place when I was at the Stack. I should have asked Piper if Dean was with her in the afternoon. I doubted it very much since Piper generally worked all day on Sundays and Dean didn't hang around the Stack too often.

Piper never liked her men to bother her at work. She liked to keep her attention on her customers, and boyfriends often seemed to have the impression that they were the most important customers of all. During business hours Piper did not agree with them. For her, every customer was the most important customer. Piper's food was great and the atmosphere was a delight but it was Piper's warm and friendly welcome and personal attention that really kept her in business. Which would be hard to provide with a needy boyfriend hanging around clamoring for attention.

I pulled into the parking lot at Village Hardware and slid into the spot right next to Dean's electric blue Jeep. I expected to find him slouched over the counter as usual, working a sudoku puzzle but found him instead in the gardening aisle sweeping up a pile of spilled fertilizer from a split bag. The air reeked of the chemicals and Dean didn't look too happy with his task. I expected he wouldn't be too happy with me before too long either if I didn't figure out a way to poke into his business without letting him know why I was asking.

"Hey, Dani. Did you need something?" he asked, stopping his sweeping in mid swish. With service like that I hated to suspect him of anything worse than not being the right guy for Piper.

"I wondered if you have any of those timers for electronics. You know, the kind you plug a lamp into so it will turn on when you aren't home but want to make it look like you are?"

"Now why would you want a thing like that? Someone's always home at your house." Dean looked genuinely surprised.

"It's for the sugarhouse. We've had a break-in." I watched his face carefully, looking for signs of guilt. I wished I had thought to bring either Grandma or Celadon along for the questioning. No one spots the faintest flicker of guilt like a mother. I've gotten better over the years, with all the babysitting I do for my niece and nephew, at noticing signs of a troubled conscience but I still consider myself an amateur. Grandma has a black belt in lie detection and Celadon is catching up fast.

"A break-in? Here in Sugar Grove? That's crazy."

"There have been a lot of unusual things going on lately."

"Tell me about it. Knowlton was in talking about the dummy dangling in the barn up at their place. Frank went and got himself murdered. What's next?" I wondered if I should flat out mention the vandalism at Kenneth's to try to gauge his reaction. I might learn that he already knew about it but I would give him more negative things to say about the cooperative if he didn't. In the end, getting to the bottom of the trouble at the Shaws' was more important so I decided to risk it.

"The Shaws' Maple Museum was vandalized, too." I kept my eyes fixed firmly on his but I felt like I had no idea if he was truly surprised or just faking it because he seemed excited more than anything else.

"No way! Not the Shaws. It took some kind of guts to mess with old Ken's place." I wasn't sure if Dean was admiring someone else or bragging about himself but I was sure I had never before heard anyone call Kenneth Shaw *Ken*. He wasn't a nicknames guy. I had heard people occasionally lengthen his name to Lord Kenneth or His Majesty Lord Shaw. I had even overheard someone mentioning the possibility that Kenneth thought Shaw was really Shah like it was in Iran.

Dean's attitude reminded me that he had been in the same grade at school with Kenneth's son, Jeremy, and that the boys had gotten into some trouble together as teenagers. Maybe Dean was still resentful. After all, Jeremy was raised by a pair of well-respected parents with a great deal of money and Dean navigated the potholes of adolescence with the help of a grief-stricken older sister barely above the poverty line. There may have been more hostility pointed at the Shaws than I had first considered.

"Especially on a Sunday. I think crimes on a Sunday get extra badness points."

"Yesterday, huh? It must not have been a football fan doing the damage."

"Why do you say that?"

"Every football fan I know of would have been home watching the games. The Super Bowl's coming up soon." I'm not a big television sports fan, I never have been. The only function of sports on television as far as I'm concerned is to give a good excuse to make couch-friendly snacks. That means things that don't require flatware and shouldn't be likely to leave traces of themselves on the furniture. Sports snacks require creativity and I like that. But I could not care less about the competition or the rules or the sweating. The sweating actually puts me off my snacks and I am definitely not a big fan of losing my appetite.

I'm too scared of wasting away to nothing to want that to happen. Don't get me wrong, I loved gymnastics as a child. I love to ice-skate and to go hiking. I love all sorts of physical activities. What I don't love is sitting around watching others being active.

"I guess that includes you then." Maybe I would be able to find out what he was up to without coming right out and accusing him of the vandalism. Or Frank's murder.

"I was glued right to my television from noon until well after nine last night."

"That's a lot of hours. And I thought baseball games took forever." As a kid I spent endless hours climbing around on the bleachers at Loden's interminable ball games, trying to outwit or outrun hoards of blackflies.

"I was hopping around to different channels catching the action on different games. Then there are the commentaries afterward. Plus, I spotted a horror movie on one of the classic channels that I couldn't pass up the chance to watch."

"Jill doesn't mind the television being on for so many hours in a row? I know my family wouldn't be able to stand it." That was the truth. We hardly ever had the thing on. As a matter of fact we had the smallest television of anyone I know and it is left in the draftiest, least comfortable room in the house. The television room actually makes Loden's train room seem well thought out and comfortable.

It's down at the end of the back hall on the first floor. The fireplace is the only source of heat and the chimney that serves it doesn't draw right so the smoke has a tendency to back up into the room. The only furniture allowed in there are pieces cast off from other rooms. Consequently, all the chairs have broken springs and the tables have wobbly legs. We don't have any of the cable or satellite services so reception is terrible at best. The only time I really ever watched television was over at Piper's house when we were kids. I have no interest in it now. Maybe it's one of those things you have to develop a taste for, like Moxie.

In contrast, the family library is toasty in the winter, cool in the summer, and is furnished with the most comfortable seats in the house. Wingback chairs with ottomans and big squishy sofas dot the room. Floor-to-ceiling gleaming maple bookshelves line the walls and are simply stuffed with books of every genre. The floors are carpeted with wool rugs in rich, deep colors.

In a newer wing of the house, positioned far away from the library, so as not to be disruptive, there's also a game room with a regulation pool table, casino tables, and a dedicated puzzle table. Any board game, card game, or nonelectronic table game you might wish for is available. My grandparents love fun, they just don't like television. I almost forget it exists.

"Jill wasn't home. She was off shopping all day with a friend from out of town. They went all the way to the mall in Nashua. Which is a place you might have to go to find the timer device you are looking for since we don't have one here."

"Thanks anyway. I'll keep looking around closer to home first." Nashua is over an hour away and I had no desire to head out of town if I could spend my dollars in the community instead. Back in the Clunker I had to decide what my next move would be. It wasn't going to be easy to prove Dean hadn't been watching the games. All the scores were available online along with commentary on the highlights. Besides, he could have recorded anything he wanted and watched it later. No one had to watch anything in real time anymore.

But Jill wasn't home and no one else lived with them so he could easily be lying. I didn't feel like our conversation had been all that helpful but at least I hadn't gotten his back up. I needed to think a bit more and I also decided to drop in at the police station to report the break-in at Greener Pastures. I wanted to put in a claim to the insurance company in case the computer needed to be replaced rather than repaired.

Myra was stationed at her desk in her typical style, eyes and ears peeled for gossip and drama, arms and legs exposed by her choice of stretch knit shorts and tank tops no matter what the weather. She looked up with that hungry glint in her eye I've seen her get at community events and the post office. She has an otherworldly knack for scenting news before it takes wing. I could just tell she was smelling it on me like I had rolled in something dead.

"So what brings you in today, Dani? Conscience get the better of you and you're here to confess to murder?" She pitched her voice low like she didn't want to share the moment with Mitch if that was the reason for my visit. Myra was wasted on the phones. She ought to be the one out doing the investigating instead of Mitch, or even Lowell if he had been home to fulfill his duties instead of sailing the high seas with my mother.

"No, sorry. I would like to file a report concerning some property damage."

"The Shaws have already taken care of their own report. Mitch is up there right now investigating." So she hadn't been trying to keep Mitch from hearing her. I wondered who else might be in the office instead. "No need to be a busybody now is there?" That took some gall coming from her. Maybe I ought to give her a bit of a tease.

"Actually it was for some business of my own but if Mitch isn't here, I guess I'll have to come back later."

"Oh you poor thing." Myra came out from behind the desk, her flabby thighs rubbing together below the hem of her shorts as she hurried to steer me into the chair opposite her desk.

"It's fine. I can just drop in another time. I'm sure I can contact the insurance company without a police report filed first." I could almost see the holes in her ears stretching and straining, waiting for the news. If ears could grumble like stomachs do, she would have lost an eardrum from the racket.

"Park it, short stuff. Mitch will be here soon. I know he wasn't planning to stay a minute longer than he can help. Kenneth makes that boy sweat." Myra pushed down on my shoulders to stuff me into the visitor's chair and then pushed it toward the desk like she was moving a child close enough to reach the table at dinnertime. If she wanted to remind me of how easily she could push me around, she had surely done so. I gave up.

"The sugarhouse at Greener Pastures was broken into."

"Anything stolen?"

"Files and catalogs, any printed materials to do with the cooperative I've been trying to start to support the local sugar makers."

"Somebody was going on about that at church yesterday. I can't seem to remember who though. Why would anyone want all that stuff? It doesn't seem valuable."

"It isn't, in itself. The catalogs are all available for free. Anyone could get them. The bigger problem was the theft of the printouts I had prepared for potential members about the cooperative. How it would work, what the costs would be, that sort of thing."

"Can't you just print out another batch of papers? That doesn't seem like something to go wasting police time about when we're shorthanded and in the middle of a homicide investigation."

"I would if someone hadn't gone and cut off the power cord to my computer."

"Well why didn't you say that first?" Myra dug into a desk drawer for a box of chocolates. She lifted the lid and slid it across the desk at me. "Have one. It'll make you feel better." I looked over the selection hoping for a dark chocolate covered caramel.

"I am kicking myself for not taking the problems at Tansey's and Jill's seriously enough to at least bother to lock the door to the sugarhouse."

"I don't think you ought to be so hard on yourself. You know almost no one locks their doors around here. We're experiencing an unprecedented crime wave. If I didn't know better, I'd think Mitch was behind it all just to have something to brag about to Lowell when he gets back."

"You don't really think that, do you?" I hadn't even considered the sabotage could involve Mitch. Not even in my wildest imaginings. I didn't want to have anything to do with him romantically and our interactions tended toward the hostile but I wouldn't have ever expected criminality from him. Or that much creativity and craftiness.

"I would if Frank hadn't ended up getting himself killed. Mitch is a boy with a lot to prove but he wouldn't kill anybody to do it."

"I don't believe Mitch would kill anybody either. And I don't think he's behind the vandalism."

"Probably not. Got anyone else in mind?" Myra pushed the chocolate box in my direction a little more forcefully. I knew a bribe when I saw one. Myra might be eager to hear everything but that meant she probably had heard some things I hadn't.

"I think I heard someone mention it could be Dean Hayes," I said. Myra raised her eyebrows and nodded her head slowly.

"He might be sick of waiting for Jill to give up on the sugaring and just sell the place. I know Frank was interested in buying it."

"Frank might have already been dead when the vandalism occurred at Kenneth's and I think he might have been when the dummy was strung up at Tansey's, too."

"Do you know what Dean was up to yesterday?" Myra tapped her long, magenta nails on the desktop.

"He says he was watching a whole lot of Sunday sports programing but no one was with him to back up his story."

"Exactly when did he say he was watching?" Myra's

posture had stiffened like a dog breed that points. Something was jangling her about Dean's story all right.

"He claimed to have been at home parked in front of the tube from noon until around nine last night, when Jill got back."

"I saw him pulling out of the Mountain View Food Mart at just past one."

"Are you sure?"

"Of course I'm sure. He climbed into that bright blue Jeep of his and took off."

"Did you see where he went?"

"No. I was going into the store as he was coming out. But I can tell you he headed west on Main Street."

"He would have gone east to head back home."

"But not if he was going to the Shaws' instead."

"We don't know for sure that he went to Kenneth's though. All we know is that he wasn't where he said he was. There might be a lot of people with a grievance against the Shaws or any of the sugar makers in town."

"Including you." Ouch. I liked to think I was thought of well enough in town that no one would target my business or me but obviously that was wishful thinking since someone had. It was still easier to consider it was aimed at the entire group rather than me personally.

"I guess I do have to consider that. Not everyone likes me or my ideas. After all, Frank set his dog on me after I approached him about joining. That was a pretty good indication that he didn't hold me in high regard."

"I wouldn't take that personally. Frank set his dog on lots of people. Just ask Byron. He's got a list so long you could paper a powder room with it." I grabbed one more chocolate after explaining I couldn't wait any longer for Mitch and hit the road. Byron was exactly whom I wanted to talk to next.

Seventeen

The Clunker gave me a perfect excuse to call on Byron. Not only did I have a legitimate reason to nag him about my MG Midget, which was still in his shop for repair, the Clunker was starting to make the noise that gave the vehicle its name. I chugged into the parking lot at Sugar Grove Auto Repair at half speed. Byron stood bent over a station wagon I knew belonged to Felicia Chick, co-owner of the local bed-and-breakfast. Why Felicia's station wagon was more urgently in need of repair than my Midget I was unsure. This was not starting out as auspiciously as I had hoped.

"Does this mean my Midget is ready to drive off and use?" I asked, sliding out of the Clunker and crossing the lot.

"Nope." Byron yanked a rag from his back pocket and

slowly wiped his hands on it. "Just trust me a little longer and I know you'll be happy with the results." He had been good to me for the past several years since my father stopped being able to take care of the car himself. I was being a bit hasty perhaps. And it wasn't as if he didn't have any other clients needing service. There was no reason for my impatience. I decided to blame it on too little sleep and too much worry over the past few days.

"I know you always do right by your clients. I actually came by to ask you to take a look at the Clunker. It's making a weird noise. I think it isn't liking being driven as much as it has been over the last few weeks."

"I promised Felicia I'd have her car back to her this afternoon. Do you think it is a serious noise or just a low-level concern?"

"Probably it isn't too pressing but better safe than sorry, right? I can come back later when you have more time."

"Time is something I never seem to have enough of lately. Between my animal control officer duties, my regular clients and the new restoration business, I've been up to my eyeballs in obligations." Byron did look a little tuckered out now that I bothered to notice.

"You're not the only one connected to the police department who's been putting in extra hours lately."

"Hell of a time for Lowell to finally up and take a vacation wasn't it?"

"I'm sorry about your friend."

"Thanks for saying so. I know you weren't exactly a fan of Frank's. I also understood you found his body."

"That's right, I did, and as much as I wasn't happy to be the one to find him, I'm glad it was me instead of Phoebe."

"Pretty banged up was he?"

"Just around the back of his head but still, no one should see a loved one like that. It's hard enough to look at their body after it's been cleaned up by the undertaker." Sometimes I worried about Loden and the image he must carry in his mind from finding our father, sitting leaned up against a tree in the middle of his sugar bush, all signs of life floated up and out like chimney smoke in a stiff breeze. "As much as finding him spooked me, the hardest part is knowing whoever killed him is still wandering around Sugar Grove."

"Why do you think that has to be the case? He could have just interrupted a burglary in progress."

"When I found him he was in the sugarhouse and Beau was inside. If he had heard something don't you think he would have sent the dog out after the person?"

"I don't know about that. Your run-in with him didn't mean he always handled intruders by siccing the dog on them."

"I heard there were a bunch of people in at the police station complaining about Beau lately. Anyone besides me get on the wrong side of Beau's flapping jaws?"

"Knowlton was one. Mindy Collins was another. I believe Beau had even been prowling around on Jill Hayes's property, too. But she just called him in as a loose dog. She didn't say Beau was bothering her."

"But the others did?"

"Knowlton made a pest of himself complaining about Beau. He said Frank was making a point of harassing him."

"What did you do about it?"

"I told him to man up and deal with it himself. Privately though, I spoke to Frank and told him to reign Beau in before Knowlton got the notion to stuff his dog and put him on display somewhere." As much as I didn't share Knowlton's passion for taxidermy, I had to agree that a stuffed version of Beau sounded a lot more appealing than a mobile one. That reminded me Bob Sterling had mentioned Knowlton sneaking off Frank's property the day he was killed. I decided to go looking for him as soon as I finished up with Byron. He was usually at the Stack for lunch.

"What about Mindy?"

"Mindy was harder to calm down because she was upset about that dog pestering her kids. And for her, that meant her own as well as all the kids involved in the Squirrel Squad. She was over here or calling in a complaint at least once a week and more often if it was a school vacation. Liked to drive me nuts with all her nagging."

"If Frank had sent Beau after Hunter or Spring, I would have parked out on your sofa until you locked him up. Do you even care at all how frightening that can be?"

"I do care and I took her concerns seriously. It was just that answering Mindy's calls was becoming a full-time

job and like I said, I've got more than one job already. I
didn't want to make time for driving all the way out to
hell and gone just because Beau was pacing back and
forth on his own side of the property line."

"Do you think she was aggravated enough about it to
kill Frank?" Mindy was one of those mothers who people
describe as being like a bear. She loved her kids with a
ferocity that seemed almost obsessive. I wouldn't want to
be the one to cross her over anything to do with them. It
was intimidating enough just being in her orbit where the
kids were involved. I couldn't imagine having her turn
all her intensity on me if I threatened them in any way.

"I still think it was a burglary gone wrong."

"Frank's place didn't seem like he had anything worth
stealing. The yard is so heaped up with junk it looks like
he started a satellite town dump."

"You'd be surprised what Frank had of value on the
property. And he knew where everything was, too. There
was an order to his madness."

"I can't believe that. From what I saw he couldn't even
keep a neat woodpile." I mean really, how hard is it to
stack wood neatly and pull pieces from the top and work
your way down. You had to be some kind of a slob to have
a messy woodpile. That seemed to have grabbed Byron's
attention more than anything else I'd said.

"What do you mean his woodpile was a mess? You
mean the one out back of the sugarhouse?"

"Yes. I assumed it was the one he used for his sugaring,

and from the looks of the sugarhouse itself I was kind of surprised to see it all tumbled around like it was. The yard was a disaster but everything associated with the sugaring operation was as neat as it is at my place."

"I think I may have been right about it being a burglary after all."

"Why?"

"Frank never trusted anything to do with the government or social security numbers. So, he didn't believe in banks. One of the places he kept his considerable stash of cash was the woodpile next to the sugarhouse."

"Did you mention a theft angle to Mitch?"

"No. I had no idea anyone had messed with one of his stash spots. I guess I'd better give Mitch a call right away." Byron lowered the hood on Felicia's station wagon and dug a greasy cell phone out of his pocket. I thought of something just as he started poking at the keys with an oily thumb.

"Byron, who else knew about Frank's stash besides you?"

"Not too many people, I don't think. There was Phoebe, of course, and his late wife, Iris, would have known. I guess I'm not sure that anyone else did." Byron turned back to his dialing and I got into the Clunker. As I pulled away I thought about how likely it was that an opportunistic burglar would have known where to look for Frank's hidden cash. I also considered the money Myra mentioned Phoebe had been spending lately and what the source of her wealth might be.

* * *

Knowlton was at the Stack just where I expected to find him when I dragged myself through the door hoping to refuel with carbohydrates and caffeine. He was sitting perched on a stool right near the door as if he was waiting for me. Which he probably was if he had heard anything about my camping trip with Graham. Knowlton and I had camped together as kids when we were young enough to be in the Squirrel Squad ourselves. It wasn't as romantic, I am pleased to say.

Even then, Knowlton tried impressing the girls with his plans for stuffing dead creatures. I remember one trip quite vividly where he found a cardinal lying on the ground, its neck broken and its lifeless eyes fixed like it was staring at the sky. I wanted to bury the poor little thing but Knowlton had other plans. He scooped it up with a trowel and tucked it into his backpack.

Later he gave it to me as a Valentine's gift because it was red and he thought restoring it to a lifelike pose was as close to bringing it back as he could manage. It was sweet in its own way, if a little grotesque. It was the most unusual Valentine's Day gift I had ever received. It remains that way 'til this day. It was probably the most thoughtful, too.

Which makes the whole Knowlton thing so hard. He tries and almost succeeds but somehow the desired effect is just never quite acheived. It really ends up boiling down to the fact that I don't want to date someone because he tries hard and I feel sorry for him. I just don't think that is the best basis for a relationship.

But I needed to ask Knowlton about his run-ins with Frank's dog, Beau, and there was no time like the present. And a heaping helping of whatever Piper was serving up as the special ought to make the medicine go down a lot more easily. I hoisted myself onto the stool right next to Knowlton, which raised his eyebrows and brought a smile to his face. Piper, nearly as astonished as Knowlton, bustled over, dropped her order pad on the counter, and pressed the back of her hand against my forehead.

"I don't have a fever."

"You seem a little warm to me. Are you sure you wouldn't be happier sitting over there in a booth, where you might not get anything contagious on Knowlton here?" Piper pointed to my favorite spot in the corner.

"Anything Dani wants to share with me is fine as far as I'm concerned." Knowlton leaned toward me and lifted his arm and draped it over my shoulder. I took the opportunity to snitch one of the sweet potato fries from his plate. There were far too many of them for him to eat on his own with the history of heart disease that plagues his family. Really, I was doing him a big favor by taking some of them for myself. His arm started getting heavy in a hurry though.

"Knowlton, I can't concentrate on your lunch if you keep touching me."

"Sorry, Dani. Is that better?" He pulled his arm away and pushed his plate closer. Sometimes I just hate myself for the way I take advantage of his affections. Then I noticed him trying to look down my shirt. I grabbed a half dozen more fries as payment. I ordered the special and Piper went off to help someone else. Now was the time to get information from Knowlton.

"So I hear from Byron that you and I have something in common."

"That's what I've been telling you for years. We have almost too much in common. But you'll always be an exotic creature to me, Dani." He went all goo-goo eyed and mushy and I thought I could see him imagining me stuffed and posed and standing in front of the stove in his kitchen. Or sprawled out on the top bunk in his child-hood bedroom at Tansey's. Or even worse, posed over a cradle, my hand laid against a doll's cheek. I shuddered. "Are you cold? You can borrow my jacket." He started to slip his arms out of the sleeves.

"No, just a goose running over my grave. I'm warm as toast."

"Running hot is something else we have in common." Knowlton winked at me as he said it and I fought down a second shudder.

"I was thinking of our run-ins with Frank's dog, Beau."

"That thing is top on my list of creatures I'd love to stuff."

"He isn't one of my favorite dogs either, at least not as long as Frank was ordering him to chase me or Hunter off his property." I looked up as Piper plunked a steaming bowl in front of me. The special was cheddar cheese and caramelized-onion soup with a crusty roll on the side and I was looking forward to every bite. She stood there looking at me, waiting for my verdict on the new recipe.

"But Frank isn't ordering anyone around anymore, now is he?" Knowlton smiled at me again and actually chucked me under the chin like a baby. Despite the smells wafting up from my bowl I was losing my appetite.

"I wanted to ask you about that. Someone said they saw you in the area around Frank's place the day he was killed."

"Who said that?"

"Bob Sterling. He said when he arrived at Frank's to talk to him about the property line dispute he saw you slipping off into the woods. Heading away from the sugarhouse."

"Nope. It wasn't me. I was nowhere near Frank's that day." Knowlton tucked both hands under his rump and sat on them.

"He's lying," Piper said. Piper is like a human lie detector. She's a crack cardplayer and is astonishingly good at noticing tells, especially the most minute of them. But even I recognized Knowlton always sat on his hands when he told lies. It was as if he thought by gesticulating with them like he usually did he would give himself away.

"You wouldn't want to hurt my feelings by lying to me now would you?" I felt dirty, playing that sort of card myself but I needed to know why he was there and he didn't seem inclined to just offer it up.

"You know how I feel about you, Dani."

"Yes, you've never lied about that."

"Myra was in here on Saturday night talking about you going on an overnight camping trip with that game warden guy."

"Graham."

"Yeah, that guy." Knowlton scowled and I worried for a second he was actually going to spit on the floor right there in the Stack.

"How does this explain your visit to Frank's place?"

"I thought if I could find proof that Frank was sabotaging the sugarhouses to try to stop the cooperative you'd think I was a hero. Then maybe you'd go camping with me instead of that other guy."

"Aw, Knowlton, that's really sweet. Did you see anything that linked Frank to the vandalism?"

"No. I didn't. I was sneaking around all quiet-like looking for clues but there wasn't anything to see but a bunch of broken-down junk in the yard and a messy woodpile."

"The woodpile was in disarray when you were there?"

"Yup, it sure was. I remember thinking Frank wasn't much good in my opinion but I wouldn't have thought him so low as to not bother stacking his wood properly."

"What time were you there?"

"Around noon, I guess."

"You guess?"

"I don't wear a watch and I don't have a cell phone so I usually rely on the sun. I think I remember it being about as high in the sky as it was going to get."

"Was anyone else around? Did you run into Frank?"

"Nope, I didn't see anyone until Bob Sterling drove up

like a race car driver. No wonder he got hired to drive the ambulance. That guy can move."

"So Frank never caught you sneaking around?"

"No. As a matter of fact, after a while I kind of forgot about being quiet. Then all of a sudden I heard Beau barking and clawing at the door from inside the house. But no one let him out to chase me." Either Frank was already dead or Knowlton was lying up a storm. It was hard to tell since he was only sitting on one hand. If he was desperate enough to impress me that he would try to pin the vandalism on Frank was he also willing to bump him off to win my favor? Watching him watching me adoringly as I took a sip of my soup, I really couldn't be sure. Even Piper didn't offer an opinion.

Eighteen

After lunch I set out to break Dean's alibi. Mountain View Food Mart is the largest seller of foodstuffs in Sugar Grove. In the growing season the farmers market has a larger offering of produce, meats, and even locally crafted cheeses but in the dead of winter it was the only game in town. The store has three checkout lanes and two aisles of beer and wine. Most of the prices are higher than you'd find down at a store in Concord or Manchester but most locals shop here anyway. The effort to go that far out of town isn't worth the bother to most people and the community does like to support their own.

It was quiet. I only saw two other cars in the parking lot when I pulled in and one of them belonged to Tish Paquette, the cashier flicking through a magazine at checkout lane two. Tish had been in high school at the same time as Piper and me. She had started out two grades ahead and ended up graduating with our class.

Unluckily for me, she had been a bully who went out of her way to push me around all the years we were in elementary school. When I finally stood up to her one day on the school bus she lost her temper and bashed me over the head with her lunch box. The bus driver happened to look up just in time to see it. Tish was suspended for a week and her parents made her come to the house to apologize. She never forgave me.

Getting her help was going to require a little gray lie. I hurried to the bakery section and picked out a cranberry scone. I added a French cruller for good measure and waited until the only other customer in her line finished before approaching.

"Hey, Tish, just the person I wanted to see." She held up the bag and counted the baked goods inside before punching some keys on the register.

"Why's that?" Tish couldn't have looked more bored if she were a fish in a bowl.

"I have a bet going with Dean Hayes." That got her attention. Tish had dated Dean in high school and rumor had it she had expected them to marry as soon as she graduated. By the time she finally earned enough credits Dean had left his high school sweetheart far behind. "He says you have a memory like a steel trap. I said I didn't believe him. He bet me you'd remember exactly what he bought in here on Sunday afternoon, right down to the very last item. I said no way you could do that."

"How much did you bet him?"

"Fifty bucks." Tish smiled with the same sort of glee she always had when she was about to dunk my head in the toilet or throw my homework in the cafeteria trash can.

"Say good-bye to your money, honey. He was in here right around one o'clock and bought a big bunch of fuchsia carnations, a bottle of our cheapest pink champagne, and a twelve-pack of our bargain brand of condoms."

"Are you sure you aren't making that up just to lose me my money?"

"I can find the register receipt and the store surveillance tape if you don't believe me." Tish crossed her arms across her ample chest and batted her clumpy eyelashes at me, all innocent-like.

"That won't be necessary. I'll pay up."

"Be sure to tell Dean if he can't think of a place to spend your money, I'd be free for dinner tomorrow night." Tish turned back to her magazine and I grabbed my bag of baked goods. It was time to go looking for Dean.

Dean's bright blue Jeep is easy to spot anytime of year but it really stands out against the snow. I had no trouble at all driving around downtown and finding him at the gas station filling up. I pulled into a spot near the gas station convenience store and waited for him to head inside to pay.

One of the things I didn't like about Dean was his way of getting into trouble with money. He didn't have a credit card because his credit was so poor, so I knew he'd be paying cash inside instead of at the pump like most people. Sure enough, he returned the nozzle to the pump and made for the store. I caught up with him at the back as he was stirring creamer into a jumbo cup of take-out coffee.

"Hey, Dean, coffee up at Piper's not good enough for you?" I asked. His hand holding the cream shook and he spilled the powder all over the coffee station. It seemed like a guilty, startled reaction to a fairly innocent question. I had to wonder if anything else about my best friend wasn't good enough for him anymore. Time to start digging.

"Now what makes you say that? I was here and needed a caffeine fix. This was just convenient." Still, he didn't meet my eyes when I grabbed a couple of napkins and handed them to him to facilitate the cleanup.

"I am just wondering if maybe you are not so happy with all the hours she works. A man can get pretty lonely spending his day off without the company of his girlfriend."

"Nope. Piper is worth waiting for no matter how long we go between visits. Besides, I always have plenty to do on my days off without her." He swept the creamer into a slim hand and made a show of focusing his attention anywhere but on me.

"So I've heard."

"What do you mean?" Dean finally snuck a look at my face.

"You were seen at the grocery on Sunday when you said you were home watching the game. You bought a bouquet of carnations, a bottle of pink champagne, and a twelve-pack of bargain brand condoms."

"Oh that. I forgot to mention going on a supply run before Piper got out of work. I wasn't gone more than forty-five minutes, tops."

"You headed out of town in the direction of Kenneth Shaw's place."

"Says who?"

"Are you denying it?"

"Maybe I am. Are you trying to blame me for the damage at the Shaws' Maple Museum?"

"Should I be? I guess I'll ask Piper how much she enjoyed the flowers and champagne."

"Are you calling me a liar?"

"You are either a liar or the world's least observant boyfriend. Piper is almost as allergic to carnations as she is to cheapness. You had no hope of needing that third purchase if you didn't know not to make the first one. Or maybe you were trying to please someone else entirely."

"I don't have to talk to you about any of this."

"No, you don't. But as her best friend, I will have to talk to Piper about it. And I am going to assume you have no reason to try to stop me."

"Don't talk to Piper." Dean's skinny shoulders slumped. "I wasn't buying anything at Mountain View for her."

"I thought as much. So who was it for?"

"Chelsea Forcier. She lives over at Gull's Rest." New Hampshire is a state with a bit of an affordable housing challenge. We don't have a broad-based tax of any kind. Not a sales tax, not an income tax. This makes the property taxes sky high in most communities. We do have a lot of mobile homes to serve the needs of people who just can't afford that kind of taxation. Trailer parks like Gull's Rest are easily explained. The interest in naming them things that are totally unsuitable for a landlocked housing development are not. All the names of the streets in Gull's Rest are nautical, too. Streets like Rigging Road, Landlubber Lane and Anchors Away Avenue divide the large complex.

"You're sneaking around on Piper with someone else?"

"It's not quite like that exactly. Chelsea and I were together before Piper and I started seeing each other. I ran into her at the hardware store a couple of weeks ago and one thing led to another."

"Does Piper know?"

"No. I don't want to tell her anything until I decide if Chelsea is really the right woman for me."

"Don't you think if Piper was really the right woman for you, you wouldn't have had any interest in giving a relationship with Chelsea a second chance?"

"I'm not ready to decide."

"Well, I am. If you don't tell Piper yourself by the end of the day, I'm going to. And don't think shoving off that task onto me is going to make things any easier for you. Either way you will get an earful from Piper for being a cheating weenie."

"If I didn't know better, I'd say you were happy that

I'll be getting the boot from Piper." Dean crossed his skinny arms over his chest and scowled at a woman who was trying to fix herself a cup of coffee at the counter.

"I'm never pleased to hear someone has betrayed my friend. But you're not right for Piper and this will get her to realize that faster than just about anything else would have. I have to congratulate you on being efficient. No other boyfriend has managed not to last the whole winter." With that I stepped away, leaving room for the poor woman who seemed to need her java. I was back in the Clunker before I had a sinking feeling. Just because Dean admitted to being with another woman on Sunday didn't mean he hadn't made time to stop in at the Shaws' and do some damage.

I called Myra on the nonemergency line at the police station and asked her for Chelsea Forcier's address. Myra wouldn't give it to me until I promised to stop in later with a cruller from the Stack and news from the investigation. I toddled along with only the odd shudder coming from the wretched vehicle despite potholes and frost heaves that would count as sledding hills in parts of the Midwest. Within ten minutes I had rattled to a stop in a well-cleared driveway in front of a decently maintained trailer.

A young woman with a baby on her hip answered the door. The child was wrapped up in a fleecy garment my grandmother would have called a creeper. It held out its chubby little hand to offer me a soggy, bitten cracker. I had worked on my story on the way over, thinking I was going to feel hostile on Piper's behalf. But all that evaporated and I decided the truth was the best strategy.

"Are you Chelsea?" I asked.

"I am. What can I do for you?" She tucked a stray bit of dirty-blond hair behind her ear and then hugged her baby closer to her chest.

"My name is Dani Greene and I am working with the police on a case. I wondered if I could speak to you for a moment to verify some information we've received." Okay, maybe I wasn't going to stick only to the truth in the very strictest sense. I may not have been working with the police but doing Mitch's job for him was almost the same thing.

"Come on in. I just started a fresh pot of coffee. Do you want some?" She stepped back to allow me to enter and I nodded. "Hold Cyan for a minute then while I fetch it." She handed the baby to me who surprised me by snuggling in close and giggling. I love my niece and nephew but I never think of myself as all that maternal.

The sudden tugging around in the area I assumed held my heartstrings was unexpected and disconcerting. If I didn't know better, I'd swear I heard a ticking noise Celadon would be sure was a biological clock. She'd be wrong of course. It was probably indigestion. Chelsea returned with a tray heaped with cups of coffee, cream, sugar, and a plate of cookies. They looked homemade.

"Thanks. You didn't need to go to so much trouble." I tried handing the baby back but Chelsea shook her head.

"He likes you. Hang on to him until he starts to fuss. And don't worry about the snacks. It's my pleasure. I was going a little nuts on my own with the baby. Its nice to see another adult even if it is part of a police investigation." Chelsea looked young and sweet and lonely. I was sorry to be thinking bad thoughts about her on the drive over. "So what did you need to ask me?"

"I was talking to Dean Hayes just now at the gas station in town and he said he was here with you on Sunday afternoon. Is that right?"

"Sure, Dean was here. And I was glad to see him. We both were, weren't we sweetie?" Chelsea made little smoochy noises at the baby who giggled again in that abandoned way some babies have.

"Can you remember anything particular about the visit? Like what time he was here? When he left?"

"He got here some time around two, I guess. He played with Cyan and tried sweet-talking me with flowers and champagne. I told him it was going to take more than that to get back in my good graces. He was going to need to pay his back child support." She made another silly face at the baby. "Isn't that right, Cyan? Daddy has been a lousy, naughty boy and he won't get off so easy." I was stunned. All this time Dean had been keeping company with Piper and he had a baby with another woman. And one he wasn't taking care of, to boot. I wouldn't want to be Dean when Piper found out about Cyan. Cheating on her, she wouldn't like. Cheating a baby would make her homicidal.

"So Cyan is his son?" I asked, trying to keep my voice neutral.

"I got the blood tests to prove it and everything. He's been ordered by the court to pay support but so far he hasn't contributed anything but a package of diapers and that stuff he brought with him on Sunday. I told him it wasn't nearly enough. And it certainly wasn't going to get him back into my bed. Cheap champagne and promises is how that little one got here in the first place. Not that I'm complaining."

"Was he here long?"

"Not too long. He played with Cyan and tried to tell me he thought he'd be coming into some money soon. He said something about being sure his sister was finally going to sell the family home and that he would get his cut. But I didn't really believe him or care."

"So would you say an hour? Less?"

"About an hour, I think. He seemed to be more taken with the baby than he expected to be. Kind of like you." Chelsea smiled at me. I felt naked and uncomfortable. "Cyan has that effect on people. He just radiates fun and love."

"Did he tell you where he was heading when he left here?"

"No. I assumed he was either going home or out with the woman who owns the Stack. I know he started seeing her a while back."

"Do you want him back?" I was surprised to hear myself ask. It wasn't my business but curiosity got the better of me.

"How is that part of a police investigation?"

"It isn't. I was just thinking about how important fathers are and whether or not you think Dean would be worth it."

"He might be if he could grow up a little. When he has bothered with him, he is very good with Cyan. And boys need a father."

"I expect you're right about that. I should go." I handed back the baby after untangling his sticky little fist from my hair. "I really hope you work things out with him." I waved at them both as I backed out of the driveway and headed toward the police station.

Nineteen

When I showed up at the police station with Myra's cruller, Mitch looked about as happy as a kid faced with a plate of lima beans. Phoebe followed him out of Lowell's office, twisting the fringe on her scarf around and around with her fingers. I watched as he tried to catch her eye but she kept hers firmly fixed on the floor.

"Am I free to go now?" she asked.

"Please, Phoebe, you know I have to do my job." Mitch grabbed at her hand but she pulled away.

"Am I free to go?" Phoebe asked again. Mitch nodded and she hurried out the door, leaving a chill in the air that had nothing whatsoever to do with the temperature outside.

"I hope you're happy," Mitch said to me as he headed for Lowell's office. I followed him in and sank into the chair opposite the desk.

"Were you asking her about Frank's money?"

"I was."

"I take it things didn't go all that well."

"Would you like it if the person you were dating started grilling you about the source of your income and the whereabouts of a murdered man's money?"

"No, I wouldn't. Especially if it made it sound like I had killed him for it."

"She said I didn't trust her. And I wouldn't have had to ask her about that if you hadn't poked your nose in talking to Byron about money stashes and to Myra about Phoebe's flashy new wardrobe. You just won't be content until you ruin things for me with her, will you?"

"I'm going to ignore that since you are obviously having a tough day. What did she say about the money?" It wasn't really any of my business but Mitch looked so sad and helpless I couldn't stop myself.

"She said there were a couple of places Frank always stashed his money but she wasn't sure where they were."

"Didn't he trust her with knowing where he put his money? I mean, what if something happened to him?"

"You mean like getting himself killed?"

"That's exactly what I mean. When your money is in the bank your family has a fairly easy time finding out about it. If you just stick it in hidey-holes all over your property, things are going to be pretty hard on them."

"She said he was worried about her safety if she knew where he put all his cash."

"He really was paranoid, wasn't he?"

"You know from your own experience how he treated intruders."

"Do you think someone was trying to rob him and Frank caught them? Could that be why he was killed? He walked in on a robbery in progress?"

"That is one of the scenarios I'm considering."

"But Frank was so vigilant about anyone being on his property. You would have thought an intruder couldn't have gotten very far before Frank spotted him or her."

"That's one of the things that makes this look worse for Phoebe. She was already on the property and the dog would have never given her a second glance." Mitch looked even more miserable.

"How did she explain her sudden upswing in spending?"

"She didn't want to. She said the money was hers and she didn't have to explain to me where she got it from."

"But did she answer you when you pressed her?"

"I was just doing my job but she got really defensive and angry. I've never seen that side of her before. She's usually so sweet." Mitch looked like a small boy whose ice cream cone had just landed on the sidewalk. I felt sorry for him until he spoke again. "Unlike some women I've dated." Mitch managed to squander any soft feelings he dragged up in me almost as soon as they came to light.

"If Phoebe really cares about you, she'll come to realize you have to do your job no matter what. If I hadn't brought any of this up would you have just swept it under the rug?"

"Of course not." Mitch rubbed his face with his hand

and tipped Lowell's chair back on its rear legs. "I just care about her a lot and don't want her to be angry with me. I really thought we had a chance at something long term."

"I'm sorry, Mitch. Maybe if you decide to stop worrying about me borrowing Lowell's cruiser, I could talk to her for you." The words were out of my mouth before I even realized what I offered.

"Even if I could convince myself you aren't a carjacker, I'm not sure you would be the best advertisement for me when it comes to relationships."

"Just because I don't want to date you doesn't mean I think no one else should want to either. Besides, Phoebe always looked up to Piper and me in school, remember?"

"So what's that got to do with anything?"

"She values my opinion and if I tell her how sorry you are about having to do your job, she just might listen to me."

"Do you really think so?" Mitch dropped the chair back onto the floor with a bang and leaned across the desk.

"I'm pretty sure. I can at least try."

"Then what are you still doing here? If you hurry, you might still catch up with her."

I had a pretty good idea of where Phoebe might go after an upsetting time with Mitch or anyone else for that matter. Phoebe was a reader, always had been. When we were kids she was the one who was sitting on one of the swings in the playground with her nose in a book while everyone else ran around playing tag and jumping rope. I pulled into the library parking lot right next to her car.

Felicia Chick sat behind the desk checking out a stack of picture books for a young mother and her two toddlers. I gave her a wave and headed to the back of the adult-fiction section. Far in the back corner, tucked up in a cushy chair, Phoebe hunched over a paperback novel with a dragon on the cover.

I slipped into the seat next to her and cleared my throat to get her attention. Not that she hadn't noticed me. She clearly had from the way she raised the book up in front of her face to block me out. Or to hide from the embarrassment she felt from me having been privy to the scene at the police station.

"Phoebe, I want to talk to you," I whispered loudly enough to wonder if Felicia was going to come on over and threaten to kick us out.

"Go away."

"I want to talk to you about Mitch." She lowered the book ever so slightly.

"I don't want to talk about Mitch."

"Well, he can't stop talking about you."

"I bet. He thinks I'm a murderer. And a thief."

"No, he doesn't. He was just doing his job. You wouldn't respect him very much now, would you, if he was the sort of policeman who put his personal feelings before his duty." Phrased like that there was no way someone as basically nice as Phoebe could say she would resent him.

"I guess not."

"And you certainly want him to get to find out who hurt Frank, right?" I felt a little silly softening the question so much but I couldn't bring myself to say *murdered* to Phoebe.

"Of course I do. I want whoever killed him to get what they deserve." Phoebe hugged the book to her chest and I wondered if she was feeling scared for her own safety as well as angry.

"Besides, if he didn't question you, how would it look later?"

"What do you mean, later?" Phoebe dropped the book all the way into her lap.

"Well, say the two of you got married someday and had a family. Don't you think it might spoil your happiness if people said Mitch had let a criminal go unquestioned because he wanted to marry her?"

"Of course I wouldn't want people to think something like that. Do you think Mitch is really interested in a long-term relationship?"

"I know Mitch is really sorry to have hurt your feelings and that he is very interested in continuing your relationship. I think you two have a real chance of going the distance but not with the sort of dishonesty that has been rearing its ugly head lately."

"I don't know how to fix this."

"You could start by telling the truth about Frank's money. Where he got it, where he kept it, who knew about it."

"I told Mitch about Frank's money, how he hid it around the property."

"Did anyone else know about him stashing his money instead of putting it in the bank?"

"Frank was always spouting off about how he didn't trust banks. And he would get to drinking a bit too much from time to time at the VFW hall. He liked to brag about how much money he made from his sugaring or from logging or from selling stuff other people thought was junk. He made it sound like he was rolling in dough."

"That wasn't very smart, was it?"

"No. He ended up moving his money around to new hiding places after every time he'd been on a bender. Sometimes I'd wonder if even he knew where he'd put it all."

"Are you sure you didn't remember a place Frank had forgotten?"

"Are you accusing me of helping myself to Frank's money?" Phoebe tried to meet me in the eyes but she couldn't. Her hand holding the book began to shake and she shifted in the seat, untucking her legs and placing them on the floor like she was preparing to flee.

"I was just talking with Byron the other day and he mentioned you were one of the only people who might know where Frank kept his stash of cash."

"Did Byron also tell you he has plenty of reasons of his own to have killed my father?"

"No, he didn't. He just said they were friends." Interesting. Phoebe was riled up again. For the second time in only a few days her voice was loud and her tone strident. She jabbed her arm in the air like she was swatting invisible flies.

"He had about a hundred thousand reasons to want him dead." Phoebe leaned back and crossed her thin arms over her chest.

"Are you talking dollars?"

"Of course. Byron borrowed one hundred thousand dollars from my father to branch out into the restoration business. They were friends and Dad wanted to help Byron out."

"How does this make Byron a suspect?"

"Byron wasn't making any money in the business. He bought a bunch of old cars that needed fixing up and he had big plans for them. But when push came to shove Byron wasn't getting orders completed or there weren't any buyers. There was always a reason he didn't have the monthly payment for Dad they had agreed upon."

"When did all this start?"

"About a year ago. Byron came to Dad with a business proposition but Dad wasn't interested in being in the car business. He offered to just lend Byron the money instead at a really low rate."

"And Byron agreed?"

"He jumped on the offer."

"Did they put anything in writing?"

"Not that I know of. Dad was a handshake kind of guy.

"Even for a sum that large?"

"Especially for a sum that large. He would never have loaned that much money to someone he didn't trust without reservation."

"Still, it seems like a bad idea."

"I said so myself but he just told me that it would all be fine and if there was no paper trail the government couldn't interfere and ask for income tax from the interest he would earn from the loan."

"You still haven't explained where Frank would have gotten the money to loan it to Byron in the first place."

"We had a nest egg from the life insurance money from when my mother died. And I know the syrup business did well over the last couple of years."

Frank had a large holding and he was a good sugar maker but if he was pulling down that kind of money and was able to just lend it to someone else, I would be really surprised.

"He sold a bunch of syrup over the Internet and through a catalog. And at farmers markets."

"Still, a hundred thousand dollars is a lot of money. Did the loan leave you high and dry?"

"What do you mean?"

"I mean was Frank worried about the cost of groceries or the electric bill all of a sudden when Byron didn't pay him back on time?"

"No. Nothing changed. Dad was worried about Byron and then as time went on he became angry because he felt betrayed by a friend."

"What did he say?" Now, we might be getting somewhere.

"He said a man had to live up to his commitments and he asked Byron to come up to the house on Saturday night."

"Did he show up?"

"He did. I was worried about Dad so I canceled my date with Mitch and stuck around to hear the conversation. I felt bad about eavesdropping but I was worried about the situation so I did it anyway."

"And? Did you hear anything?"

"It was ugly. You know how my father was when he got going." Everyone in town knew how Frank was when his dander was up. He was one of the reasons Lowell set up a police presence at all select board meetings. Before that, Frank could be counted on not only to start a screaming match but to quite possibly throw things that were either putrid or heavy or both at the members of the board. Especially at Kenneth Shaw.

"What did they say exactly? Do you remember?"

"Dad said Byron had not lived up to their friendship and he wanted to know what was really happening to the money. Byron said sales were just slow and his other commitments made it hard to get the restorations done. Dad said that wasn't his problem and that repayment was due no matter what. He wanted Byron to give him back the bulk of the money right then and there."

"What did Byron say about that?"

"He said he had no way to pay that month or any of the previous months either. He said the money was all tied up in cars and parts and advertising and he didn't have it. He said Dad would have to be patient."

"Frank wasn't exactly a patient man."

"No. And telling him to be one always made things worse."

"This situation would make more sense if your father had killed Byron in a fit of rage," I said but Phoebe shook her head.

"Dad's bark was far worse than his bite. He never would have killed anyone. And besides, if he had killed Byron, how would he have ever gotten his money out of him?"

"But since there was nothing on paper, if Byron killed Frank, then it would be like the loan had never even happened. Did Byron know you knew about the loan?"

"I have no idea. I wasn't there to see the transaction take place if that's what you are asking. Dad told me about it later."

"Did they ever speak about it in front of you? I mean that Byron would have known about?"

"I don't think so but I can't be sure. It had been a while." So if Byron needed to cancel out his loan he might think canceling out Frank would be the best way to do it. Especially if he thought no one knew about it but himself and a dead guy.

Twenty

 The phone in the hall rang just as I shucked my boots into a tray to dry. My mother's voice came over the crackly line.

"Dani dear, just the one I wanted to speak with." My stomach sank. Her last call had been accurate enough to worry me about another. I told myself maybe she just wanted to get in touch. Maybe she missed us. Over the years I had noticed she was easily distracted. Maybe it would work now. Although I realized a lack of knowledge about the future didn't mean it wasn't going to occur anyway.

"How was the belly-dancing lesson?"

"It works wonders on the sacral chakra. When we get home I'll be sure to show you and Graham some moves. Excellent for opening you to your sexuality." My mother had never been one to feel intimidated by the birds or the bees.

As a matter of fact, every time Grampa carved a roast chicken in front of her or someone slathered honey on a biscuit in her presence I held my breath waiting for her to be reminded of just such things. Her ability to judge other people's comfort with the topic was negligible. Or maybe, she thought she was doing them a favor by running roughshod over their sensibilities. I think there's every possibility Celadon's first marriage ended because our mother embarrassed it to death.

"I'm not sure Graham would be into that sort of thing."

"Don't be silly. All men love belly dancing. It's primal. But that's not why I called." Suddenly the sound of her voice was more muffled and I heard her giggling. I didn't really want to think about what she and Lowell had been up to with their chakra tune-ups. I was tempted to hang up on her before she decided to share her itinerary. "I've had another vision."

"Two in less than a week. Wow."

"It's the sea air. All the negative ions, I think. I do have a lot more visions than I share with the rest of you. I know they upset you so I keep them to myself."

"I appreciate that, Mom." And I was surprised. I hadn't realized my mother came out of her spiritual bubble long enough to notice how her proclamations affected the rest of us. Maybe I was the one who wasn't doing the noticing.

"You've always been an appreciative girl, Dani. Your father was saying so just last night." My mother thinks my father drops by to chat with her from the great beyond, apparently on a regular basis. I had no idea until a few months ago when he sent a message for me that turned out to be important. Still, it wasn't always easy to credit. And if I was being entirely honest, I was disappointed that he had never gotten in touch directly with me.

"Dad dropped by for a visit while you were on vacation with another man?"

"Why wouldn't he? Your father always loved to travel." As strange as the idea was, I felt a bit better about what she and Lowell were up to if my father was happy to stop by for a visit.

"Speaking of travel, don't you need to get back to some shipboard activities?"

"Not until I tell you why I called. That was the real reason for your father's visit. He wanted me to tell you something."

"Wouldn't it be easier if he tried getting ahold of me directly?"

"What makes you think he hasn't?" Her sigh came through the phone so clearly I wondered for a second if Celadon had picked up the extension and was adding her own two cents. "You aren't always the most open to unexplainable experiences."

"You're right. Tell him if he visits again that I'll try harder to hear him. What was it he wanted me to know?"

"He says to eat more cake, especially at night. And he says not to be scared of the dark."

"I eat cake as a midnight snack all the time. And I

haven't been scared of the dark since I was eight. What did he actually show you?" My mother receives her communications as images. Her interpretations are where things seem to break down.

"He was holding out the pieces of that night-light you had when you were six."

"The one shaped like a unicorn with the horn that lit up?"

"Exactly. Remember how upset you were when Loden backed into it and snapped off the horn. You told him you didn't love him anymore." I'm not sure when I started having night terrors so intense I thought I'd die of fright but they all went away when Grampa brought home that night-light one afternoon, plugged it in, and showed me how to turn it on. Loden had been so distraught at breaking it he snuck into my room after bedtime with a flashlight he had found in the junk drawer. He spent the whole night leaned up against the wall in my bedroom with it switched on.

"How could I forget?" I looked down at the jagged scar on my finger. I had picked up the broken unicorn horn and had cut myself badly enough to need stitches. "That's it? Dad showed you the broken night-light?"

"There's more. Then I saw a little candle, like a birthday candle flickering in the dark. The light from it was very weak but it bobbed slowly through the air toward a giant heart-shaped card."

"A broken bit of childhood, a candle, and a card?" I paused to think of what it could all mean but didn't have a clue. I hated to ask but I heard myself doing it anyway. "What do you really think it means?"

"Maybe to never give up on love because it cuts like a knife through the vast darkness of life."

"Even from beyond the grave you think Dad is giving advice on my love life? If he keeps showing up on the cruise with you and Lowell, I'd think he'd be more interested in giving you advice."

"Who says he doesn't?" That was unsettling. I had never appreciated until that moment how complicated things could get if you really could have dead loved ones dropping in unannounced. Maybe I didn't want to hear from my father directly after all.

"Things have been pretty busy here lately. Do you think it could mean anything else?"

"Maybe he wants you to buy your brother a lamp for his birthday."

Feeling unsettled after disconnecting with Mom, I decided to shove Dad's message to the back of my mind and to focus once more on what brought me home in the first place, information about Frank's financials. I found Grandma in the laundry room sorting whites into the washer. Laundry isn't anyone's favorite task but our laundry room is one of the demonstrations of Grampa's love for Grandma.

Before they were married he offered to hire help for all the housework, including the laundry. Grandma refused, saying as soon as they were married she expected to be the only woman to ever get her hands on his underthings. So, he got the ahead-of-his-time notion to move the washer and dryer to the second floor to be closer to all the clothing and thus most of the laundry. He and his own father converted a bedroom into a laundry room extraordinaire.

He added oversized windows for light, custom cabinetry to hold the soap and other supplies, and pull-out wooden drying racks for those days when you want to air-dry but it is raining. There's a pair of rockers and a braided rug and a counter for folding. The ironing board pulls out of a cabinet in the wall and an upright steamer sits in a closet in the corner. Everything is neat, tidy, and well thought out. Grandma always says that so goes the laundry room so goes the rest of the house. Hers is always shipshape.

"Do you know anything about Frank's wife's life insurance policy?" I asked as I picked through a basket of clean laundry to help match the socks.

"There wasn't one."

"Are you sure? Phoebe seems to think there was."

"No. Frank was in rough shape when Iris died. He had a devil of a time keeping Phoebe and himself fed. His name appeared on the annual report for people whose property taxes were in arrears for three years in a row. I thought they were going to lose the place for sure." Grandma measured soap into the washer, the emerald in her engagement ring sending sparkles of light bouncing around the room. Grandma's nails were beautifully manicured and even though she was only doing the laundry she wore lipstick and a dress most people would think was too formal for church these days.

"That's terrible."

"It was. And the whole thing was made worse by his total refusal to accept any form of help. He qualified for assistance for heating oil and even for the local food pantry but he wouldn't hear of it. I don't know how he managed to make it."

"How did he turn things around?"

"I guess the biggest difference was that Phoebe got old enough to stay on her own after school. Frank had only worked at jobs that provided mother's hours so Phoebe wouldn't be a latchkey kid when she was very young. You can imagine how that cut down on his ability to produce enough income. Once he started working full-time they got back on their feet just fine. It never seemed like they had a lot of extra, but they had enough."

"From what I'm hearing from Phoebe, his financial situation had changed drastically. She says he lent one hundred thousand dollars to Byron for his vintage-auto restoration business." Grandma dropped one of Grampa's holey undershirts into the washer and gave me her complete attention.

"That's a great deal of money. Are you sure?"

"I just heard it from Phoebe. She says Byron and Frank had a verbal agreement about the loan."

"I'm sure I never heard about it if they did."

"Phoebe says she thinks no one else knew. You know

how private Frank was about his life. He wouldn't have been inclined to tell anyone about a thing like that."

"I suppose you're right. But I can't imagine where he could have gotten the money in order to lend it."

"Phoebe said the syrup business was doing well and also that they had money from her mother's life insurance."

"Unless Frank's trees are producing a lot more sap than is normal, I'd be very surprised if he could make that kind of money from his operation."

"That was my thought, too. And if there wasn't any life insurance, how can it be explained?" I asked.

"I don't know. You said the agreement with Byron was verbal. If he doesn't repay the loan now that Frank's dead, Phoebe may be right back where she and Frank were when her mother died."

"That makes it sound like Phoebe has less of a motive to murder Frank."

Grandma paused thoughtfully before saying, "But it puts Byron right near the top of people who might have had a very good reason, now doesn't it?"

I hated to ask Byron anything that might get his back up before he finished rehabbing the Midget but the paint job on my car seemed like it ought to take a backseat to murder. I managed to track him down at Stems and Hems, the local florist and combination bridal-tailoring shop. Not that it's much of a trick to find him. Every Tuesday Byron heads into the shop to pick up a bouquet for his live-in girlfriend, Luanne.

At first it seemed like the shop was empty. With my lack of height I couldn't see past urns full of flowers and mannequins modeling the latest in wedding dresses. I paused for a moment in front of a dress draped with enough lace to make a mosquito net for a king-sized bed. Even if I ever found myself in the position of shopping for a wedding dress, I couldn't imagine I would choose one that looked at all like that. Besides, my mother would be crushed if I didn't allow her the pleasure of creating one for me herself. Mom always made all our special-occasion clothes.

When Celadon and I were small she made us matching dresses for all the major holidays each year. At Easter she even made bonnets, too. I never liked getting dressed up but I had liked matching my big sister, especially since I knew it drove her crazy. I squeezed between two more voluptuously frothy gowns and ran right into Priscilla Martin, the shop owner.

"Should I assume from your presence here that you've decided to follow the game warden home for sausage every night?" Priscilla loomed down at me and winked in a way that made me wonder if she had taken lessons on lewdness from Mindy.

"No. I'm just here looking for Byron." I did my best to keep a smile plastered on my face. Priscilla had been trying to get me to put a deposit on a wedding dress ever since

Celadon had, of course, asked Mom to make hers. The whole family had tried to make up for the slight by purchasing flowers year-round, even when our gardens were bursting with blooms, but Priscilla was never truly appeased.

"I should have known. Well, once you finally need a dress come back in and see me. Not only do we have the most beautiful dresses you'll find anywhere, we have undergarments to fix anything. Say, for instance, your topographical map looks like Kansas. Our patented line of bustiers will resculpt your meager assets into the Rocky Mountains." Priscilla stared at my nonexistent bustline and gestured disturbingly with her hands.

"I'll keep that in mind." I hurried deeper into the store, hoping to locate Byron. Even asking him about his loan from Frank seemed like more fun than talking fashion with Priscilla. I caught up with him at the glass cooler case reaching in for a mixed bunch of calla lilies. He was humming to himself and I hated to throw a damper on his good mood.

"Has Luanne said yes yet?" I asked, chickening out and delaying just a bit longer.

"Not yet, but I haven't given up. One of these days I'm going to wear her down." Byron had been asking Luanne to marry him once a week for the past four years. He thought the flowers would help but I wondered if maybe Luanne worried he was a spendthrift. Perhaps that was the way to introduce my questions about the loan.

"Maybe she's worried about all the long hours you work. Between your animal control duties, the garage, and now your restoration business, you've got to be stretched pretty thinly. Have you thought about cutting back?"

"No need to do that. Luanne understands. She realizes the business is important for our future."

"Maybe it's money. A lot of women think seriously about their financial future when they consider settling down." I felt bad even mentioning it but it if Phoebe was telling the truth, Byron was in over his head.

"Money's not a problem."

"Is that because with Frank being dead you think you don't need to repay what he lent you?" I asked. Byron squeezed the lily stems and I heard the cellophane crinkle.

"What loan?"

"The hundred thousand dollars Frank loaned you for your restoration business. You know, the loan you were having so much trouble paying back."

"Where'd you hear that?"

"From Phoebe. With Frank dead, she says the money you borrowed will be owed to her instead."

"She says that, does she?"

"She does. That's a lot of money. And it's been a bad time to start up what most people would consider to be a luxury business."

"I don't have to talk to you about my business."

"That's true. You don't. But Phoebe is in the hot seat for Frank's murder and she is sure to want to put someone else in it instead. Right now you look like a good substitute."

"Phoebe can say anything she wants. But can she prove it?"

"I don't know. But she can certainly cast a long shadow of doubt. Are you sure there isn't anything you want to tell Mitch before Phoebe gives him her side of the story?"

"I don't want to talk to Mitch about anything outside of the Patriots' chances at the Super Bowl."

"So you weren't up at Frank's arguing with him on Saturday night about not repaying your loan?" Byron's face went white then red.

"Dani, if you want me to work on your car before you reach retirement age, you had better change the subject." Byron stood up a little straighter and loosened his grip on the bouquet. One calla lily flopped limply against the bouquet wrapper.

"You know, I've had just about enough of being threatened. I've put up with it from Frank and his dog, from whoever wants to stop the cooperative, from Bob Sterling, and now from you. I don't think I'm going to take any more. I'll have the Midget towed off your property and I'll find someone else to handle the repairs." I was so surprised at myself it was like having an out-of-body experience. I heard the words coming out of my mouth but it was hard for me to believe I was forming them. The events of the past few days were giving me a crash course in assertiveness. Even though I should have felt powerful and proud of myself for not biting my tongue and making peace, I didn't. I just felt crummy.

I think we were both surprised by what had just happened. Byron had been my mechanic since my father died and I took over driving his favorite car. It had been hard for me to trust someone to work on my father's car since he had always done it himself but Byron had risen to the challenge. When you think about crime you don't necessarily think about all the little ways it will tear things up. If you had told me a week earlier I would have been looking for a new mechanic, I would have laughed in your face.

"If that's the way you want it." Byron stood up even straighter, turned on his heel, and marched out of the shop. A break in my friendship with Byron wasn't what I had wanted at all. I wished more than ever that Lowell would get back and put things right but at that moment it felt like some things were broken beyond repair.

Bingley raced up to the Clunker as soon as he heard me pull in. I stepped out into the driveway and the smell wafting off the dog hit me from several feet away. Bingley smelled like low tide and death. He pounced on me with his filthy front paws and I gagged. Bingley and I have had a long-standing relationship that has included ear rubs and two-handed belly scratches. But not today. When it became clear to him that I wasn't going to give him any physical affection he ran off behind the sugarhouse. Determined to see what he had gotten into, I followed.

It was no surprise, considering the smell to find one of the Shaws' trash barrels overturned, the lid removed and trash spilling from a ripped bag. Bingley gave me a goofy dog grin then turned back to rolling around in the pile of stinking refuse. There, amid the plate scrapings and plastic wrap were a couple of lobster carapaces.

"No wonder you smell so bad," I said to the cheerful dog. "We can't just leave this for Kenneth and Nicole to come find." I left him to his fun while I went into the sugarhouse in search of a new trash bag. My stomach fell again just like it had the last time I was here listening to Kenneth blaming me for the vandalism visited upon his property. I looked over at the wall where the antique sap buckets should have been and was relieved to see the red paint was gone.

I looked all around the main part of the sugarhouse and found no trace of trash bags or cleaning supplies. I walked to the back of the building and tried the office. Kenneth's desk, his chair, and bookshelves were all neat and tidy. I tried a door in the back of the office and found it led to another, much larger room. It looked like a storage space for finished syrup and also for supplies.

This room was not on the official tour of the sugarhouse during New Hampshire Maple Weekend. It was far too functional to be interesting and was certainly not used for the production process. The Shaws prided themselves on having the prettiest, quaintest sugarhouse in Sugar Grove for the festivities each year and this room wouldn't have helped with that image.

Very little light filtered in through only a small window. I felt along the wall for a light switch but managed to bark my shin on something big and cylindrical before locating it. My eyes searched the room for supplies but instead noticed barrel after barrel hugging the perimeter of the room and crowding all available space on the floor. The Shaws must have had a phenomenal year of sugaring or were hoping to in the future.

Each barrel would hold forty-five gallons of the sweet stuff and I estimated at least fifty barrels. I had no idea the Shaws were making so much syrup. With the amount of supplies they must need, the cooperative would really benefit from their participation. I felt even more strongly that I needed to convince them to stick with it. Maybe pitching in with their stinky dog would help get me back in their good graces even if I never located the vandal.

I squeezed through a narrow corridor left between barrels and made my way to a metal shelving unit that looked like it held cleaning supplies. As I drew closer a heavy, chemical smell filled my nostrils almost as intensely as the rotting lobster outside had done. Sure enough, a cardboard box of trash bags sat next to a package of paper towels and a bottle of glass cleaner.

I pulled out the box and was reaching into it for a bag when I noticed a milk jug with the top hacked off. A length of wire, like you might cut from a coat hanger, spanned the top of the jug. The wire was threaded through the hole in a paintbrush. My grandfather did the same thing when he wanted to clean a brush but didn't have time to take care of it right away. The jug was filled with a reddish liquid.

I moved the jug aside and spotted a quart-size can of paint. I slid it forward and checked the label. It was the same kind they used at Village Hardware and looked brand new other than a few drips of crimson clinging to the side of the can. Where better to hide the paint used in the graffiti? No one could trace it to the vandal if it was left at the scene of the crime.

Dean was climbing even higher on my list of suspects. He never mentioned anyone buying red paint at the hardware store when it came out that the Shaws had been hit by a vandal with red paint. My mind roamed its way over to Chelsea and her baby and I didn't really want Dean to be guilty, at least not for their sakes.

I pushed the paint can back onto the shelf where I'd found it and moved the milk jug back into place. I even abandoned the thought of tidying up the trash. Kenneth would care more about me getting to the bottom of the damage to his sugarhouse and the theft of his valuable items than he would about a bit of a mess in the yard. I hurried back out and climbed into the Clunker with every intention of confronting Dean.

Twenty-one

I pulled in at the Hayes place hoping to find Dean. His Jeep was gone but Jill's car was there. Jill answered the door before the second knock landed. Her coat was zipped and her purse perched on her shoulder. She clutched a ring of keys in her gloved hand.

"Hi, Jill. I was hoping to find Dean at home." I didn't think it likely but there was no harm in asking. After all, if anyone had expected not to find me home because my Midget wasn't there, they would have been wrong most of the time for weeks.

"Sorry. He's over at Piper's. He said there was something he needed to tell her." I wondered if Jill had any more of an idea about Dean's baby than Piper did but it didn't seem like my place to ask. "I'm just on my way out myself." Jill stepped out onto the stoop and pulled the door shut behind her.

"I wouldn't want to hold you up. While I've got you for just a minute though, I wanted to ask, have you had any more damage to your trees?"

"I haven't bothered to check since Frank died. After all, he's the one who was causing all the problems, right?" Jill pushed past me and started down the steps. "I've really got to go. I'm late for an appointment with the bank to talk about my mortgage. Wish me luck."

"I hope it goes well. Do you mind if I check your trees myself?"

"Knock yourself out. I can't imagine there will be anything to find but it never hurts to look, I guess." Jill climbed into her car and putted off. I fished around in the back of the Clunker and found the pair of extra snow boots I always take with me from November until tax day. You never know when you'll need to walk through the snow and it's always easier if your feet stay warm and dry. I pulled them on, checked that my cell phone was charged up, and yanked my hat down around my ears. The temperature had been low all day and the wind was starting to pick up.

I made my way through the trees, checking carefully for signs of disturbance. I reached the trees that had previously been damaged without spotting any new problems. I looked at the bridge grafts Jill had attempted and hoped they would take. Running my mittened hand over the bark on the largest tree I sent up a little wish for healing and hoped both the tree and something bigger than us both would hear me.

Up ahead, a bit closer to Frank's property line I saw trampled snow at the base of more trees. As I drew closer I could see more girdling. I followed what seemed like a path of damaged trees deeper and deeper into the sugar bush. As I walked my uneasiness grew. Now and then a twig cracked or a startled bird burst into the air and I jumped out of my skin. I looked around me but saw no one and told myself I was just imagining things. I was at least as worried about running into Beau as I was a murderer. Even with Frank dead that dog was a menace.

I wasn't sure where the property line was exactly and I kept going until I thought I spotted some movement through the trees. My heart jumped into my throat. Whatever it was, it was too tall to be Beau and the figure just sort of popped up out of nowhere. I wanted to turn around and pretend I had never seen anything worth investigating. But the look on Jill's face as she mentioned her banker flitted through my mind.

If someone was still fooling around, hampering the cooperative, I wanted to know who and why more than I wanted to turn tail and run. I still couldn't shake the feeling of being watched as I picked my way through the trees, hoping to sneak up on whomever I has seen. I wished Graham were with me this time as I crept quietly along. I wondered briefly about guardian angels and what they might look like and whether they ever went on vacation.

Things in the woods have a certain wildness to them, a character of naturalness that humans never seem quite able to duplicate no matter how much we try. Something up in front of me had the look of falseness, or artifice that is a sure sign people have been there. I stepped closer, around a pile of hemlock branches and almost fell down into what looked like a cellar way with no house on top of it. Rough wooden doors sagged open on either side of the stairway.

I didn't hear anything coming from underneath me so I eased myself down the stairs, one step at a time, pausing on each to listen for noises from either below or above. The earth at the sides of the stairs was held back by lengths of logs sunk deep into the soil. At the bottom, another door, this one made of heavy steel, stood slightly open. I pushed it open slowly and peeked around.

The lighting level was low and seemed to be coming from a single source in a corner. I wished I had a flashlight. I swung the door open widely to let in more light and stepped all the way into the underground room. The first thing I noticed was the tidiness of it. Shelving lined the walls and supplies of all sorts filled every inch of space. Food, bottled water, beer, books, batteries, and toilet paper crowded together in row upon row. The space was enormous. Forced to guess I'd have said it rivaled Grampa's cow barn for square footage.

It looked like something you'd see on the news after the FBI raided a cult compound. The only things that looked out of place were a couple of boxes stacked on the floor. I lifted the flap on the top one to reveal crumpled newspaper carefully wedged as cushioning around tree taps, sap buckets, and even an old hand auger for making holes in a maple tree. It looked like exactly the sort of things missing from Kenneth's sugaring display. It was packed like someone was moving their best china cross-country in a covered wagon.

The second thing I noticed was that I recognized the place. I turned my head around slowly and stepped farther into the room to explore, trying to remember where I had seen it before. An old metal flashlight lay on its side on a table next to a pile of fabric and just within its beam of light I saw Phoebe sagging in a chair. Her legs were tied together at the ankles and her arms were lashed to the arms of the chair with what looked like torn strips of fabric. She appeared to be asleep.

I laid my hand on her shoulder and gave her a little shake but she didn't rouse. I picked up the flashlight and pointed it at her to get a better look at her face. Most of her hair was stuffed up in a baseball cap but the little bit escaping on the right side was matted and sticky. I touched it and checked my fingers. Blood. I shook her again but still got no response.

I touched her wrist, checking for a pulse and felt one thrumming away. Not that I was any kind of an expert but it seemed fairly strong. I bent over to begin wrestling with the knot binding her ankles when it occurred to me there was no way I was going to be able to drag Phoebe out of the bunker, let alone carry her to safety by myself.

I had to get her to wake up. There was only one thing for it. I started singing.

I may be small but my voice is not. My pipes can rattle the chandelier in the opera house if I take the notion to do so. Now I'm not saying this is a case of good things coming in a small package. Just about anyone who has heard me lift up a joyful noise has asked me to stop doing so immediately.

Celadon told me once my singing sounds like a cross between cats brawling and a high-speed train collision. For the first time ever, I was hoping she was right. No one who wasn't dead ought to be able to remain in the land of Nod with me serenading them. I dug deep and let out a noise loud enough to deafen myself. Which explains why I didn't notice someone creeping up behind me until I felt something hard pressed against the back of my head.

I felt my voice choke off in mid note. I tried to turn around but a strong hand gripped the back of my neck and pinned me in place.

"Well, this is unfortunate." Kenneth Shaw's voice filled the room and I noticed Phoebe's eyes fluttering. "What brings you by?" He squeezed even harder on my neck.

"I was checking for more damaged trees up at Jill's place and I thought I saw something moving around over here. With everything that's been going on I thought I'd better check it out. What are you doing?" I asked.

"I'm tying up loose ends." He shoved me toward a second chair and pushed me into it. Grabbing the flashlight from my trembling hand, Kenneth placed it on the table facing the fabric. Keeping the gun in his other hand trained on me, he began tearing strips from the fabric, which looked like a bedsheet, with the help of his teeth. Once he had three strips he stopped. "Now unless you want me to shoot you, I suggest you tie your ankles together, just like your friend here did." Kenneth tossed one of the fabric strips into my lap and waggled the gun at me.

"I'm a loose end?" I had no idea what he was talking about. I racked my brain for how he could possibly be involved with what was going on. Then I remembered the boxes. The items from the Shaws' place had been too carefully packed to be the handiwork of someone who didn't care about them. "You're the vandal, aren't you?" Kenneth shook his head sadly at me and gestured at the fabric in my lap with the gun.

"Please, just get on with it."

"But why? Why would you do something like that to your neighbors? To your friends? It wasn't the competition, was it?" I bent down and started fastening my ankles together, hoping he would start talking if I started cooperating.

"Of course it wasn't the competition. I sell more syrup in a month than most of the rest of the producers in town sell in a year. Now, I'm going to put the gun down to tie up your hands. I'll still be able to get to it faster than you if I need to. If you give me any trouble, I'll shoot Phoebe. Do you understand?" I nodded and held still while he tied each of my wrists to the arms of the chair. Finally, after all these years it was like Phoebe and I were wearing matching outfits. If only she were awake, she might be pleased.

"What was it then?"

"The cooperative. You just had to try to solve someone else's problems. I swear it's a genetic thing with all of you Greenes. It's like you are chromosomally unable to mind your own business if you see any problems in the community."

"But you are a community leader yourself. Why wouldn't you want the cooperative to go forward?"

"The inspection."

"But you run a first-rate place. You would have easily passed the inspection and it isn't as if the five-dollar fee would have been a hardship for you."

"Oh it would have passed for quality but then I would have needed to explain all the syrup we were storing." I thought back to all the barrels in the back room at Kenneth's place.

"You do have a lot more in storage than I would have thought." Kenneth gave both wrists a tug to verify the bonds were secure.

"Now how would you know that?"

"I stopped by today to verify Dean's alibi. I thought he might have been the one who took your valuables. While I was there I noticed Bingley had gotten into the trash and made a mess of the yard. I let myself into the sugarhouse to look for a new trash bag to clean it all up."

"What did I tell you about compulsive do-gooderness?"

"I spotted the paintbrush you must have used to deface your own wall and a whole lot of barrels. That still doesn't explain why you're doing this."

"The syrup didn't come from my own trees. And the inspectors would have been suspicious of all the excess and where it came from. I couldn't let them into the facility. I couldn't explain to you why I didn't want to participate so I decided to sabotage all the sugarhouses to make it look like joining the cooperative was a bad idea. Then when I chose not to be a part of it no one would think twice."

"Where did all the excess come from?"

"You must have heard of the warehouse heist up in Canada." I felt my jaw drop, just like in a cartoon.

"You mean the robbery at the syrup reserve a couple of years ago? The syrup in the barrels came from that?" The vast majority of the world's maple syrup supply comes from Quebec. Even though syrup's per-barrel price is approximately thirteen times that of crude oil, security and inventory control at the warehouse had been low-key. Unfortunately, someone had taken advantage of that fact and had used trucks to make off with around eighteen million dollars worth of syrup, wholesale. It was one of the biggest agricultural heists in world history.

"Exactly."

"But why would you do a thing like that? I thought you loved making syrup?"

"*You* love making syrup. I'm sick to death of the work and the unpredictability of the whole business."

"But what about the tradition? Your family has been doing it at least as long as mine."

"But unlike your family, mine has no interest in continuing the tradition. Both of the kids have moved away and have lives of their own. It's not like I'm going to ask an oral surgeon and an aviation engineer to drop their careers to park in the woods and draw fluids off of trees for a few weeks each year."

"You could have just stopped sugaring if you were sick of it. You didn't need to do any of this."

"You're wrong about that, too. We've been barely keeping up appearances for years. Most of our wealth was tied up in stocks and real estate. You must have heard how well all of that's been doing lately. And the kids' college costs just about did us in. When someone in the business offered to sell me a whole lot of the stolen syrup at a deep, deep discount. I took all the cash I could get my hands on and bought it. We're finally getting back on our feet because of the tremendous profit." My head was reeling, trying to reconcile what I thought I knew with what I was being told. The Shaws couldn't be thieves or saboteurs, could they?

"How did you expect to move enough syrup to make it worth the risk without attracting attention?" Unless their foot traffic was a lot heavier than ours I couldn't imagine how what he was doing could have paid off.

"I set up an agreement with a major restaurant chain a year or so ago. I've been selling it to them in bulk ever since."

"And they didn't ask any questions?"

"No, Dani. Unlike you, they knew when to stop asking questions." Which only brought another one to mind. One I really didn't want the answer to but couldn't keep from asking.

"Did you kill Frank?" I felt queasy and dizzy enough that I was almost glad to be lashed to something more stable than myself. Phoebe's eyes opened wide just in time to hear the answer.

"It couldn't be helped. He caught me in his sugarhouse starting to sabotage the place."

"Why would you sabotage Frank's if he wasn't going to join the cooperative?"

"Because I hated his guts for all the harassment I've had to endure from him all these years. He showed up at every single board meeting I was a member of for as long as he lived in Sugar Grove. That man made a hobby out of giving me grief. So I figured, if I was damaging properties of people I liked, why wouldn't I go ahead and throw Frank in for good measure. Besides, damaging his place might have made people even more unsure about joining if they weren't absolutely positive about where the danger was coming from."

"So you decided to kill him?"

"I couldn't let him live anymore than I can let the two of you. What he knew would have led straight back to investigating my property and I would have been out of business and in prison instead. And now, I need to get my boxes and get on the road before Nicole gets home. She hates it when I'm late for dinner."

"You wouldn't really just leave us here like this." I tried to sound convincing instead of terrified and whiny but I don't think I quite managed it. I felt my voice sliding and cracking as the words slipped out and even with my ankles tied, my knees were knocking like I was a one-woman band with a tambourine strapped between them.

"You're right, I almost forgot something." Kenneth started patting down my jacket and I suddenly worried he was a dirty old man in addition to all his other faults. In response to a jingling he reached into my pocket and pulled out the keys to the Clunker. "You must have parked at Jill's if you were checking her trees. I'll need to get rid of that sorry excuse for a car if I don't want anyone to find you. But don't worry, I've got a couple of places in mind to stash it." He patted the top of my head, grabbed his boxes, and left. I heard the metal door clanging shut and then nothing but the sound of Phoebe starting to sob.

Twenty-two

 "It's okay, Phoebe. We'll get out of here." I tried using my babysitting voice, the one I use with Hunter and Spring when they stub their toes or pinch their fingers in a kitchen drawer. It didn't seem to work as well on Phoebe as it did on the kids. I would have scootched my chair closer to hers but just like always, my feet didn't even come close to reaching the floor.

"No, we won't."

"Someone is bound to come looking for us. We just need to wait it out." And try not to think about the need to use the bathroom. My bladder isn't any bigger than the rest of me. I'm like a toy dog that way.

"It won't matter if they do. This is a survival bunker and it's meant not to be found. Frank built it secretly more

than ten years ago and no one has ever got wind of it."
That explained all the food and water and other supplies.

"But surely it shows? Or someone can hear us if we
yell loudly enough." I started singing again. Phoebe
yelled even above my racket.

"It's soundproofed and the whole place is hidden under
the brush entirely if you just cover it over with the
branches we keep piled up nearby."

"Cut branches should dry out and leave this place exposed after a
while."

"It's winter. You know how long a wreath stays fresh-
looking on a door in this kind of weather. The same can
be said for hemlock boughs."

"But eventually they'll wither."

"And so will we. You and I will have died of thirst
long before this place is easy to spot. If we're lucky, someday they'll find our bodies." Phoebe began to sob again.
"We're going to die completely surrounded by survival
supplies. How ironic is that?"

"If it's so hard to find this place, how did Kenneth do it?"

"He told me he saw it the night he was out girdling
Jill's trees. I left the brush pulled away and the outer doors
open when I ran back to the house to get something. I
wasn't here and he checked it out and left."

"But why would he put his stuff in here?"

"I guess he had the stuff in the back of his SUV when
he drove up here to vandalize the sugarhouse. He wanted

to get his things back so he remembered this place and he left them here for safekeeping. I guess he thought either they would go unnoticed or someone would call the police and they would find their way back to him in the end."

"So he was here checking up on them since you didn't call the police?"

"Exactly. I came in and found him in here. He hit me on the head. I was sort of stunned, I guess, and he took advantage of that in order to tie me up. I kept drifting in and out of consciousness as he kept coming back and forth for his boxes and yelling at me for being here and forcing him to hurt me."

"Was today the first time you noticed Kenneth's boxes?"

"No. I spotted them when I was here yesterday."

"Why didn't you call Mitch?"

"Because people would be even more inclined to think Frank was the vandal. And this proved to me he wasn't. Besides, I couldn't let Mitch see this place."

"Why not? It's a little kooky but it isn't anything to be ashamed of. I bet Mitch would actually think it was pretty interesting."

"He does."

"If he doesn't know about it, how can he think it's interesting?" I looked around trying to think what she could mean. In the dim light from the flashlight Kenneth had been gentlemanly enough to leave, my eyes made out a vintage New Hampshire vanity license plate with the word GEEZER from Backwoods Bruce's videos. "Wait a minute, was Frank Backwoods Bruce?" Phoebe shook her head.

"No, he wasn't."

"You are. That's where all your money has been coming from."

"That's me. When I first came up with the idea for the videos, I thought Frank would be the star of the show. It turned out he got completely tongue-tied. We even tried disguising his appearance and using a voice changer. I thought anonymity might put him at ease. Eventually, we decided since Frank had already taught me everything he knew about the woods and survival skills, maybe I could host it instead. We didn't think most of the viewers would be as willing to listen to advice from a young person, and a young woman at that."

"And you already had been trying to disguise Frank so why not try it on yourself."

"That's right. I realized I loved being in front of the camera and the videos went viral. Before long, Backwoods Bruce was a huge hit and we had sponsors and advertisers streaming in."

"Is that what you and Frank were arguing about Friday when I drove up to accuse him of vandalizing the Midget?"

"It was. He wanted me to stop disguising myself and to let everyone know who Backwoods Bruce really was. I told him we couldn't risk it. I loved my job and didn't want to lose it because viewers wouldn't take me seriously. Besides, I didn't want Mitch to know."

"But I bet Mitch would think it was a turn-on to find out he was dating a celebrity."

"I don't think he'd understand me pretending to be a man."

"I think you might be underestimating him."

"He's always going on about how pretty he thinks I am and how much I make him feel like a gentleman," Phoebe said.

"You know things didn't work out between Mitch and me."

"Everyone in town knows about that." Phoebe was right. Everyone in several surrounding towns probably knew about it, too.

"So you know I don't always have a lot of good things to say about him."

"I've never heard you say anything good about him. Even when you were dating him."

"I guess you're right. But one thing I can say is that he isn't a sexist. If he respects something, he respects it and it wouldn't matter to him whether an expert at something he was interested in was a man or a woman. Knowing Mitch, I think he'd find the whole thing pretty hot."

"I don't know. He likes my long hair and my lip gloss. He loves it when I wear heels."

"And he loves hunting, fishing, and running all over God's creation on a snowmobile. If he thought you were not only someone who would share his love of those pastimes but could teach him a thing or two, I think he'd be overjoyed."

"Really?"

"I wouldn't steer you wrong. And I think it would be a lot better to risk it than to leave him wondering if you killed Frank. As much as he likes you and wants to invest in your relationship that is going to be a hard thing to get past."

"I'm afraid my sponsors and advertisers will stop ordering ads on the program and the blog if they know I'm a woman."

"Think about it. Your viewership is bound to increase if you go on camera and let everyone know who you are. Everyone loves a big reveal. The guys who watched for the tips will keep coming. Guys who like to watch pretty women will start coming. Women who are proud of you for making it in a man's world will start watching. You'll attract an even larger viewership once word gets out Bruce is really a woman and advertisers love that. It'll be the best thing that could happen."

"It doesn't matter though, does it? We aren't going to get out of here." Phoebe pulled up in her arms and kicked with her legs. I tried the same. Over the course of the next couple of hours I managed to shout myself hoarse and Phoebe just got really quiet and withdrawn. I had a lot of time to think about roads not taken and words unspoken. I wished I had been nicer to Knowlton. I wished I had time to be closer to my sister. I wanted to get married and maybe have a cute baby of my own like Cyan. I wished I could tell my mother I believed her psychic shenanigans.

Which got me to thinking about how my mother's shenanigans were not always as silly as they seemed. I tried to remember our phone conversation. Something about the dark and never giving up as long as there was light. That even a flicker of light was like a knife through the darkness and would lead back to love. So what did it mean? Just thinking about it made me angry. If things beyond our regular senses wish to be taken seriously, they ought to actually make sense instead of mucking around with all the flowery language and fluffy imagery.

"This is ridiculous. Phoebe, you're an experienced survivalist. What should we do?"

"I don't know. I really don't." I thought she was going to start to cry again. With the way she was making a habit of weeping she was going to die of dehydration before the night was out.

"What would Backwoods Bruce do? Come on, think."

"Bruce is imaginary. This situation is real."

"But the principle is the same, right? I mean, Frank would have taught you some strategies for Bruce to share." Phoebe stopped crying and sniffed.

"Evaluate all the things in your environment. Take an inventory of anything and everything available. The odds of survival in any situation increase with your ability to adapt and think creatively."

"So what have we got?" I looked around.

"We've got chairs and sheets and we're both wearing clothes," Phoebe said. "There's the flashlight and a bunch of supplies we can't get to while we're tied up."

"The flashlight. It looks old."

"Everything in here except the food and water is old.

Frank didn't believe in buying new if you could reuse something you already had or someone else was getting rid of. Why do you think we have so much junk lying around the place?"

"Could it be old enough that the lens is made of glass?"

"Absolutely."

"Can you use your feet to drag yourself over to the table and grab it? If you can, I think I have an idea." I explained the plan and Phoebe nodded and began the slow process of hauling her chair, inch by inch, to the table. The sound of the chair legs scrapping the concrete floor was as least as unpleasant as my singing but within a few minutes she had gotten there.

"Now what?"

"Can you reach it?" I kept hoping I had figured out what my mother had been talking about. Broken lights and knives in the dark. I still wasn't sure about the heart-shaped card. I held my breath while Phoebe stretched her slim fingers out. I heard a little grunt that probably got squeezed out of her by some of the skin on her arms rubbing off on the sheet ties.

"Ten years of piano lessons," Phoebe said managing the impossible. "I never thought I'd be glad I took them. Now what?"

"Can you keep ahold of the flashlight and drag yourself next to me? I'd take a turn with the moving but my feet don't reach the floor." Phoebe nodded and started back toward me. Within just a few minutes, by working together, we had managed to unscrew the top and to get the glass lens out of the flashlight. Phoebe rapped the lens against the arm of her chair and broke off a jagged bit, exposing a sharp edge.

"I'll saw you out first," I said holding the bit of glass gingerly between my thumb and index finger. "Tell me once I've broken through to the fleshy bits. I can't see very well."

It took some doing but before what seemed like too long I had freed her nearest arm. She took over with the untying and sooner than I thought possible Phoebe and I were both on our feet and stumbling. I'd like to say we ran triumphantly for the stairs but the truth is our legs were stiff from all the sitting. We tripped and limped to the stairwell and staggered up, hesitating near the double doors at the top.

I couldn't speak for Phoebe but I was scared. Scared Kenneth was still up there waiting for some reason. Scared Beau had gotten loose once more. Scared the ghost of Frank would saunter up and clap us both on the back for a situation well survived. But a desire for freedom and, even more important, a bathroom won out and we shoved the doors open together.

Dusk was gathering, the temperature was falling, and I heard a throat being cleared. Knowlton stepped out from around the corner of the bunker like he had been waiting around for paint to dry.

"See, there you go again, spoiling everything," Knowlton said, crossing his arms across his puffy down-filled jacket.

"Knowlton, what are you doing here?" I asked.

"I followed you here from Jill's place." That didn't explain why he had left us in the bunker.

"Why didn't you come see what was keeping us?"

"Well, I stood outside listening and watching after you went in. Then Mr. Shaw went in and I listened even more carefully. Mother always says I should mind my manners around Mr. Shaw and his wife." Knowlton paused for dramatic effect before continuing. "I heard him threatening you and arguing. I hightailed it and dove for cover before he got back to the top of the stairs."

"Why didn't you come down and rescue us? We thought we were going to die down there." Phoebe was yelling now. Mild-mannered Phoebe had completely lost it. She thought she had the strength and she tried to haul off and deck him. Fortunately for Knowlton, the adrenaline had robbed her of normal muscular capacity and instead of connecting with his jawline she knocked herself off balance and sagged to the ground.

"I thought if I waited long enough, you would get really worried and think of me as even more of a hero." Knowlton shook his head at her then turned toward me. "I thought you'd be grateful."

"You thought wrong. A gentleman would never have left us in such a predicament in order to inflate his importance." I was working myself up, too. Usually, I made a point not to give etiquette lessons. I left that sort of thing to Celadon and occasionally Grandma. But I found myself beginning to need a lesson of my own as the pitch of my voice started raising up into the echolocation territory and my fists were aimed toward Knowlton's face.

"Would a gentleman have captured the guy who trapped you down there?" Knowlton asked. My fists dropped and a shriek died off in my throat.

"You caught Kenneth?"

"I've got him tied up to a tree in front of Jill's sugarhouse."

"How did you manage that?"

"I followed him back to Jill's. You know how quiet I can be walking through the woods when I set my mind to it." Which was true. Knowlton had a terrifying ability to appear out of nowhere when I was enjoying a walk through the sugar bush. "When Kenneth stopped in Jill's driveway I hit him over the head with my walking stick. He crumpled like a piñata in the rain."

"You hit the chairman of the select board over the head?"

"I did. Then I tore the clothesline down, dragged Kenneth to a tree, and tied him to it. I guess that makes me a hero after all." Knowlton draped an arm across my shoulders. "You'll have to be nice to me now." He pulled me just a little closer. And that's when I realized Knowlton was the heart-shaped card.

"You were just doing your civic duty. It wasn't like you did me a personal favor." He was managing to press himself against the length of my side. I wasn't sure if it was shock setting in or the idea that Knowlton was trying to get me to be grateful in a highly demonstrative way but I was starting to feel dizzy.

"It was more personal than that. I stopped him just as he was trying to push your car over the edge of that steep drop-off near Jill's driveway. If I'd been any slower, the Clunker would have been a goner for sure."

Twenty-three

Two weeks later the opera house was full once more. The crowd was even bigger than it had been for meat bingo. Tonight instead of the bingo ball cage sitting up on the stage, a projector screen stood at the ready. All around the hall people whispered and shuffled their boots against the worn hardwood floor. Jackets rustled and the wintery smell of damp wool scarves and mittens filled the air. Phoebe climbed the short set of stairs to the stage and gently tapped the microphone. The noises in the room died off and all faces turned toward her.

"I wanted to thank you all for coming this evening. I wasn't sure if anyone was going to make it, what with the snow and all." Phoebe dipped her head shyly and glanced off to the side, where Mitch stood giving her a thumbs-up. "I hope you enjoy the show and the refreshments that will be available afterward." Phoebe hurried down from the stage and took a seat close to where Mitch was standing. I couldn't imagine how awkward it would be to watch all your friends and neighbors watching you. The houselights went down and the screen lit up. And then there was Frank's survival bunker, mostly like I remembered it, but without anyone tied to a chair.

The camera panned around and then settled on a figure wearing a cap and sitting on a stool, back to the camera. A hand reached up and pulled off the cap and then the head shook and a cascade of blond hair tumbled down. Phoebe spun around on the stool and faced the camera, a great big smile on her face.

"Welcome to today's episode of *Backwoods Bruce*. I'd like to dedicate this show to my dad, Frank Lemieux. Frank taught me everything I know about the woods, survival techniques, and being yourself even when you think it might not be a popular choice. Frank thought I should go ahead and trust people to like my program whether I was Backwoods Bruce or Backwoods Brenda. I didn't decide to trust my viewers until it was too late for Frank to know how it turned out." Phoebe's voice broke a little on the screen and I noticed everyone in the hall turning to see if the real-life Phoebe was starting to cry, too. She wasn't. She was just sitting there peacefully, hanging on to Mitch's hand. "Frank never got to see me do a show as myself and that is my biggest regret in my life so far. I hope all my viewers decide to risk living their own dreams before they run out of time."

People all over the opera house leaned toward each other. I saw more than one person elbow another in the ribs. If I were close enough to Loden, I would have been one of the elbowers. He was sitting a regrettable two rows behind Piper. But Dean was sitting three rows back on the other side of the hall with Cyan in his lap. Chelsea sat at his side, watching like she was worried he'd drop the baby and run.

Celadon was discreetly waving a finger in my direction like she wished she could tap me on the forehead with it. I thought back to what Graham had said about the state of Celadon's marriage and I wondered if Phoebe's message grieved her at all. I smiled at her before shifting my attention to my mother and Lowell. They were gazing at each other in a way that looked to me like they were congratulating each other for being bold, for pursuing their heart's desire. With their unseasonably tanned faces they looked like people who had snatched happiness from the jaws of too late and knew it.

You know that soreness that comes from a strenuous workout? That tight feeling in your muscles that twinges but makes you feel alive and virtuous? That's how I felt looking at my mother and Lowell. It still stung a bit seeing them together but the ache felt good, too. Like I was stretching a muscle that had forgotten how to be used but appreciated being remembered.

Things were different, there was no denying that. Things with my mother, things with my business, things with my impressions of the town around me. It was disillusioning to realize the people who had been in charge as long as I could remember weren't always what they seemed. Mothers had love lives, classmates had secret identities, and respected townspeople had killer instincts. Things certainly weren't the same, but then I wasn't the same either.

Only a few weeks earlier I had stood quaking in front of Kenneth Shaw hoping he wouldn't send me home with my hat in my hand and my tail between my legs. And I would have thought seriously about calling on Grampa for backup if he did. Now I had a few more survival skills of my own under my belt and the confidence that went with them.

Up on the screen Phoebe was demonstrating the pros and cons of a quality flashlight. She was just starting to mention how a flashlight could come in handy if you found yourself unexpectedly tied to a chair when the door to the opera house creaked open. In the dimly lit space a figure crept quietly around the back of the hall and then slipped into the empty chair next to me. Graham leaned in close and whispered in my ear.

"I had a call about a some out-of-control snowmobilers. I hope I'm not too late." I felt someone staring at me and looked over to see my mother winking like she knew just what I was thinking. I reached out for his hand and felt his cool fingers wrap around my warm ones.

"I'd say you're right on time."

Recipes

Grandmadama Bread

Makes 2 loaves

This is Grandma Greene's variation on the New England classic, anadama bread. Subtly sweet with a moist, nubbly crumb, this bread is sure to please your family as much as it does the Greenes. Try to use Grade B maple syrup if possible. The maple flavor will be more pronounced.

½ cup yellow cornmeal
2 cups water
1 package active dry yeast
½ cup lukewarm water
½ cup Grade B maple syrup (if Grade A must be substituted add ½ -1 teaspoon of maple extract when maple is added to other ingredients)

2 teaspoons salt
2 tablespoons softened butter
3½ cups all-purpose-flour
½ cup whole-wheat flour
½ cup oat flour (you can make this at home by
        grinding old fashioned oats in a food processor
        or blender until pulverized to a powdery
        consistency)

Place the cornmeal in a heat-safe bowl. Boil the 2 cups of water and pour over the cornmeal, stirring with a whisk to eliminate lumps. Leave soaking for half an hour for cornmeal to soften.

Grease two loaf pans with nonstick baking spray. In a small bowl dissolve the yeast in ½ cup lukewarm water and let stand five minutes. Add yeast, maple syrup, salt, and softened butter to the cornmeal and blend until smooth. Add the flours and mix thoroughly. Divide batter equally between prepared pans and allow to rise in a warm place until loaves are doubled in size. Preheat the oven to 350 degrees F and bake for 40-45 minutes or until bread's internal temerature registers 190 degrees on a instant read thermometer. Tip out of the pans and cool on racks.

This bread is especially delicious served still-warm and slathered with Dani's Maple Butter.

Dani's Maple Butter

Quantity varies

With a metabolism like a hummingbird, Dani is always trying to slip a few extra calories into her diet. Even if you aren't faced with the same problem, this sweet and creamy spread is just the thing to slather on warm bread on a cold day.

In a small bowl mix five parts softened butter to one part maple syrup. Spread generously on toast, muffins, and even saltines. Kids, especially, love this!

Apricot Maple-Glazed Ham

All the members of Dani's family love ham but this sweet, salty, and tangy combination is her favorite way to eat it.

1 4-6 pound, fully cooked boneless ham
2 cups apricot preserves
3 tablespoons maple syrup (Grade B has the strongest maple flavor)
¼ teaspoon coarsely ground black pepper

Preheat the oven to 325 degrees F. Place the ham in a shallow roasting pan. Place the apricot preserves in a microwave-safe dish and heat until mostly melted, approximately 30-60 seconds. Stir in the maple syrup and the pepper. Lightly score the top of the ham in a diamond pattern. Insert an oven-safe meat thermometer into the thickest part of the ham. Spoon the glaze over the top of the ham. Bake for 1¼ -2 ½ hours or until thermometer registers 140 degrees F.

Caramelized Peach Oven-Puffed Pancake

On a cold morning nothing beats a hot breakfast, especially if it features peaches enveloped in a sweet, buttery sauce. This recipe is almost as easy to make as it is to eat. Served with bacon or sausage this is a great breakfast to share with guests.

1 pound sliced frozen peaches
½ cup salted butter
½ cup brown sugar
1 cup flour
1 cup milk
7 large eggs
¾ teaspoon nutmeg

Preheat oven to 425 degrees F. Place peaches in a microwave-safe bowl and defrost until mostly thawed but still firm to the touch. Alternately, the peaches may be left at room temperature for several hours before use. In an oven-safe skillet melt the butter over medium heat. Once melted, remove 1 tablespoon of the butter and place it in a large mixing bowl. Add brown sugar to the peaches and stir to coat evenly. Add peaches to skillet and cook, stirring frequently, until butter and sugar have thickened slightly into a sauce that clings easily to the peach slices. Remove from heat and set aside.

Beat the milk, nutmeg, and eggs together in the mixing bowl containing the melted butter. Add the flour and, using an immersion blender or a whisk, beat until the batter is smooth. Adjust peaches so they are spread evenly in the skillet. Carefully pour batter over the peaches, trying not to disarrange them. Slide skillet into the oven and bake for 20 minutes or until the pancake is puffed and golden brown.

> "[McKinlay] continues to deliver well-crafted mysteries full of fun and plot twists."
> —*Booklist*

FROM *NEW YORK TIMES* BESTSELLING AUTHOR

Jenn McKinlay

Going, Going, Ganache

A Cupcake Bakery Mystery

After a cupcake-flinging fiasco at a photo shoot for a local magazine, Melanie Cooper and Angie DeLaura agree to make amends by hosting a weeklong corporate boot camp at Fairy Tale Cupcakes. The idea is the brainchild of Ian Hannigan, new owner of *Southwest Style,* a lifestyle magazine that chronicles the lives of Scottsdale's rich and famous. He's assigned his staff to a team-building week of making cupcakes for charity.

It's clear that the staff would rather be doing just about anything other than frosting baked goods. But when the magazine's features director is found murdered outside the bakery, Mel and Angie have a new team-building exercise—find the killer before their business goes AWOL.

INCLUDES SCRUMPTIOUS RECIPES

jennmckinlay.com
facebook.com/jennmckinlay
facebook.com/TheCrimeSceneBooks
penguin.com

M1287T0313

FROM *NEW YORK TIMES* BESTSELLING AUTHOR

JENN MCKINLAY

~~~~~~~

THE CUPCAKE BAKERY MYSTERIES

Sprinkle with Murder
Buttercream Bump Off
Death by the Dozen
Red Velvet Revenge
Going, Going, Ganache
Sugar and Iced

INCLUDES SCRUMPTIOUS RECIPES!

~~~~~~~

Praise for the Cupcake Bakery Mysteries

"Delectable . . . A real treat."
—Julie Hyzy, *New York Times* bestselling author
of the White House Chef Mysteries

"A tender cozy full of warm and likable characters
and...tasty concoctions."

HILLSBORO PUBLIC LIBRARIES
Hillsboro, OR
Member of Washington County
COOPERATIVE LIBRARY SERVICES

M1212AS1013